The Royal Palace

SIX ROYAL WOMEN IN THE BIBLE: THE GOOD,
THE BAD AND THE MISLED

M.E. MAYORGA

5 SISTERS MINISTRY
BRISBANE, AUSTRALIA

*The wise woman builds her house,
but with her own hands the foolish one tears hers down.*

—PROVERBS 14:1

Contents

Dear Reader,

I am very excited to introduce you to six royal women of the Bible. You are about to embark on a journey back in ancient times and into these women's hometowns and lives. These novelettes are short stories that will show you how those around the women affected or inspired their lives. I hope that at the end of each story you will be inspired to open your Bible and read their stories for yourself, the way the Holy Spirit originally wrote and inspired the prophets with them.

Here are the women you will read about:

Anisenath (fictional name)—the princess who saved baby Moses from the Nile

Zaria (fictional name)—the queen of Sheba who ventured from her home to find out about King Solomon's wisdom

Jezebel—the queen who introduced her husband, king Ahab, to pagan idols

Jehosheba—the brave princess who saved baby Joash from being murdered

Esther—the obedient Jewish girl who was taken from her home to become queen

Salome—the princess who asked for John the Baptist's head

Although these stories have been taken from the Bible and researched through historical content, remember, as the author I have created dialogue, additional characters, and fictional names and events to fill and move each story along.

I pray that as you read through this book, you will develop a closer connection with God as you see how these women's lives connect with yours.

—M.E. MAYORGA

One

Anisenath: Benevolent Princess of the Nile

Then Pharaoh's daughter went down to the Nile to bathe, and her attendants were walking along the riverbank. She saw the basket among the reeds and sent her female slave to get it. She opened it and saw the baby. He was crying, and she felt sorry for him. "This is one of the Hebrew babies," she said.

—EXODUS 2:5–6

Find the story in Exodus 2:1–25.

Prologue

1525 BC, Temple of Isis

As the shades of red and yellow scattered across the sky as dawn approached, Princess Anisenath went into the sacred pool to purify her body before entering the temple of Isis. The cool water of the morning made her jolt, and she shivered slightly as she moved to the middle of the pool. Inside, Ramla, the high priestess, waited for her with a cup filled with water. Anisenath inclined her head and waited as water trickled down her head and clothes. Then she dipped herself underneath and closed her eyes as she lifted her soul to Isis and asked to be cleansed from all impurity. As she came up, Ramla started walking out of the pool and Anisenath followed to dry and change before being in the presence of Isis.

Once dried and dressed in her day clothes, Anisenath walked out to where Ramla and two other priestesses waited for her. She followed them up the steps and into the main part of the temple where a shrine of the goddess Isis dwelt. Anisenath's breath caught at the sight of the goddess she adored. The statue was vast, covering almost the entire back wall of the temple. In front of the figure was a shrine with a replica of Isis but in miniature size. Tears filled her eyes as she entered her presence. Today she clung to the hope her prayers would be answered.

Ramla's tall, lean body moved through the ritual with effortless elegance—she poured water from the sacred well of the temple and replenished all the libation vessels. Soft music and chanting echoed in the background, adding to the sacredness of the occasion. As the sun rose, two priestesses drew the bolt of the door back and opened it for the light to pour through.

The princess remained bowed, waiting for Ramla to motion it was her turn.

"Princess Anisenath, Isis is ready." Ramla lifted her arms in the air and chanted a few words Anisenath did not understand and moved away so the princess could face the shrine. Anisenath took a deep breath, stood, and walked reverently toward the statue. She lit charcoal and incense in the censer next to Isis, made an offering, and took the statue before anointing it with oil and perfume. When she finished, she placed Isis back on her shrine and prayed out loud.

"Goddess Isis, I have been purified to be in your presence. I ask for you to heal my womb so I can birth many children. Listen to my prayer, oh Isis." She bowed down, took off her bejewelled collar, and placed it as a gift in front of the altar. Then she knelt down and kissed the ground. She remained there for a few minutes, basking in the rhythmic incantation nearby.

How she yearned for a child of her own. Her husband, Ini-herit, died before she could become a mother. They had tried for years to have children, yet she had been unable to conceive. She grieved his death after he came home with a rare skin disease he incurred during battle; however, having no child from him had also disheartened her. She had been begging Isis, the goddess of motherhood, fertility, love, and healing, for many months. She was not ready to marry anytime soon, yet her father, Pharaoh the king, constantly mentioned he would find her a husband. She hoped to delay his wishes for another four seasons.

A soft hand touched her shoulder. "Princess Anisenath, time is up. We do not want to tire the gods."

Ramla's voice broke through her thoughts and nodding, the princess stood and followed the priestess out of the temple and into the courtyard where six of her male servants and her carry chair waited for her. The sun was bursting with heat, slapping her delicate skin. She was glad her carry chair had a cover and she would not burn her skin under the sun's vengeance. She was eager to arrive home, take a bath in the Nile, and eat. Her body felt weary from being up too early.

Ramla stopped and turned to face the princess, giving her a gentle smile. "Isis will hear your request. It is only a matter of time."

Anisenath exhaled as she covered her womb with both her hands. "I believe she will, Ramla. Thank you for all you do for me."

The priestess inclined her head and moved out of the way so the princess could walk past and climb her litter.

Once seated, the chair was raised, and the brief journey to the palace began. Her heart felt lighter, and new hope surged through her soul.

Anisenath admired her surroundings as they passed the Nile River that had overflowed overnight. Anuket, the goddess of the Nile, seemed to be in high spirits. The princess smirked; the gods could be temperamental and so easily offended. Her eyes travelled further to the distance and stopped at the pyramids. The completed structures looked grand; even the unfinished ones looked imposing. The Hebrews were working day and night to finish the workload her father had given them. She shook her head at the thought of being a slave and a prisoner. She was a princess and treated as a goddess; they made anything she asked for possible and no one dared mistreat her or lift a finger against her. She was well aware of how privileged she was. The sound of a whip and a scream echoed through the morning, and she jumped. Up ahead, she noticed the slaves at work. An Egyptian taskmaster was beating a young man.

"You are being lazy! Work harder or you will bleed to death," the Egyptian bellowed.

The young man was hunched over waiting for the next whip lash to hit his back.

"Get me closer," Anisenath ordered her carriers.

The men moved her closer, and just as the Egyptian was about to hit the Hebrew again, Anisenath lifted her hand and shouted, "Is that the way to treat a man who is unarmed?"

At the sound of her voice, the stout taskmaster's head shot up. Immediately, he prostrated himself to the dusty ground. "Princess Anisenath!" His voice and bulbous stomach shook.

"I believe it is unjust to hit a young man who has no weapon to defend himself. I command you to let him go!" She felt her voice rise a few notes.

"But . . . my lady, he was sleeping on the job. We need to get these monuments erected in due time. Your father, our great god Pharaoh, has given us a time frame." The man remained on the ground with droplets of sweat on his bald head.

"If you resume beating him, he will no longer be able to do his work. You will be one worker less, and my father would have your head for allowing the delay." She almost felt like grinning at her ingenious comeback.

The slave master's mouth dropped. "Of course, my lady." He struggled to his feet, and with perspiration running down his face and chest, he gave orders to the young man to get back to work.

The Hebrew turned to face the princess and inclined his head. Princess Anisenath observed the young man, from his dark, curly head to the bottom of his feet. He did not look older than her twenty years. His body was well sculpted, like the pillars of the temple. He wore a dark loincloth, and she watched as his bare chest heaved with each breath he took. She felt her face heat from staring at the young man's body, but it wasn't out of lust, just curiosity. Everywhere she looked, she saw well-built Hebrews. Muscular and strong. Healthy and crimson cheeked. Even their children looked well. It was as if the gods smiled down at them and blessed them with bodies of the gods themselves. How was that possible? Should they not have protruding bones with pale skin and gaunt faces? They worked as hard as camels, yet they remained strong. She shook her head as the young man bowed and ran toward a group of slaves making bricks.

With one last glance at the young man, she motioned to her manservants to take her home. The taskmaster remained with his head bowed until she disappeared around the corner and lost him in the dust's thickness.

Her heart ached for the slaves, and she hoped that one day when she became Pharaoh, she would eradicate such cruelty.

Chapter One

1525 BC, Egypt

Princess Anisenath laughed. "I beat you again, Tanith!" She clapped her hands and stared at her friend's pretend angry expression.

"You, my dear Anisenath, cheated me again!" Tanith scrunched up her nose and threw one of the counting sticks of their senet game to Anisenath.

The piece landed on the princess's head, and both girls burst out laughing. Anisenath's black cat, Sef, stretched lazily on her lap. She ran her hand lovingly over his furry body and grinned. It was early afternoon, and Tanith's father, Amenhotep, a government official and important man of Egypt, had a meeting with the princess's father later that evening. Upon knowing that he was headed to the palace, Tanith had come along to spend time with the princess and make the most of their time before she had to leave Egypt with her husband.

Anisenath enjoyed her dear friend; she was one of the very few women she could talk to openly. Tanith's father had married her at fifteen to the son of Baako, the priest. Her father, a devout man of the gods, believed his daughter would live a prosperous and safe life under the protection of the son of the high priest. Up to the present moment, his predictions had been correct, and for the last six years, Tanith had lived a blissful life. She was planning to have babies soon, and each time she mentioned it, Anisenath could not help but feel like a dagger was pierced through her heart. Why was life cruel? Was she cursed? She very much doubted a curse hung over her head. Sef brought her good fortune, and his supernatural powers would keep her untouched. She rubbed his jewelled neck and bent down to give him a brief kiss. When he passed, she would have him mummified. He would live forever.

"The earth of the gods to the princess."

Tanith's voice brought her back to the present, and she blinked a few times. "I apologise, Tani," she said, calling her by her childhood name. She took a deep breath and detoured the conversation to something neutral. "I witnessed an Egyptian whipping a Hebrew man a few days ago. I intervened, of course." She folded her arms across her chest and shook her head. The braids on her short, dark wig bounced as she moved.

"Again?" Tanith leaned forward and lowered her voice so no one in the room would hear. She flicked her long, braided wig to one side, and her bracelets clinked with the movement. Her painted eyes narrowed. "Ani, if your father gets news that you are getting the taskmasters in trouble for hitting the slaves, he will be furious. You know how much he detests the Hebrews."

Anisenath unfolded her arms and leaned over, being careful not to press Sef. "I find it very brutal to hit someone when they have done nothing wrong. My heart breaks!" She tickled her black cat's stomach with one long, painted nail. The animal purred, and she giggled.

"Your father thinks differently. That is why they are in bondage. If these people stopped multiplying and growing stronger each day, they would be free men and women. If you ask me . . . it is their fault." Tanith flicked her head.

"They are very strong," she whispered, remembering the young Hebrew man and his companions she had seen a few days ago. "What is the mystery of their strength, do you think?"

Tanith leaned back in her seat. "I do not know. However, Amun believes it has something to do with their God."

Anisenath moved her head slowly in agreement. "Your husband is very knowledgeable, as I have thought the same . . ."

"My husband is brilliant indeed." Tanith grinned, and a shimmer twinkled in her eyes.

The princess smiled softly; it was the same look she used to see in her husband's eyes when he looked at her. Oh, how she missed him! She grimaced as another depressing thought mulled in her mind. She reached over and took her friend's hand in hers.

"Oh, Tani, I just realised that you are to leave me soon and I will be alone." Anisenath bit her bottom lip.

Water welled in Tanith's eyes as she squeezed her friend's hand. "I will miss you, my dear Anisenath. I will visit you when I am able."

Anisenath nodded and wiped the corners of her eyes. "We are like two old ladies in tears."

The friends let out a laugh and quickly covered their mouths.

"Oh, Tani, who will I laugh or talk with again?" the princess moaned. She did not feel close to anyone else.

Tanith's kohl-painted eyes widened. "I—"

Whatever Tanith was going to say next was drowned out by the sudden roar of Pharaoh. Both girls' heads shot up, and Sef, frightened by the sound, leaped from her lap and scurried off. Pharaoh, Baako the high priest, and Amenhotep, Tanith's father, sat engrossed in conversation. Pharaoh stood as he hit his fist into the palm of his hand. From where Anisenath sat, she saw his face the colour of fire.

The entire room stopped breathing.

The music died.

The dancers stopped.

The maids froze with trays of melon, figs, and dates in their hands.

Anisenath glanced at Tanith, whose face had somewhat paled. She was used to her father's angry outbursts, but it was rare for others to see him in this state. He only reacted when he was absolutely infuriated. The princess wondered who had caused his anger. She did not have to wait long, as he continued to roar.

"I do not care who their ancestor Joseph was. He means nothing to me. Peasant of a man!" The king paced around the room, running his hand over the khat headdress. "Something must be done to end them once and for all!"

Anisenath cringed. Besides slaves, peasants were some of the lowest people in Egypt. She wanted to tell her father that Joseph, the Hebrew slaves' ancestor who had migrated them to Egypt, had been a very intelligent man with powers to interpret dreams—he had also been the prime minister of Egypt and second to Pharaoh. However, she doubted it would make any impression on her father. He was in no mood for idle discussions. With his brow furrowed, his face red, and his heavy, painted eyes narrowed, he was to be left alone.

At that precise moment, he turned his eyes to the musicians and pointed his long, thin finger in their direction. "Leave!" he shouted. The three musicians bowed and, with panic in their eyes, fled the room, leaving their instruments behind.

He continued barking orders for everyone to leave. Only Amenhotep and Baako were ordered to remain. The princess looked at her friend and motioned for them to leave.

"Do not leave, Anisenath." The booming voice of her father stopped her, and she turned to look up at him with trepidation. "One day you will be the next Pharaoh, and you must learn to be ruthless in these matters."

She sat back down. "Can Tanith remain, my father?"

The king waved his hand, indicating she could. Anisenath's shoulders relaxed at the thought of having her friend there for support.

Today her father looked menacing, with his leopard-skin cape over his shoulders and a lion's tail hanging from his belt. The symbol of power was clear.

The remaining four people in the room waited for him to speak. When his furore subsided, she watched him walk to the balcony that overlooked some of the working fields. He groaned loudly.

"Look at the Israelites. The more I make them work, the stronger they are! They grow in strength!" He turned to Anisenath and extended his hand. "Come, Anisenath."

She gulped and hurried to his side. The tapping of her delicate ox-leather sandals, adorned with green precious stones symbolising earth and fertility, echoed in the room's silence.

"My Anisenath, we must make plans to stop these Hebrews from growing. They multiply by the hundreds . . . daily!"

Anisenath looked below and watched as male and female Hebrews worked like animals, building what her father demanded of them. She cringed as the slave masters lashed some for being slow. The Hebrews remained standing with fists tightened into a ball, letting the brute taskmaster hit them. As much as she wanted to turn her head away, she knew her father would never permit her being feeble. If she was to be the next Pharaoh; she must pretend to be emotionless.

Chapter Two

From the balcony, Anisenath stared at the endless number of Hebrew slaves. Her father was right: it seemed they *did* multiply daily.

"I fear if there is a war, *they* will join our enemies and defeat us." With his right hand, Pharaoh slapped the leaves of a plant that rested in a vessel near the balcony. "Taking over our land and killing each one of us!"

"Father, what makes you think they will turn against us . . . and not be on our side?" she asked, searching his face for answers.

Her father tore his gaze from the potted plant and walked back to the balcony. His eyes scanned the grounds below.

"Because they hate us, Anisenath! They have been our slaves for many years, and they would enjoy nothing else than to eliminate the superior race . . . us!" Pharaoh's fury seemed to creep back.

The minute she saw his expression change, she regretted her questions. She needed to distract him and leave the room immediately. "My father, do not overburden the energy the gods have given you on the Hebrews. Instead, why don't we take a turn around the gardens near the Nile River? The view is always wonderful at this time of the day." She rested her hand gently on his arm and smiled softly.

Pharaoh glanced at her, and his shoulders relaxed. "Oh, my beloved daughter, you are so much like your late mother. She always knew how to say the right thing and calm my nerves. The gods have blessed you with her gift. Let's take a turn around the Nile, shall we?"

She dipped her head and placed her palm on his arm and walked out with him—she turned her head and smiled at Tanith. Her friend smiled back and exhaled with relief. Anisenath wanted to laugh out loud. Tanith understood how she felt.

"Come, my friends, walk with us." Everyone stood and followed them out of the room and toward the back of the palace where the doors remained open, inviting the view of the Nile River into their space. It was one of Anisenath's favourite place. The breeze of the afternoon washed over her face, and she lifted her chin to greet it. It felt wonderful. The king, Anisenath, and their guests walked down the few steps to the garden and the water below.

"What is this?" The question from her father made her pause and look where he was pointing.

A sheepish smile crept across her crimson lips. "This miniature shrine was a gift from Ramla to keep in my garden."

"Is that not the goddess Isis?" Pharaoh inclined his head a little lower, looking down at the statue surrounded with food, plants, and jewellery. Although the smoke had died out, the scent of incense lingered in the air. "Why Isis?" Confusion dripped from his tone.

Sensing Anisenath's hesitation, he asked his guests to walk ahead.

"What is it, my flower?"

Tears welled in her eyes at the tenderness in her father's voice. "Father, I yearn for Isis to heal my womb." Her hands spread protectively over her stomach.

"Are you sick, Anisenath?" Her father's eyes filled with concern.

"Ini-herit did not make me a mother before he died. I feel the gods have cursed me." She turned her head away as a silent tear rolled down her cheek.

"Cursed? How so?" His eyebrows lifted in surprise.

"I was married for a few years, Father, yet no baby blessed my womb. I am asking Isis to heal me, and I know she will!" The certainty in her voice surprised her. She doubted the gods often for their silence, but the more she spoke, the more she believed it might happen.

"Anisenath, I believe it is time for you to marry again. You have mourned long enough." Pharaoh walked, and she followed.

"Father, allow me to mourn a little longer. I do not feel ready to forget Ini-herit." Although her marriage had been arranged by her father when she was young, she had learnt to love her husband. Even after her father had arranged for him to be embalmed, she was not ready to lay him to rest in her heart.

Pharaoh nodded briskly. "Very well. A few months longer and then I will betroth you. I know a pleasant companion for you." A small smile played on his lips, and Anisenath moaned softly. "A baby would be a wonderful addition to our palace. I like that idea very well."

Anisenath took his arm and grinned. "Maybe two, three, or four grandchildren might roam around this palace. They will multiply and bring joy to our household. The gods will hear."

"Hmm . . . multiply?" Pharaoh's voice went almost into a whisper as he repeated the words a few times.

The princess watched her father's eyes flicker with an emotion she could not read—but she knew something had just dashed into his mind. A small dread filled her chest as they continued their walk.

Chapter Three

It was midmorning two days after Anisenath and her father had conversed in the garden at the banks of the Nile, when she heard a commotion in the palace. Running footsteps and voices echoed, and she wondered what could have happened. She glanced down at Sef sleeping peacefully on her lap with no concern. Her maidservant, Onofria, was finishing putting on the last touches of her headdress. The princess lifted her hand for her to pause and turned around. "Onofria, please find out what has happened. It sounds like a disturbance has taken place."

"Yes, my lady." The middle-aged maid fixed her simple sheath dress with the wide shoulder straps and headed out the door.

Anisenath stood and placed her cat on his little golden bed by the window; then she shut the lid of her jewellery box. She had adorned herself with enough jewellery and did not need to add anymore.

She turned around when she heard the door open, and a trembling Onofria came back in.

"What is it?" Her stomach turned. "Is it my father?"

"Your father is well, my lady, but he has given a decree—"

"Decree?" she interrupted Onofria. "What decree?"

The maid did not lift her dark head to look at her—the simple ribbon across her forehead looked like it was squeezing her head.

"Onofria, speak!" Anisenath's harsh voice took her by surprise. She cleared her throat and asked again in a softer tone. "Please, what happened?"

With tears streaming down her face, the maidservant whimpered a few words that made Anisenath draw in her breath. "King Pharaoh has commanded for all the Hebrew babies to be killed!"

"No!" The princess grabbed the closest chair and flopped onto it. "No, Onofria. Tell me it is not true."

The maid shook her head.

Anisenath covered her mouth with her a trembling hand. "I do not believe it."

"He has demanded two Hebrew women to be brought to the palace to make his command official. They are on their way."

Anisenath gasped. "Quick, finish my hair. I need to be a witness to this. Hurry, Onofria!"

The maid worked faster, even as her fingers fumbled with the headpiece. Then she helped her put on her sandals, and Anisenath was off to the king's meeting room. She saw servants scurrying and whispering amongst themselves. It was noticeable everyone in the palace had heard about the verdict.

Her heart thudded in her chest as she walked down the multicolour, painted corridor walls of their palace. Today each colourful symbol gave her head pain. With each step she took, she hoped it was all a misunderstanding. Her father was not a criminal. Surely, he would not have commanded innocent children to be killed, would he? The thoughts swirled in her mind, giving her no peace or answers. How she wished Tanith was still close by and not so many miles away. As Anisenath rounded the corner toward the door of her father's meeting room, she saw two Hebrew women being escorted by two soldiers. Immediately, she hid behind the pillar and observed.

The women were dressed in simple linen-coloured tunics. They covered their heads with coloured veils and wore papyrus sandals. They did not have painted faces like she and her people did. The women's serene look caught her attention, and she wondered if they pretended to look peaceful to anger her father or if they really felt no fear. Before the women walked past, Anisenath hurried her pace and squeezed herself between two columns to shorten her path and get to the room.

There were more soldiers than usual standing guard across the main doors. Two of them had blocked the entryway with their javelins, but when they saw her, they bowed and let her through. Her father sat on his throne shouting orders to the scribes, who sat on the floor cross-legged, writing on papyrus. As she entered, he looked up, not smiling as he usually did when she entered the room; instead, he lifted his arm and motioned with his hand for her to come closer to the throne. They had placed a smaller golden chair near the pillar to the right-hand side of the king. "Take a seat, Anisenath."

She walked over, took a seat, and watched the room with concern. Amenhotep and Baako were present; so were the scribes and soldiers. No music or entertainment lightened the room. This *was* a serious matter. Her father usually had entertainment of some sort happening in the background, but no sounds of joy echoed today.

The room suddenly went silent as they escorted the Hebrew women into the room. Two soldiers stood on either side of them, waiting to be given instructions.

"Approach," Pharaoh commanded.

All eyes followed the women until they came to a stop in front of Pharaoh. They inclined their heads and waited reverently for him to proceed.

"I believe you are Puah and Shiphrah?" Pharaoh stated.

"We are," they said in unison.

"Is it true that you are midwives to the Hebrew women?" The king leaned forward, watching their faces.

The taller one with the blue veil bowed her head. "We are, my lord."

Pharaoh stood. "Listen and listen carefully." He turned to the scribes. "Write as I speak," he ordered. "From this day forward when a Hebrew woman gives birth to a daughter, you shall let her live . . . However, if she gives birth to a son . . . he must be put to death!" His words echoed in the room, and Anisenath gasped, covering her mouth with her hand. It was true. Her father was killing the Hebrew babies!

Shiphrah and Puah did not show any emotion; instead, they inclined their heads and waited for further instruction.

"Leave!" Pharaoh shouted, then turned to the scribes as the women walked out of the room. "Have you written every word I have spoken?"

"Yes, my lord god of the Nile and Egypt. It is written." The bald head of the scribe perspired, but he dared not wipe it clean in the presence of Pharaoh.

"Anisenath, from today every Hebrew baby boy will be eliminated, and their population will diminish until they cease to exist! Let it be written as I have commanded."

Anisenath felt anger bubble inside her soul. How dare he kill a living soul. A baby! Here she was yearning for a child, and he was destroying them. She wanted to lift her voice and shout with all her might, to curse the gods and renounce everything, but she could only nod and remained voiceless. For who would dare to go against the king?

Chapter Four

Slowly, the events of midmorning faded as the day progressed and the servants went about their daily work. It was early evening and Anisenath could not get the decree out of her mind. Restless, she took Sef into her arms and went outside for a walk along the Nile. The afternoon sun melted behind the horizon as dusk settled in for the night. The colours of the sunset splashed across the sky, and the landscape took her breath away.

"Sef, look at how the gods paint the sky. Isn't it lovely?" she said as she sat overlooking the scenery. Sef stretched and purred in her arms without a care about the sky. She smiled and ran nails along his head. "Sef, I wish I was a cat, with no concern plaguing my mind. Life is too difficult at the moment." She sighed.

"You wish to be a cat?"

At the sound of her father's voice, Anisenath froze. He was the last person she wanted to speak to at this present moment. She did not turn around as she heard his footsteps approach. Gradually, she lifted her head. "Good evening, my father."

"I had my suspicions that I would find you here." Her father was still dressed in his formal attire. She suspected he had been with an audience all day.

"It is the place I find peace when I feel unsettled," she replied and stood to face him while holding her cat close.

Her father reached out and patted Sef's head. "I came to speak to you about the decree I gave today. I saw your face, Anisenath, and I was not impressed at your reaction." He stared at her, waiting for a reply.

"I apologise if my face showed dismay, Father. It never crossed my mind that you would make such a command." She sighed and placed Sef on the ground. The cat leaped back up on the seat and stretched out.

"Would you have done something different if you were Pharaoh?" His eyes narrowed.

Anisenath shook her head. "I do not know what I would have done as Pharaoh." She paused, choosing her words carefully. "I have never questioned your judgement. You are wise and have made Egypt prosperous and powerful. Father, you need to understand that I yearn for a baby of my own, and hearing you speak of the death of children made my heart bleed."

She watched her father's face harden. "The gods will not give you a Hebrew baby; therefore, your heart should not bleed for them. They deserve to die! As Pharaoh, my priority is Egypt. I need to ensure the safety of *my* people. I need to secure yours!"

The princess did not utter a word but inclined her head in respect. She knew that anything that came out of her mouth would be rebuked, and she did not want him to strike her. He never had, but recently he had been acting a lot harsher than she was used to seeing him.

"Of course, my father," was all she said.

Her father looked at her for a long while; then, without another word, he spun around and went back inside.

She breathed again and sat down to admire the sinking sun, searching for peace.

Two weeks passed with no news or eradication of her father's cruel plans. The declaration remained standing, but things seemed unusually settled and quiet. It was about noon as Anisenath finished writing a letter to Tanith, who was now visiting the sacred site of the gods in Memphis, the capital of Upper and Lower Egypt. She was with her husband and her father-in-law, Baako. Anisenath smiled, thinking of how much her friend was enjoying her life. She and her husband were taking advantage of not having children to travel. Soon they would settle down and have many little ones. The princess felt only joy for them. Her dear friend deserved all the happiness. A soft knock at the door startled her concentration. Onofria, who was folding clothes, crossed the room and went to open the door.

"Yes?" she said.

"The king has requested for Princess Anisenath to come to the meeting hall immediately," the male voice answered.

Anisenath frowned, wondering why her father needed her immediately. Had something occurred? She folded her paper, stamped it, and left it on the table for Onofria to organise the delivery.

The door closed, and Onofria came back in. "My lady—"

"I heard," Anisenath interrupted. "I will make haste." She hurried to the mirror and checked her painted eyes, cheeks, and lips and fixed her plaited wig. She smoothed her pleated shawl and put on her sandals.

The princess hurried to the hall, and as she walked in, she noticed that there were even more soldiers than usual. Their faces hard like the statues in the temple. Anisenath drew in her breath as she noticed that her golden chair had been placed next to the king. As soon as her father saw her, he lifted his hand and welcomed her to his side. She gave him a shy smile and hurried to her seat. The servants and soldiers bowed as she made her way to her throne.

"Anisenath, welcome." Her father patted her hand as she took her place next to him.

She gave him a side glance and noticed that he was dressed in his usual half-pleated kilt around his body with a pleated section drawn to the front. He also wore the leopard skin over his shoulders to symbolise power, and on his head today he wore the Nemes with its striped linen headcloth tied at the back of the head. Each side of the lappets came down to his shoulders. A rearing cobra decorated the middle of the headdress.

Anisenath frowned. Her father did not wear his Nemes usually, especially with the cobra, the sign of protection for the Pharaoh. Whom would he need protection from? She was most intrigued. She noticed Amenhotep was also present. Omar, the chief scribe, sat cross-legged with two other scribes ready to take notes.

A soldier walked in and made an announcement. "Shiphrah and Puah, the Hebrew midwives." As his booming voice resounded around the room, everyone grew silent.

Anisenath's mouth rounded into an *O*. So, it was the midwives her father had called again. Had they failed their assignment? She leaned forward and watched with interest as the soldier bowed and moved to one side, allowing the women to walk in. Was Pharaoh going to execute them?

Chapter Five

The two Hebrew women walked in, escorted by one soldier on each side. Their faces were serene and their bodies poised. As usual, they seemed unafraid of being in the presence of Pharaoh. The women bowed and stood with their heads inclined.

Pharaoh leaned forward and stared down at the women. Silence resided. Anisenath shuffled uncomfortably in her seat. What was her father waiting for? She remained motionless, with a sudden urge to turn her head and see what he was up to. Finally, she heard him speak.

"Is it true?"

The princess frowned. Was what true?

The taller woman with the red-and-white striped head veil spoke first. She lifted her eyes to Pharaoh. "It is true, your majesty."

At her declaration, Pharaoh stood and roared. "How dare you!" His anger vibrated in the room—even the pillars shook. "You are letting the Hebrew boys live after I commanded you to kill them?"

Anisenath sucked in her breath. Everyone else in the room had paled, and although the scribes had their heads down, writing on papyrus and dipping their reed brushes in ink, she could see their hands tremble. Everyone seemed afraid of her father, yet these women were not. What was their secret? Maybe being Hebrew just made them brave.

Pharaoh walked down the few steps from his throne and stood in front of the women.

"Why did you defy my command? Do you not know that I will kill you for this?" His Nemes shook as he spoke.

The other woman with the darker veil lifted her head and spoke. "May I explain to you, great Pharaoh, what has occurred?"

Pharaoh did not say a word; instead, he clenched and unclenched his fists. Finally, he waved his hand for her to speak as he walked back up to his throne and sat down. He leaned forward, placed his elbow on his knee, and rested his chin on his hand.

"Your Majesty," the Hebrew woman began, "we did not intend to show disrespect by not obeying your command."

Pharaoh grunted.

"The Hebrew women are robust, stronger than the Egyptian women, and they give birth to their babies before we can go to help them." The woman paused and looked around. "Great Pharaoh, we want to obey your command but have found it difficult to follow through as the Hebrew women tend to their own births and do not need us."

Anisenath held her breath. The Hebrew woman made a great point, yet she wondered if it was true. Nevertheless, this news brought abundant happiness to her heart. The baby boys were alive! The princess turned to look at her father, who had sat up straighter.

"Is what you say true?" he asked.

The women nodded and bowed their heads. "Yes, my lord." They chorused in unison.

Pharaoh stood and lifted both his arms as if he was blessing the room. "Today I give a new command . . . write this down." His eyes stared at each person in the room, and finally his eyes rested on Anisenath. "From this day onward, as the new moon rises, every single boy child born to a Hebrew will be thrown in the Nile River!"

Gasps and murmurs erupted in the room, and Anisenath covered her mouth. *Oh, Father.* Her heart trembled to think of so many babies dying unnecessarily.

The noise died down as the king brought his arms down and turned to the women. "Let every girl child live, but destroy the boys. I have spoken. Let it be done as I say!"

Anisenath felt tears threatening to erupt and did not want to cause a scene. She turned her head away. She wanted to run and hide, but it was against the rule to embarrass the king and leave without his permission. She took a few deep breaths and fought hard to control her emotions.

With the new command in order, her father dismissed the Hebrew women and half of the room. Only Amenhotep, Omar, and Anisenath were left. Her father asked Omar to read back the notes. Omar nodded and read. Anisenath drowned the voice, not wanting to hear about the cruel command. She could not wait to be given permission to leave the room.

Three long nights went past, and Anisenath found it hard to sleep. Every time she closed her eyes, images of crocodiles, water, and crying babies invaded her dreams. With a thumping heart, she would wake up and sit in bed, unable to fall asleep.

"My lady?" The voice of Onofria, her maid, made her jump, as she did not hear her come in.

"Onofria! You startled me." Anisenath put her hand to her beating heart.

"I apologise, my lady, but I heard you scream and wanted to come and see if all was well?" Onofria moved closer to her bed with a cup in her hand.

"Oh, I did not realise I screamed." Anisenath rubbed her forehead. "I had a nightmare and now cannot fall asleep."

Her maidservant nodded and extended the cup. "I have brought you Karkadéh to drink. This will help your overall being."

Anisenath forced a slight smile. "Thank you, Onofria." She reached for the cup and took a little sip. The fruity sweetness washed over her. "Delicious," she murmured and took another sip.

Soon after she had sent Onofria to bed, Anisenath stood and walked over to the big window that overlooked the waters below. She sat on the plush seat that was placed under the window and leaned her head back, admiring the brightness of the moon.

There seemed to be a heaviness lingering over Egypt. She felt the sadness that enveloped the days, and a darkened gloom resided in her heart. She closed her eyes and let the soft breeze enter her room and run over her face. She decided that in the morning she would take a bath in her secluded area of the Nile and wash away the sadness. But before her bath, she had to burn some incense so the gods could grant her peace.

Chapter Six

Early the next morning, as the sun rose, Anisenath informed Onofria of her plan to bathe in the Nile.

The maid's eyes lit up. "That is a wonderful idea, my lady. I will prepare the oils and perfumes for you. I will also bring two other maids to assist."

Anisenath thanked her and hurried to dress in a soft linen white dress. She rubbed Sef's sleeping head and watched him nap peacefully. Two other maidservants arrived, painted her face, and dressed her head with a long braided wig. Anisenath smoothed the sides as she looked at herself in the mirror. Her dark eyes appeared bigger today as the black kohl enhanced them. She asked the maids to add a collar of jewellery around her neck and bracelets on her arms and wrists.

"Onofria, bring incense as well," she called as Onofria scurried around the room collecting all they would need for her bath. "I need to offer some scented fire to the gods. I feel they are unhappy."

"Yes, my lady." Onofria took oils and other essentials with her.

It was not long before Anisenath kneeled on the cushion on the ground, chanting and burning incense to the gods. Her weary spirit had *almost* given up the possibility of her ever having a baby. She felt a touch of resentment creep into her heart as she finished praying. She had been worshipping for years, yet they remained silent. What was she doing wrong? She closed her eyes and petitioned the gods again. After a few minutes of silence and solitude, she completed the ritual and was ready to bathe.

Onofria walked up ahead, making her way toward the secluded area where the princess took her bath away from prying eyes. Anisenath followed her down the back steps to a tranquil corner where birds flew above, squawking as they made their way south. Green bushes and long river reeds lined the banks. The Hebrew slaves had built a spacious bench and table for her mother when she was alive. They were made of limestone to prevent decay from flooding seasons and rain.

Anisenath and her mother could sit and dry off once their bath was finished and place their ointments and drying material on the table. Anisenath, with the help of Bihiti, one of the maids, removed her heavy, thick wig and cleaned her painted face. She then spread juniper oil to calm and cleanse her skin. The aromatic smell of woody, sweet scent drifted up the princess nose.

Onofria worked lotus oil in Anisenath's hair, and the welcome smell of floral and earthy aromas danced through her body. The oils always made her feel relaxed. Her problems washed away during her pampering session.

Soon, Anisenath took off her sandals and dipped her toes into the cool water. Slowly, she descended further in, until her shivering body was accustomed to the temperature. In the background, Bihiti played soft music with the arghul, a single-reed woodwind instrument Anisenath enjoyed listening to when she bathed. The princess dipped in and out of the water, rinsing off the oils on her skin. She lifted her eyes and observed the still blue sky. It was going to be a sweltering day with the absence of clouds.

She swam a little further until she was submerged up to her shoulders. The cool waters lapped around her body, and she felt the tension disperse. While she drifted into a calm place, a sudden rustling noise startled her. Anisenath opened her eyes and looked around.

She turned her head to see Onofria and Nefret busy collecting the oils and her outer clothing from the ground, while Bihiti continued playing the music. They seemed unaware of what she had heard. Maybe she had imagined the sound. She immersed her body again and washed her dark hair. It felt invigorating to wear no wig and have no paint on her body—it gave her a sense of freedom. The sound came again, and this time she felt panic begin to stir within her.

The princess scanned her surroundings, and at once she saw something floating amongst the tall grass. She squinted; from the distance, it looked like a baby crocodile. The skin looked thick, leathery, and scale like. She gave a little squeal and swam toward her maids.

"Onofria!" she shouted. "There's something in the water amongst the reeds." She pointed weakly into the distance.

Onofria and Nefret hurried to her side as they entered the waters. Bihiti stopped the music, and the princess stood close to the steps, ready to escape if needed. Slowly, Onofria walked further into the river.

"What did you see, my lady?" she stretched her neck and skimmed the area.

"It looked like a small crocodile," she said, faintly afraid of what could be lurking beneath.

Onofria reached the point where the princess pointed, and she let out a laugh. "My lady, it looks something like a child's toy. A basket of some sort."

Cautiously, the princess went to her maid and peered over her shoulder. The basket disentangled itself from the reeds and drifted out of the reefs, where it became visible.

"Oh, Onofria, you are correct, it is a basket! I do not think it is a toy." She noticed it looked a little big, and her curiosity was peaked. "Retrieve it, please. I must look inside."

Onofria swam slowly to the basket and pushed it toward the princess until it came to a stop.

Filled with awe, Anisenath stared at the strange basket made of papyrus. By the smell, it seemed to have been coated with tar and pitch. The potent scent itched her delicate nose.

Carefully, she lifted the lid and peered inside. The puckered face of a baby met her eyes, and with an open mouth, the baby began to cry, disturbing the early morning peace.

Anisenath gasped. "It's a baby!" Her throat constricted at the thought of this precious child being in the Nile's crocodile-infested waters. Who would do such a cruel act?

The child continued crying. His tiny hands balled into fists, and his fat little legs were flinging everywhere. He looked about twelve weeks old, with ruddy cheeks and little rolls on his arms. What caught her attention was the cloth, the colour of dust, which covered his body.

"Hebrew!" Anisenath breathed the words, and her eyes widened as she touched the fabric.

Chapter Seven

Her heart vibrated in her soul, and she instantly knew the story. The unknown mother of the baby had resorted to this means of hiding her baby in a basket to preserve the life of her precious little one. Tears welled in the princess's eyes as they rolled down her cheeks unashamedly.

This mother did what *she* would have done in the same situation. She would have done anything to save her child from death. From the death sentence her own father had given upon the little Hebrew boys.

Gently, she took hold of one of his chubby hands, and he grabbed and pulled at her thumb. A giggle escaped her lips. The baby was strong, just like all Hebrews. He tightened his grip on her finger. She smiled and leaned her face close to his whimpering one.

"Hello, little one," she whispered. "You are safe now." She ran her free hand over his little forehead and on one side of his face. The gentle touch and soothing words quieted his anxious spirit. He looked at her with alert brown eyes, and he cooed. Anisenath's heart melted.

"Onofria, help me take him to shore." The two maids pushed the little boat toward the steps. Anisenath lifted her drenched gown and walked up the steps as fast as her wet feet allowed. She turned and waited for Onofria to hand her the baby.

The maid's face looked perplexed, a little anxious. Anisenath waved her hand. "Do not look so concerned. All will be well." She took the baby into her arms and held him close.

"You are so handsome." She ran her index finger along the softness of his right cheek. "Would you like to live in the palace?" At the cooing of the baby, Anisenath laughed. "Of course you would. Yes, you would." Her voice had softened as she talked to him.

"He is a handsome baby, my lady," Bihiti whispered, looking over the princess's shoulder.

Anisenath grinned. "He is indeed. He will make a great pharaoh one day."

"A pharaoh?" The shock in Onofria's voice was clear.

"Yes, a pharaoh. Why are you so stunned?" Anisenath felt little bubbles of anger rumble inside. The emotion took her by surprise, but being questioned was something she could not tolerate in this moment.

"I mean no disrespect, Princess Anisenath. I only assumed you would return him since he is a Hebrew child." Onofria's voice trailed off at seeing the princess narrow her eyes.

"Are you not aware that all Hebrew baby boys are to be killed? If I return him, he will be put to death." Anisenath shook her head. "The gods of the Nile have brought me a child. He is a gift, and I will adopt him as my own." She held him close to her heart, afraid that a soldier would come and snatch him from her arms. "He will be *my* son, and my father can never lay a hand on him. He will be trained as the next pharaoh of Egypt, and he will do great things." She bent over and kissed his small face.

"Of course, my lady." Onofria busied herself with the basket.

The baby cooed, and Anisenath felt laughter erupt. "My son." She lifted him up in the air and gently swirled the chubby baby.

"My lady, should we wrap the baby in his cloth?" Onofria stepped out of the water, holding the Hebrew material in her hand. "He might get a little cold with your wet body next to his."

"You are correct! I did not realise this." Anisenath reached for the cloth and wrapped the child in it. She held him close again and admired his little face. The baby opened his mouth and moved his head toward her breast. "I do not have milk for you, little one."

Suddenly his face scrunched up again, and he cried.

"I think he is hungry." Nefret stood next to the princess. "My son cried just like him when he was around that age."

"We need to feed him . . . What would he eat besides milk?" Anisenath looked at Onofria.

"Breast milk, my lady. There is nothing else you can feed babies that small." Onofria came to the princess and leaned over to admire his face.

"I cannot feed." Anisenath worried. She did not want the baby to go hungry.

"We will need to find a nurse. Someone who has a baby of her own and can feed him milk . . . preferably a Hebrew to connect with the child." Onofria's wise words had Anisenath and the two maids nodding in agreement.

"Make haste, Onofria. Change into dry clothes and find the woman." Anisenath leaned her face on the baby's and whispered soothing words. As she rocked him back and forth, his eyes fluttered. She was so engrossed in seeing him fall asleep that the sound of a small voice startled her.

Out of the waters and coming up the stairs was a young girl with a striped blue-and-red tunic and a red sash around her waist. Her curly hair lay loose with a ribbon across her forehead. Anisenath gaped. It was a *Hebrew* child! Unable to speak, she watched spellbound as the girl came to her. The princess tightened her hold on the baby.

Onofria moved in front of the princess and looked down at the child. Anisenath touched her shoulder lightly. "It is well, Onofria. She is just a child."

The girl waited for the maid to move to the side to speak. "My lady, I was playing amongst the reeds, and I overheard you need a nurse for your baby. Shall I call a nurse of the Hebrew women so she may feed him?" The little girl inclined her head, but her eagerness and breathlessness told Anisenath another story. The girl was lying about something.

Finding her voice, Anisenath finally spoke. "What is your name?"

"Miriam, my lady."

"Why did you play amongst the reeds? Do you not know that the Nile is dangerous?" Onofria's sharp tone startled the little girl, and the child stepped back.

"Yes, but I often . . . forget," Miriam stammered, giving a slight side glance at the baby, her big brown eyes softening.

"Onofria, please." Anisenath pursed her lips and watched her maid's angry face.

"I beg your pardon, my lady. I have concern for children playing near the . . . crocodiles," she added lamely.

Anisenath turned to the child, who had her eyes fixated on the baby. Her heart tightened. This *must* be the baby's sister. Had she been keeping an eye on her baby brother? Tears welled in Anisenath's eyes and she looked away.

"I know a nurse who can feed your baby, my lady. Would you like me to bring her to you?" The girl stared at Anisenath with wide eyes, waiting eagerly for her answer.

Anisenath's mind swirled with turmoil. She did not want to hand over the child, yet she knew she could not feed him. He was too small and could die if someone did not give him proper food. Besides, she reasoned, he would soon be in her arms again. It would only be for a little while.

She planted a smile on her face and turned to Miriam. "That is a very fine idea. Please bring the Hebrew woman to nurse my son." Anisenath reached out and tugged a curl from the girl's hair. "You are a very good . . . little girl."

The girl's shoulder relaxed, and she grinned. "I will return as fast as I can."

"One more thing." The princess lifted her finger. "Do not meet me here. Come to that area over there with the big pillars. I will wait in the garden for your return." Anisenath pointed to the palace.

The little girl gulped and nodded. Giving the princess one more bow, she ran off behind some tall grass further down the banks.

The four women watched in silence as the girl disappeared. Anisenath turned to Onofria and enveloped the baby further into her embrace. "I need to change out of these wet clothes. Let us make haste before they return!"

Chapter Eight

For the next hour, her room was chaotic. Clothes, makeup, wigs, sandals, oils, and perfumes were pulled out from her elaborate ivory storage chests. Luxuriously scented oils were lathered onto her skin, and the three maids worked frantically.

The baby had been dressed and was wide awake, moving his little arms and legs in unison. Each time Anisenath looked over at the bed, she felt a surge of joy take over. Sef growled at the tiny human and watched from afar.

The princess laughed. "Sef, you better like him because he is my son! The *next* pharaoh." Pride tinged her tone.

He hissed and scurried out the door. She chuckled. Maybe he was jealous. The baby began crying again.

While she finished dressing, Bihiti took the now whimpering baby in her arms and rocked him back and forth until he fell asleep.

"My lady, you are now ready," Onofria said. "You are a vision of beauty." The maids stood back, admiring their work.

Anisenath stood and glanced at herself in the mirror. She nodded in approval. She *had* to emphasise her position by dressing in her finest. The Hebrew woman needed to see she was indeed a princess and the utmost care had to be given to her son.

She smoothed her fitted white linen gown adorned with tiny precious stones all over. A thick jewelled collar with an intricate design rested around her neck, rings on her ears, and bracelets on her arms complemented her elegant look. Onofria had decorated the princess's head with a vulture-gold headdress over her long wig. Anisenath leaned closer to the mirror and looked at her face. Even her painted face looked more delicate than usual. Her maids had outdone themselves.

Satisfied, she looked at the three women in the room. "I am now ready to go . . . but first . . ." She paused and looked around. "I need a scribe. I need to get a document done immediately. Nefret, get a scribe."

While the maid rushed off, the princess opened a small jewellery box and rummaged through her gold finery. "Onofria, do I have a small bracelet?"

"Yes, my lady." She hurried to an adjoining room where Anisenath kept a few other belongings and came back with a wooden box. She lifted the lid and pulled out a tiny gold bracelet. "This box has the bracelets you used to wear as a child."

Anisenath gasped. She had forgotten she had those. Reverently, she took the bracelet and walked to her sleeping baby. "Bihiti, place the baby on the bed." The maid did as she was told. Ever so gently, the princess opened his little wrap and exposed a tiny arm. She rubbed the bracelet between her hands and blew on it to give it warmth. Then she put it around his little hand and nuzzled it all the way to his upper arm. "There . . . now everyone will know he is the son of a princess."

As she finished wrapping the baby again, Omar the scribe strode in with wide eyes. He held papyrus in his hands and a reed brush behind his ear. Nefret followed close behind. Omar stood with his head inclined, waiting for the command.

"Omar, thank you for coming." Anisenath moved toward her writing desk and motioned for him to sit. "I need a brief letter written urgently. I write my own letters, but I do not want to get ink on my dress."

Omar nodded and ignored her gesture to sit at the desk; instead, he moved away from the door and sat on the floor. He looked up at her. "Yes, my lady?"

Anisenath paced the room. "Write the following." She cleared her throat and began.

"I, Anisenath Nashwa Jendayi, princess of the Nile and daughter of the divine intermediary ruler of gods and Egypt, the great Pharaoh, declare that in this Hebrew household, my son, the child I drew out of the waters, a gift from our goddess Anuket, will be taken care of while he is nursed. No hand or decree can touch him. If you dare disobey, you will die under the hand of Pharaoh. Let it be done as I, Princess Anisenath, have commanded."

Anisenath's voice cracked with emotion at the thought that she could save one Hebrew baby from death. She was even more determined to adopt her son.

Omar's eyes flickered with confusion as he looked up at the sleeping baby in Bihiti's arms. Quickly, he lowered his head again and finished writing the last words. He added the royal symbol and rolled up the paper into a scroll. Omar stood and handed the paper to Onofria and bowed.

"Thank you, Omar," Anisenath whispered and turned to Onofria. "It is time." She turned to her other two maids and said, "Onofria, you will carry the note. Bihiti and Nefret, you will be my sunshade bearers. The heat will be too stifling, and I do not want the baby to burn his delicate skin." Her maids bowed.

Anisenath took the sleeping baby from Bihiti's arms and walked ahead, followed by her two maids. Onofria followed farther behind, holding the papyrus roll. The heat of the day seemed to suffocate the princess as she stepped outside.

The sun was bright and burning strong. She moved the baby closer to her chest and pulled the cloth to cover his little face. Her maids moved closer to her, each holding a long pole topped with feathers. Instantly, the shade brought relief to her body. As the princess lifted her head, she saw a woman and a child standing in the garden where she had asked the child to come. Her heart thundered in her chest. She felt scared. *Stand strong, be brave, do not weaken,* she told herself with every step she took. As soon as she reached them, both the woman and child bowed. She looked at the woman dressed in a simple white tunic and blue veil on her head. A sash of green adorned her waist.

"Thank you for coming," Anisenath spoke as Onofria moved to one side while Nefret and Bihiti stood still, covering her and her child. "I understand you can nurse my son?"

The woman nodded, and her eyes travelled to the baby who lay covered in the princess's arms. "It would be an honour to take care of your baby," she whispered.

"What is your name?" Anisenath asked.

The Hebrew woman looked up as her light brown eyes glimmered. "Jochebed, from the tribe of Levi, wife to Amram, the Hebrew slave."

Anisenath noticed Jochebed had the same serenity as the Hebrew midwives. What was their secret? Their God?

"I need the greatest care for him." Anisenath looked down at the stirring baby. "I will pay you well for his care, and you will no longer work as a slave."

Jochebed's brown eyes flickered with emotion. "I will do as you request."

Anisenath watched the woman's face and noticed how her eyes softened and lingered on the sleeping baby. Eyes filled with love? The princess tilted her head to one side. As she opened her mouth to speak, the baby squirmed. His little mouth opened, and he wailed.

"He is hungry." Anisenath uncovered his wriggling body. "I will not make him wait any longer. Please take great care of him." Her eyes filled with tears as she bent over and gave the baby a light kiss on his cheek. She handed him over to Jochebed and watched as the woman welcomed him into her arms. The baby twisted his little head to her chest, and his mouth went straight to Jochebed's breast.

"There, there, little one. I will feed you soon." Jochebed touched his forehead with one finger. Instantly the child stopped crying and looked around until his face met Jochebed's.

Anisenath watched as he cooed and smiled with the Hebrew woman. Love radiated from her face. The familiarity between them was undeniable.

The princess gasped and covered her mouth with her hand. This *was* the baby's mother! Anisenath wanted to cry with joy. The gods were good; they had reconnected a mother and son. *Her* son now.

"I have a decree for you to take and keep safe. No soldier can touch him. My father's decree does not affect him." She motioned for Onofria to hand over the paper.

"Miriam, please take hold of that document." Jochebed smiled. "Thank you, my lady. I have no words to express my gratitude for delivering this little boy who was sentenced to death. On behalf of his mother, I thank you."

She watched as the mother touched her son's upper arm and ran her finger over the bracelet.

"That is a symbol that he belongs to me and he is royal. No hand can be laid upon him."

Jochebed nodded with tears spilling down her face. "May the God of Abraham bless you for your compassion and kindness, and may he shine his face on you today and forever."

Anisenath gaped at the beautiful blessing she had received. Never had words to a god sounded so musical. She inclined her head and smiled. "Thank you." Her voice cracked, and she quickly cleared her throat.

Composing herself, she gave a few more minutes of instructions, kissed the baby good-bye, and watched as Miriam, Jochebed, and the baby left the Egyptian grounds and went to theirs. With their backs toward her, Anisenath let the tears flow freely, her heart yearning to have her baby back.

Her only consolation was that he was safe and death could not touch him. She lifted her eyes to the sky and whispered a thank-you. With one last glance toward the disappearing figures in the distance, Anisenath turned back to her palace and went in search of her father.

She knew it would elate him to know that the gods had granted her wish and she was finally a mother. She wiped the tears away as a laugh escaped her lips. She could not wait for her son to be back home. He would make a magnificent Pharaoh, she was sure of that.

Epilogue

1509 BC, Egypt

Princess Anisenath stood behind the opened doors of the meeting hall, watching her son standing at the balcony looking below. He was leaning over in a pensive pose as a tinge of sadness and anger washed over his face. She knew that look too well.

Jochebed, his birth mother, had taught him he belonged to the Hebrews and how his God had saved him from death when he was a little boy. The look on his face was of pain and sorrow that his people were suffering while he lived in the splendour of the Egyptian court.

"Anisenath! Why do you hide behind the door?"

At the sound of her father's voice, the princess twirled around, her hand to her heart. "My father, you startled me! And I am not hiding. I am watching my son."

Pharaoh stopped next to her. "He is a handsome boy, is he not, my flower?" he smiled. "The gods blessed you with a true warrior and strong young man. The Nile produced a fine pharaoh."

Anisenath grinned, and her heart expanded with love for the boy. "How is he doing in his studies?" she cocked her head to the side and looked at her father.

"He is receiving the highest civil and military training. He is a natural military leader and may I add a favourite amongst the army." Pharaoh laughed. "The wisdom he speaks with is remarkable. He has a noteworthy character. A fine, fine king."

Anisenath felt pride take over her heart. With his eyes still on her son, Pharaoh walked out to the balcony and grabbed the boy by his shoulders.

"My son! How is the next pharaoh faring?"

Moses turned around and laughed. "Grandfather Pharaoh, it is good to see you today. I'm faring well."

Anisenath watched the lovable exchange between her father and Moses and slowly came out and onto the balcony. It had been so many years ago that she had saved him and adopted him as her own; she often forgot he had not been born of her. She felt he was part of her very being.

From the first day she had found him in the basket to now at sixteen years old, she felt he was indeed a real gift. She had drawn him out of the waters and had named him Moses. Even his name felt musical and unique, like her boy. She walked over to stand next to Moses and looked below. Her heart constricted seeing the taskmasters whipping the slaves.

She wondered if amongst the slaves were his brother, Aaron, and sister, Miriam? His parents as well? Her heart went out to him and knew how he felt; she too, despised the cruelty. She looked away from the sad scene below and turned to look at him—his eyes met hers and he smiled. Her heart melted. He was the only one who could melt her heart, which he'd been doing since he was three months old. She had refused to marry again and instead chosen to become Moses's mother. Her father miraculously had not objected.

After much talk between the three of them, Pharaoh left, as he had to meet the high priest Baako in the temple.

"By the way," her father stopped at the doorway. "Amenhotep says Tanith is coming to visit you today."

"Tani is in Egypt?"

Her father nodded and, with a final laugh, left the room.

Anisenath turned to Moses with much joy in her heart. "Oh, my darling, it will be so good to see Tani today."

Moses frowned. "Mother, did you not see her last month?"

The princess laughed. "Last month? Are you sure it was only then?"

He groaned and rolled his eyes. "I better disappear and practice my javelin. I am being tested tomorrow."

"Tani is not here yet, darling. Stay a little longer and tell me about military school."

He chuckled and agreed.

They talked about many things: war, school, girls, and God. At the mention of God, Moses paused. "Mother, do you truly not mind that I worship a different God than you do?" His light brown eyes flickered with concern.

"In Egypt, my son, you can worship *any* god that takes your fancy. I do not object to yours." She gave him a sheepish smile. "I should confess that I like your God too."

His boyish face lit up. "You do?"

She walked to the other side of the balcony and nodded. "He brought you to me, remember?"

He sighed. "My mother . . . I mean, Jochebed always said that God had a purpose for me and that is why I was saved."

Anisenath took his strong hand in hers. "It is okay for you to call Jochebed your mother. She bore you. She saved your life by putting you in the basket. I do not mind." She leaned her head against his shoulder. "My son, you will be great one day. I feel it."

"I hope so, Mother. I hope so." He looked down from the balcony again. "One day, the hand of my God will free my people!"

Anisenath lifted her head and watched his determined face harden. She knew he was right. He was destined for greatness. Maybe even beyond being a pharaoh. With a little squeeze of his hand, she agreed. "And I will be right beside you the whole time," She muttered.

Two

Zaria: Purposeful Queen of Sheba

*When the queen of Sheba heard about the fame of Solomon and his
relationship to the Lord, she came to test Solomon with hard questions.
Arriving at Jerusalem with a very great caravan—with camels carrying spices,
large quantities of gold, and precious stones—she came to Solomon and talked
with him about all that she had on her mind.*

—1 Kings 10:1-2

Find the story in 1 Kings 10:1-29 and 2 Chronicles 9:1-31.

Prologue

969 BC, Sheba

Queen Zaria closed her eyes for a few minutes, basking in the coolness of the natural pool behind her palace. Beautiful tall palm trees and greenery imported from Mesopotamia surrounded the area, bringing in a fresh breeze and respite from the heat of the desert. If only she could stay there forever and forget all the diplomacy and business she needed to face now that she was queen. Zaria opened her eyes and sighed.

It's not that she did not know she would be queen one day, but she did not expect to be queen so soon. Her father had been killed in battle twelve months ago, and the weight of ruling the kingdom was heavy on her shoulders. She still remembered her sister, Naja, begging their father to stay home and let the soldiers battle the war themselves, but he had insisted that he needed to be present and see up close how things were progressing.

"Father, we need you in the kingdom. You cannot be gone for so many months while the battle is raging. Who knows how long that will be?" Zaria crossed her arms, feeling a little angry inside. She was afraid that something would happen to him.

"A king always thinks of his people before himself." He touched her chin gently. "I will be back soon, my darling. All will be well."

"What if something happens to you?" Naja asked as her big emerald-coloured eyes filled with tears.

"Oh, my little Naja, nothing will happen to me, my love. No need for tears." He wiped her tears with his thumb, then gathered both girls in a tight embrace.

Zaria and Naja held hands as they watched him ride off into the desert with an escort of soldiers. Their hearts heavy.

Eight weeks later, news arrived from the war front. Zaria was sitting with Jaleel, her teacher, learning about the importation and exportation of goods.

"This is so very confusing, Jaleel," Zaria exclaimed as she ran her hands over her thin light blue veil. "I cannot understand the calculations of how we can make money with this."

Jaleel tilted his turban-wrapped head to one side and smiled patiently. "Princess Zaria, give yourself time. All will be clear in due time. Your father has many years of reign. However, it is very important for you to learn."

Zaria exhaled. That was true. At nineteen she still had a lot to learn. She hoped she would be at least forty by the time she became queen, and if anything happened to her, her sister, Naja, would be queen—but at fifteen she was far too young to ascend.

Just as she opened her mouth to reply, Ehsan, the palace news bearer, barged into the study room.

"Princess Zaria!"

The agitation in his voice made hers and Jaleel's head snap up. Her heart beat faster as she looked at the boy's pale features.

"Yes?" she said.

"Commander Najib, representative in battle of the royal guard would like to see you." The young man kept his head inclined until Zaria talked to him.

"Commander Najib? Here?" This did not sound good. "Take me to him, Ehsan."

"Yes, my lady."

She followed the servant boy down the long ivory-coloured corridors of the palace—its walls painted with elaborate illustrations of the desert and palm trees. It was a beautifully coloured wall that Zaria loved to admire each time she walked past. But today her heart worried.

What news could Najib have brought? Had something happened to her father? Her chest constricted, and she took a deep breath. *Calm down*, she told herself. Commanders usually visited families to bring updates from their family members fighting in battle. Maybe he brought a letter from her father. She smiled and hurried her pace. She could not wait to read her father's letter, if he had sent one.

Ehsan opened the door to the reception room, where the princess's father did all his meetings and negotiations. It was a room that frightened her because one day it might be hers. The servant held the door open while she walked through. Her face lit up when she saw Commanders Najib's back toward her. He faced the vast window that overlooked the luscious garden her father had created for his pleasure. He said he did not want to have the view of the vastness of the desert. The water fountains, palm trees, and greenery created a wonderful oasis for him and anyone who visited.

"Commander Najib?"

At the sound of her voice, Najib turned and bowed. He moved from the window and went toward her.

"Princess Zaria."

"How is my father?" she blurted.

The commander glanced at Ehsan and motioned with his head for him to leave. "Please close the door."

Ehsan bowed and did as he was asked.

By now Zaria's apprehension was building. Something was not right. She watched Ehsan leave. As soon as the door clicked shut, she turned back to the commander and asked, "Is my father injured?"

Najib came over and took her slim hands into his calloused ones. Her hands stiffened under his touch. No man was allowed to touch her or her sister. This was against the law. She studied the commander's face and saw no malice on his face. Instead, his eyes glistened as he spoke.

"Your father is dead, Princess." The grip of his hands tightened.

Suddenly the room spun as she felt the blood drain from her body. "Dead?" She grabbed the commander's hands with all her might and waited for the dizziness to subside. She must be in an unpleasant dream. She closed her eyes and opened them again. But her bad dream was real. Her father was *dead*.

"How?" Her voice shook.

"An arrow from the rival army hit his chest." Najib cleared his throat. "The wound was fatal, and he bled to death . . . everything was tried, but it failed."

Zaria tore her hands from Najib's grip and ran to the door. Opening it, she stuck her tear-strained face out the doorway and saw Ehsan standing outside. "Call on Naja immediately!" she shouted.

The boy bowed and ran down the hallway. She did not bother to close the door; instead, she leaned her head against it.

"Princess Zaria, come and take a seat. You can tell Naja gently while sitting here."

She could hear Najib's voice, but she did not turn her face to see the chair he pointed to. Instead, she shook her head and stood at the door, waiting for her sister. Having the door open made her feel less like she was being buried alive.

"Zaria?"

The soft voice of her sister broke through her haziness. "Naja." Sobs tore through her body as she wrapped her arms around her younger sibling. "Father has been killed."

The pain in Naja's cries ripped at Zaria's soul as the girls stood at the door wrapped in each other's arms, weeping.

Life would no longer be the same for them.

Chapter One

966 BC, Sheba

It was a hot evening as Zaria and her sister sat in Zaria's room talking about King Solomon, a great and wise king of the North. Naja was convinced that he was perfect, but the queen was not so sure.

"Naja, do you believe all that you read?" Zaria laughed at her sister and turned back her attention to her personal maidservant, who was untying her elaborate hairstyle and getting her ready for bed.

"Not that I believe everything I read, Zaria." Naja moved over to sit on a little white cushioned chair that had been imported from Persia. "I hear the talks and rumours from servants and from government officials and merchants I see in the markets." She flicked her lustrous black hair and smoothed her white luxurious pyjamas she had bought from a merchant of the North.

"You need to be careful what you pick up." Zaria glanced at her younger sister and sighed, Naja could be so innocent at times. "Although I have heard of King Solomon from the north, I do not believe the illusory stories of his great wisdom *or* wealth."

"I do not understand why not. This man sounds absolutely wonderful! Can you believe his father chose *him* to be king over his brother?" Naja's unusual emerald-coloured eyes sparkled, her lovely face lost in the wonder of King Solomon. "And his father, King David, said *he* would build the temple. Which is a great honour. Their temple means everything to them."

Zaria wondered how a father could choose between two sons and give the kingdom to the younger one. It would be as if her father had chosen Naja to be queen instead of her. At the thought of her father, her heart saddened.

It had been four years since his death, but to her it felt like he had only been gone a few weeks. She missed his gentle, kind face, his wise words, and his presence. After their mother had died during Naja's birth, the girls had been raised by their father, who doted on them and did not mind that they were girls. He believed that the rightful heir to the throne could be a male or female. He believed in equality, which was rare in her part of the world. She was already beginning to feel the difference between how her father was treated and how she was perceived, especially by Alim, the vexing advisor to the kingdom.

"Relax your back, my lady," Yara, her maid, instructed as she massaged her shoulders. "There is a lot of tension. I will run a bath for you and add frankincense oil to soothe your body." Yara finished brushing her wavy long hair and hurried to the other side of the room where her father had had a room installed for them to bathe in privacy away from prying eyes. Zaria loved her bathing room.

"Thank you, Yara," she called as the short maid dressed in a blue tunic and gold headdress disappeared into the room.

"Oh, and you should hear the latest story I have read in *Sheba's Periodical!*" Naja stood and ran to her sister's side waving the country's most loved and read scroll. Zaria grabbed the ivory hairbrush with one hand and began running it through her hair. "Would you care for me to tell you the story while you bathe?"

Zaria was about to say no, but the excited look on her sister's face made her only nod. She knew her sister meant well. Besides, a good story always helped her forget the present.

Once in her bath of frankincense-scented water, Zaria closed her eyes and let the water alleviate her tired body. She had been in and out of political and financial meetings all day, and her brain hurt. No wonder the tight shoulders.

"Are you ready?" The sound of her sister's voice made her open her eyes and smile as Yara vacated the room and left them in solitude.

"Yes dear, I'm ready."

Naja took a seat on a stool that was at the foot of the bath. "This one is a story of how King Solomon saved a baby from being killed!"

"Oh?"

"Wait till you hear the details!" she rubbed her hands together. "It's about two women who were harlots. They—"

"Naja, what kind of story is this?" Zaria interrupted, horrified, leaning forward from her relaxed position, water splashing onto the marble floors.

"No interruptions, Zaria. Trust me, it's a great one, and there is nothing inappropriate about it."

Zaria pursed her lips, leaned back into her bath, and closed her eyes as her sister began the tale.

King Solomon lifted his eyes to the God of Abraham and opened his palms in prayer and asked God to give him wisdom as he faced the courtroom.

"God of my father, David, please hear my prayer. The courtroom is filled with people who need help and resolution. I cannot do this on my own, Lord; fill me with the wisdom you promised, and may you speak through me. Amen." Taking a deep breath, the king pushed the door open and went to his throne.

Silence descended as he took a seat and motioned for the first case to take place. He was intrigued at some problems that had arisen; some involved land dispute, while others were about dowries that were not fulfilled. One case in particular made him smile, as a child of about seven told him he was upset because his goats kept running away. The young boy did not know how to handle the situation. Solomon solved the problem for the boy by telling him to build a fence with his father to prevent them from going away. He would allow the young child to gather wood from his own lands behind the palace. The boy and his father went off gleefully. Hours later and feeling exhausted, the king stood, ready to retire for the day.

All cases were closed, or so he thought. The shouts of people and the cry of a baby outside the courtroom caught his attention. He squinted to see what was happening. One of his advisors entered the room and approached his throne tentatively.

"My lord, we have one more case which—"

"Can it wait until tomorrow?" Solomon interrupted, hoping to leave so he could rest.

"No, my lord. This situation is . . . delicate." The man cleared his throat uncomfortably. "It's regarding two . . . harlots."

Solomon's eyes widened. *Harlots? Oh, dear Lord, this does not sound good.* "Allow them in." He walked back to his throne and took a seat.

In minutes, the room was filled. Soldiers, spectators, the king's advisory team, and the two women walked in. As soon as the king saw them, he drew in his breath. They were dressed in ladies-of-the-night attire. Low-cut dresses showing more than what was appropriate, splits on the sides of their dresses, heavily painted faces, unveiled heads, and coarse-looking jewels. The one dressed in crimson held a basket in her hands. A tiny baby lay sleeping. Solomon could only wonder what these women's dispute was all about.

He lifted his hands and asked for silence. "Your names?"

The woman in red spoke first. "I'm Noa and this is my baby." Her dark eyes filled with disdain turned to the other woman. "*That* woman is Keziah."

The woman wearing the yellow dress whose name was Keziah narrowed her eyes and glared at Noa. Solomon was intrigued.

"What problem has arisen between you?" His voice rang loud and clear, and the room quietened.

Keziah's long, curly hair cascaded to her waist; she flipped a few curls out of her face and began to talk. "Pardon me, my lord. Both Noa and I had babies a few days apart from each other. I had my child first, and three days later Noa also bore a baby boy." The woman paused and swallowed. "We share the same house, and no one else lives with us. Therefore, there are no witness to what I will tell you." Keziah glanced at Noa, who remained silent and had placed the baby in the basket on the bottom step of the king's throne. "One night, while your servant was asleep, in the middle of the night, Noa accidentally lay on her baby and killed him!"

A sob escaped from Noa's lips, and shaking her head, she covered her face. "Not true. That is not true!"

King Solomon lifted his hand. "Noa, I will ask you to speak later. Please allow Keziah to finish."

Noa nodded slowly and wiped her face. Makeup ran down her cheeks.

Keziah cleared her throat and continued. "When she saw her baby dead, she took *my* son from my side while I slept and put him by her breast, and the dead son she placed next to me." Keziah turned to look at the audience when murmuring erupted. She nodded. "The next day, when I woke up, I noticed in the morning light that he was not the baby I had borne. It was *not* my little boy but *hers*!" Keziah almost screeched the last words and pointed a long painted nail to Noa.

Noa fell to the king's feet, sobbing, "No! My lord, my king. The living son is mine; and the dead one is hers. She lies!"

"Noa, you know you lie! You will go to Hades for such a lie. This baby is mine!" Keziah's jewellery jiggled as she moved her hands in crazy motions.

The whispers in the room increased with each woman's screams and accusations, as did Solomon's heart and confusion. How was he to know who was speaking the truth? Who did the baby belong to? His thoughts tangled together. What was he to do? Then he felt a whisper saying, *Remember me.*

Lifting his hands up in the air, Solomon asked for silence. A hush fell over the palace room. Closing his eyes, he prayed a short prayer. When he finished, he got back to the matter at hand.

"Keziah claims the baby is hers, yet Noa also claims that this baby belongs to her." Solomon pointed to the basket at the foot of the throne, with the sleeping baby unaware of what was happening. "I have made a decision." Solomon watched as people leaned forward to hear what he was going to say. Both women glared at each other, then turned their attention to the king.

He stood. "Bring me a sword," he commanded.

A gasp rippled through the room. Even his soldiers, who never looked his way or reacted to anything that happened in the room, turned their heads with widened eyes. Keziah gaped, and Noa's hand went to her throat. Solomon frowned. Did they think he was going to kill *them*?

One of his servant boys brought a sword on a pillow. He bowed to the king. The blade shimmered with the sunlight as the king raised it toward the sky.

"Azriel," Solomon called to one of his robust soldiers with a hard face and a scar that ran from his forehead to his throat.

"My lord." He inclined his head and waited for the command.

"Take my sword and cut the baby in half. Give half to Keziah and half to Noa." With that last command, Solomon sat back on his throne to let the scene unfold.

Gasps, murmurs, and shock reverberated throughout the palace room.

Keziah screamed. "No, my lord! No!" She prostrated herself at the king's feet, sobbing uncontrollably.

Solomon pretended not to look at her, but inside his heart cried. Instead, he focused on Azriel carrying the baby, who had awoken and was crying.

Noa moved away from the basket and the soldier.

Solomon felt someone pull the hem of his robe. "My lord, please do not kill the baby. Please let him live." Keziah looked up at him with tears streaming down her face and clothes.

"No, my lord." Noa moved forward, both hands on hips. "Neither I nor Keziah should have him. Cut him in two!" she scowled.

"My lord, I will be your servant until my dying days. Just give the baby to Noa. She can have him." Keziah cried softly now, sitting on the marble floor with her hands covering her face as black tears stained her yellow dress.

King Solomon stood and walked down the steps of his throne. Everyone watched in silence.

Azriel stood with a crying baby and a sword waiting for the king's last command. The king walked over to Azriel and took the baby in his arms. The tiny baby continued wailing.

King Solomon looked down at Keziah and said, "The baby will not be killed! This baby belongs to Keziah. She is his real mother."

Keziah's face melted, and standing up, she fled to her baby and tore him from the king's hands. She showered him with kisses and thanked the king for his kindness over and over again.

Solomon felt tears wet his eyes as he witnessed the love of a mother. So pure. He turned to Noa, but she had fled the room.

The wisdom of the king spread throughout Israel, and they held the king in awe because he had wisdom from God to administer justice.

It was hours before Zaria could fall asleep. The story her sister had read to her played in her mind. There were parts that rang with truth, but others were too fantastic to consider. Being a queen and an inexperienced one at that, she was not to be easily swayed and must always keep her wits alert.

Chapter Two

By midmorning the next day, Zaria sat in the study with Jaleel, learning about trade and political matters. There were things she understood, but there were others she did not understand clearly. Rubbing her temples after many hours of learning, she asked Jaleel if she could take a break.

"You look perplexed, Your Highness." His kind light brown eyes softened as he watched her face. "How can I help?"

Zaria gave him a weary smile. "I cannot fool you, Jaleel." She exhaled. "My mind is filled with confusion." Besides her inability to comprehend all of the trade and political matters, Zaria's thoughts were filled with the king of the North. Solomon. "What do you know about the king of the North?"

"King Solomon?"

She nodded.

"I have heard many great things about him. His wisdom, the way he rules his country." Jaleel's eyes brightened with excitement. "I have been told that he has also built the first known marine fleet for trade on the Red Sea!"

"How is that possible?" Zaria stood and motioned for Jaleel to follow her. "Let us walk in the garden. My mind clears when I am outdoors."

Jaleel opened the back doors that led to the garden, and she stepped outside into the heat of the midmorning sun. "Oh." She wriggled her nose as the humidity struck her face.

"It is too hot, my lady. Let me get the parasol."

Soon they were strolling the garden under her favourite parasol—a gift from her late father. A slight breeze refreshed her face. She was glad she had put her hair up today and worn a simple gown of white with gold and blue fringes.

"As I mentioned before, my lady, the king of the North, has done incredible things for his country. He is not only wise but also extremely wealthy."

"Do you know how Solomon got his wisdom?" She was not sure what intrigued her about this foreign king with his strange ways and unknown God.

"I do not know. However, I believe it has something to do with the God he believes in."

Zaria pursed her lips. "Do you think . . . do you think if I ask to meet this king, he would accept an audience with me?"

"My lady?" Jaleel stopped walking and turned to face her.

"It might sound like I have lost my mind, but I wonder if I may visit this man. I could talk to him and discuss the economy of Sheba." Zaria squinted. She liked the idea very much.

"Hmm." Jaleel started walking again. "Why not discuss the economy with me or some of our educated men?"

"Jaleel, I believe you and my advisors are intelligent, and you know many things. There comes a time when one must seek a wider view from someone outside his or her own country." Zaria rubbed her hands together. "It would be a good idea to have an outsider give me a different perspective."

"You make a valid point," Jaleel said.

"My father was a wise and cultured man. Sheba prospered under his care. We have silver, gold, precious stones, oils, food, and the list is endless." She took a deep breath. "Simply put, the success of Sheba is because of my father's guidance." Zaria lifted her hand when she saw Jaleel open his mouth to protest. "You must admit, I do not have the business or political brain he possessed. Therefore, I must work harder so my beloved country does not crumble . . . under me," she added softly, with a forlorn look on her face.

She watched Jaleel smile and bow his head. "I think you are a wonderful queen. You have more to learn, but you are on the rise to greatness."

She touched his arm and chuckled. "Thank you, Jaleel. I owe it all to your impeccable and, may I add, *patient* teaching." They both laughed, remembering the laborious hours spent repeating the same lessons twice, three times, or more.

"Just so you know, my lady, Jerusalem is at least three thousand miles away, and you would have to travel tortuous roads. It does not sound safe to me."

Zaria harrumphed. "Are you suggesting, because I'm a woman, I cannot make the trip?"

"Oh no, Your Majesty, that was not my intention at all!" Jaleel looked horrified, and he stopped walking again. "I simply wanted to inform you of the distance between us."

Zaria paused and studied his concerned face. "Very well," she said. "What do you suggest I do?"

"We could look at the map and trace the journey from Sheba to Jerusalem, just so you could have a clear idea?"

Her eyes twinkled. "I would like nothing more."

They continued speaking of many things, but especially the wonders and greatness of King Solomon.

That evening during dinner, advisors and noblemen of the region surrounded Zaria, discussing politics and trade. The subjects fascinated her, but she found it hard to comprehend. She knew there must be a way to trade and grow and have her country at the centre of exportation. She sighed deeply; she had almost forgotten she had this high-profile dinner to attend that evening. The last thing she needed was to be sitting there discussing the future of Sheba. She felt tired and needed a few days away to rest and invigorate her spirit. Right now, though, all she wanted was to take a bath and have Naja read her some more stories from Jerusalem. Yet here she was, on duty again, entertaining the government.

Alim, her chief advisor, leaned over to her and whispered, "Your Highness, are you understanding the discussion, or would you prefer the subject changed?"

Zaria stared at him for a few seconds before replying, "Alim, you are too kind to be thinking of me, but please do not use me as an excuse to change the subject. If *you* do not understand the topic, speak of other things."

Alim's eyes flashed, clearly taken aback by her response. "I apologise if I have offended you, my lady," he mumbled. "I wrongly assumed females disliked politics and business trade topics."

"I am *not* a woman, Alim." She grinned. "I am a queen." With that, she flicked her long dark hair and turned her attention back to Halim, a guest who sat on her right. When she looked up, she noticed that Jaleel had a little smirk on his lips; Zaria believed he had seen their interaction, although he sat a few seats away from her.

Queen Zaria knew Alim did not revere her, not on the same level as he had treated her father. He found her incapable and was constantly questioning if she understood what was being discussed in meetings or in banquets.

She was aware she was not of the same calibre as her father, but she was determined to succeed and refine her ruling. In her defence, she had been ruling for only four years and still had much to learn. Her eyes turned to Jaleel, who watched her intently. She smiled to assure him she was fine. Why couldn't Jaleel be her advisor instead of Alim? She cocked her head to one side. Could she replace Alim? She was the queen, after all; she was sure something could be done. Her heart fluttered with excitement. Jaleel was wise. He understood her and respected her as a woman, especially as a queen. He always encouraged her and never made her feel incompetent.

Yes, she could definitely grow and flourish under Jaleel's wise guidance and love. *Love*! Why had that thought entered her mind? She felt heat rise to her cheeks. Jaleel was her teacher, and a relationship beyond a teacher with his student would be forbidden in their culture. As queen, she was to marry an equal. From under her long dark lashes, she watched Jaleel speak and behave like a true nobleman—he *was* equipped. The sudden mention of King Solomon made her look up and sit up straighter.

With great interest, she joined the conversation and asked many questions about the king of the North. Even Alim joined in with excitement, saying there had never been a king like Solomon. Queen Zaria was impressed. Alim did not speak highly of anyone. Maybe Solomon's importance was correct. The more she thought about Solomon, the more her heart told her to visit him. Tonight she would discuss it with Jaleel. Her heart flipped with anticipation—although she was not sure if her excitement was because she would visit Solomon or because she would visit Jaleel.

Chapter Three

Later that night, after the dinner party had ended, Zaria went to see Jaleel. She knocked on the study room door and waited for him to open. He often went to bed late, as he prepared many programs for the following day. She hoped tonight he had remained there.

The door opened, and his eyes brightened when he saw her. Opening the door wider, he gestured for her to come in. He was dressed in a simple sand-coloured tunic, and his turban was off his head, giving him a more relaxed and less professional look. His dark curls cascaded a little to one side in an unruly manner. His hair looked soft. She wondered how it would feel to touch. Zaria drew in her breath and cleared her throat.

"How can I help you, Your Majesty?"

Zaria blinked. "Jaleel, I have decided to call upon Solomon!" she exclaimed excitedly as she paced the room. "After tonight's conversation, I realise I need to talk to this man. I *need* to know his secret to wisdom." She turned to look at her teacher, who had remained quiet as she spoke. "Well? What do you think? Do I have your blessing?"

Jaleel let out a breath and walked over to her. She stopped pacing and faced him. "I suspected as much, my lady. I believe you should go. Let no one, such as Alim, tell you otherwise. You *are* a great queen. Never doubt. And . . . you have my blessing."

Her heart skipped a beat and reached for his hands. "Thank you, Jaleel, but I will not go without you." His hands felt strong under her slim ones. She did not know what possessed her to take hold of his hands, but she did not want to let go.

"Me? Are you sure?" In the soft light of the lanterns, she watched his eyes flash with uncertainty.

"I am. Otherwise, I will not go." She squeezed his hands. "I feel safe with you. Please, do me the honour of accompanying me to Jerusalem." She spoke softly and liked the idea of having him beside her.

"I will be honoured, my queen." With a hoarse voice, Jaleel inclined his head.

Her heart rejoiced. "Thank you! Shall we go over the map?"

Slowly, he pulled his hands from hers and walked across the room. He opened the door of a tall wooden cabinet and retrieved a long scroll. He waved it in the air. "At your service." He chuckled.

For the next hour, they went over the trail they would take from Sheba to Jerusalem. Zaria felt overwhelmed, for it was many miles, as Jaleel had pointed out during the walk in the garden earlier that day. The journey would be arduous, long, dusty, and hot. However, her desire to meet this mysterious king made the trip worthwhile. She had to know if he was all they claimed he was.

After many weeks of preparations, Queen Zaria was finally on her way to visit King Solomon. They had sent messengers weeks in advance to prepare the king for her arrival. The last thing she wanted was to offend His Majesty by turning up unannounced. From her covered seat high above on the camel, she admired her magnificent caravan of camels, carrying spices, large quantities of gold and precious stones, frankincense, and myrrh in abundance for the king.

There were many travelling with her to Jerusalem. They had eight cooks and the caravan master, like a captain of a ship, who guided the caravan's travel schedule. She had over eighty soldiers guarding her every move and monitoring danger lurking in the desert. Ehsan, the news bearer, his assistant, camel pullers, and Jaleel also accompanied her—as well as her personal maids, Yara and Kalila. Although Naja had wanted to go with her,

Zaria knew she could not leave the kingdom with no royal family present. Naja would have to stay and take on duties Zaria could not attend to. With a teary good-bye, the sisters had embraced for a long time before Zaria began the strenuous journey through the Arabian desert. Zaria glanced down from her seat and grinned when she saw Jaleel look up at her. His eyes looked like the colour of honey under the brightness of the sun. He smiled back and gave a little wave. Feeling at peace, she leaned against her seat and enjoyed the rich reds of the scenery.

The first night in the desert was freezing. Makeshift tents had been erected for their nightly rest, and Zaria, wrapped in warm clothes made of thick animal material, fell asleep almost immediately, weary from the many hours of travelling. Each day was long, scalding, and dusty, and every night was cold, short, and dangerous as predators lurked in the dense darkness of the night.

Even though Zaria had Yara and Kalila assisting her, her consolation was Jaleel. He checked on her in the mornings, during the day, and at nights before she went to sleep. His presence brought her great comfort, and with each passing day, he stole a little more of her heart.

One frosty evening, after many weeks of travel, Jaleel gave her the delightful news that they would arrive in Jerusalem in the morning. After months of anticipation, she was finally close to meeting King Solomon. After he bid her good night, a thought crept in her head.

"Yara," she said as the maid brushed her hair, "please tell Jaleel to send Ehsan ahead with the news that I will arrive in Jerusalem in the morning. I want King Solomon to be ready." Zaria paused. "Do not send the boy tonight. He can go early tomorrow with an escort of soldiers."

"I will do as you say, my lady." The maidservant finished brushing her hair and went off to look for Jaleel.

Although Zaria crawled into bed fatigued, sleep was slow to come. Excitement and trepidation filled her restless night. She yearned for her trip not to be in vain. She did not want to be disillusioned, but above all she did not want to have put her people through this arduous trip because of her childish whim. Sighing deeply, she put her animal covering closer to her head and closed her eyes. She had to make herself sleep; otherwise, she would look an absolute mess in the morning.

The bright light seeping through the tent and the sound of shouting woke her up with a start. Zaria sat up and looked around. In the corner she saw Yara packing up her belongings in the trunks.

"Yara, what is going on? I can hear shouting."

"Good morning, my lady." The maid's older face wrinkled as she grinned. "Do not fret, my lady. King Solomon has sent a great escort of soldiers to accompany you into Jerusalem."

"He did?" Her voice was incredulous.

"Jaleel sent Ehsan and his assistant to Jerusalem, and the boys did not return. Instead, an escort of about thirty soldiers on horseback arrived and will take you into the city of Jerusalem. Jaleel is organising all the details and departure time." The maid busied herself as she continued packing.

At the mention of Jaleel's name, her heart jumped. What was wrong with her? She could not be having romantic notions about her teacher. What would he think of her? She shook her head and got ready for the meeting.

"Your bath is ready, my lady. It's time to freshen up before the king has the honour of meeting you." Yara continued talking as Zaria took off her sleeping clothes and got into the warm water pleasantly scented with oils. "Kalila is outside getting a few bags with your belongings. I believe you need the finest jewellery and dress."

"Thank you," Zaria whispered as her body relaxed in the tub. She could not wait to arrive in Jerusalem.

Chapter Four

Two hours later, Zaria bopped up and down as the camels made their way into Jerusalem, riding behind King Solomon's army escort. She glanced over the horizon and out of the corner of her eye saw Jaleel riding close to her camel at her request. She had confided in him that she was anxious and needed him to remain close. He had kindly obliged.

"Are you feeling better, Your Majesty?" he whispered as he got as close to her as he could. His face had tanned over the last few weeks due to the brutal rays of the sun and the burning heat.

She smiled. "I feel safe with you," she whispered, regretting the words the minute they left her mouth. *What would he think of her?* She felt mortified.

He grinned. "That makes my heart very content." His eyes softened, and the way he looked at her made her feel weak in the knees. Instantly, her hands flew to her face as she felt heat creep up. Her heart raced. What was the meaning of all this? Was something happening between them? Could it be possible that he felt an attraction toward her?

The deep, long sound of a shofar broke through the many questions and lack of answers in her head. Up ahead, one of King Solomon's men was blowing the shofar, announcing their entrance into Jerusalem.

"We have arrived, Queen Zaria." Jaleel pointed up ahead.

She craned her neck as her caravan entered the city's fortified gates. She drew in her breath as she admired the incredible architecture of buildings and domes that greeted her. Townspeople stopped to watch the mighty procession with perplexed looks as her camels continued toward the palace.

At the first sight of King Solomon's palace, her mouth was agape. The grandeur of the palace grounds and the colossal pillars took her breath away. She felt small as they entered the courtyard that could easily fit her entire palace inside.

Her party and escorts came to a stop, and they instructed her camel to lie down. It was time for her to descend and meet the king. She smoothed her gold-coloured dress and fixed the transparent veil that cascaded past her knees. Kalila had brushed her hair into a high elaborate hairstyle and finished the look with golden jewellery on her neck, ears, wrists, and arm cuff. She felt very much like a queen. Jaleel helped her descend from her camel and onto solid ground. She gave him a tiny lopsided smile as nerves crept into her stomach. She was not ready for this!

Jaleel must have sensed her uncertainty because his hand lingered on her arms and he whispered, "You can do this, Zaria. I have complete faith that you will make a wonderful impression on the king. Besides, I will be by your side the entire time."

Hearing him call her by her first name made her heart flutter. "Thank you," she managed to say.

"Queen Zaria?" Interrupted by the voice of Kalila, the queen tore her gaze away from Jaleel and turned to look at the girl. "I need to fix your veil and headpiece before you enter. The king awaits."

Zaria nodded, and when Jaleel moved away, her maid finished the last details of her look. The shofar blew again and then again and again once more.

Finally, left alone with Jaleel, the maids, and King Solomon's royal announcer, Zaria closed her eyes briefly, took a deep breath, and waited for the elaborately decorated doors to open. The palace's royal announcer signalled for the doors to open. The doors were pushed open, and splendour greeted her eyes. The entranceway was impressive with floors of ivory so polished she could see herself in them. Intricately designed golden walls carved with battle scenes and lions added opulence to the room. The exotic plants adorned throughout made the room feel warm somehow. Instantly, Zaria felt the presence of peace in the room. She frowned, unsure of why. The announcer and two soldiers escorted the visitors to the throne room where she was announced.

The throne room was ivory with elaborately carved pillars and shiny marble floors. Rugs of different colours and patterns adorned various parts of the room, and thick, expensive draperies of purple and blue adorned the ceilings and added elegance. The room was bright with lights illuminating every corner, and people dressed in their finest met her gaze and bowed as she walked down the pathway toward the throne. Music played as dancers twirled in one section of the room. The whole ambience made her feel comfortable and welcomed.

As her eyes scanned the room, they came to a stop on the impressive figure sitting on his throne. His extravagant tunic of blue with gold on the collar and hem glistened in the sunlight. His red cape was clasped with a golden lion-head brooch. His crown was short but adorned with jewels, and his beard was trimmed neatly. He smiled at her, and she smiled back. His eyes spoke kindness.

When she arrived at his feet, she bowed low and watched as Jaleel inclined his head and kept it there reverently. Her maids had been escorted to another side of the room, away from the throne. She almost gasped as the king stood and towered over her. His physique was impressive.

He bowed and beamed. "Queen Zaria of Sheba, welcome to Jerusalem. I am honoured to have you in my palace." He inclined his head again.

"Thank you, Your Majesty. It is an honour for me to visit your beautiful country." She felt her hands a little sweaty. "I would like to present my advisor during this trip, Jaleel. The palace cannot do without him." *Or I*, she wanted to add.

The greetings continued for a few minutes, and she enjoyed their pleasantries. The king introduced her to everyone present in the room, including some of his striking wives who were seated together in the right wing of the hall, wearing gowns of rare material she had not seen before. Their jewels and hairstyles added to the magnificence of the palace walls. She wondered how emotionally difficult it must be for these women living in the king's harem, all vying for one man's attention. Zaria knew it was common for kings to have queens and concubines, but her father had refused and only had their mother. He did not marry again after she passed. Zaria believed in being faithful to one only. From the corner of her eyes, she looked at Jaleel and felt he was *her* one.

The king revealed they had a grand banquet prepared for her the next evening, but for today he would give her a tour of the grand palace. Zaria enjoyed everything he showed her. They walked the splendid corridors filled with tapestries depicting battles won. Other paintings on the walls had drawings of King Solomon, and one particular wall in the king's prayer room caught her attention.

The entire room was the colour of the moon—it had minimal furniture and soft cushions in an array of colours scattered across the room.

"This is the prayer room." Solomon's voice held a tone of pride. "It is where we communicate with our God."

Zaria felt the reverence. "I do not see any images of your God." She looked around. The only thing she could see were inscriptions on the walls. Beautifully written in elegant ink.

"Our God is invisible, my lady," Solomon said simply.

Zaria glanced quickly at Jaleel, who looked as perplexed as she felt. "Invisible? I'm intrigued." In her palace, they had many gods according to their needs. The goddess of fertility, the god of war, the god of rain and field, the goddess of love, the god who brought healing. Statues of gold, silver, and ivory adorned every corner in her palace.

"Our God is the most powerful God. The God of the universe. He created nature and humans."

"He sounds grand . . . but why not showcase his greatness for all to see?" She felt confused.

"Our God forbids it. He wants us to love him and communicate with him through prayer. He does not want anything made of gold to represent him. Nothing can compare to him." Solomon continued walking around the room and showing the letterings on the wall.

One caught her eye, and she stopped to read it out loud. "The law of the Lord is perfect, refreshing the soul. The statutes of the Lord are trustworthy, making wise the simple. The precepts of the Lord are right, giving joy to the heart. The commands of the Lord are radiant, giving light to the eyes. The fear of the Lord is pure, enduring forever. The decrees of the Lord are firm, and all of them are righteous. They are more precious than gold, than much pure gold; they are sweeter than honey, than honey from the honeycomb."

Queen Zaria exhaled. "Such an exquisite poem."

"My father, David, wrote this. He was a poet and songwriter. He wrote many lyrics about our God."

"What does *the commands of the Lord* mean?" She did not think her gods had commands. Did they?

"The Ten Commandments are rules that were given to the people of Israel via Moses many years ago. It is ten ways we should live on this earth. For example, one says to honour your father and mother. Another one says you should not murder or commit adultery."

Zaria was mesmerised. Those rules were common sense rules to live by. She liked those ten rules. At her request, King Solomon continued reciting the commandments.

Many hours later, as the moon shone high in the sky, Zaria sat outside in the quiet garden contemplating everything the king had spoken about. The more she spoke to him, the more she liked what he said. Every word that came out of his mouth seemed flawless and wise. Tomorrow she must ask him where he got his wisdom from.

Chapter Five

The next evening, the queen sat reclined against one of the luxurious seats amongst soft cushions, admiring the entertainment and enjoying the lovely music. She smiled at Jaleel, who sat next to her enjoying the festivities along with her. The king also sat with them, along with his Egyptian queen and a few other noblemen of Israel. Zaria noticed his queen wore one of the many jewels with precious stones she had brought to the king as gifts. She was delighted.

Earlier, the king had profoundly thanked her for the gifts she had brought from the South. She felt it was the least she could do after being received and welcomed so warmly into their country. During dinner they spoke of many things, but one question remained unanswered to her.

"Your Majesty," she began, "in Sheba you are well-known and respected as the wisest man who has ever existed. If it is not a secret, may I ask how you got so wise?" She held her breath.

"My lady, I would be honoured to tell you what God did for me."

Everyone at the table got comfortable. Zaria leaned forward and listened intently.

"I was in Gibeon in the early times of my reign. I had gone up there to sacrifice and burn the offering. A gift to my God. That night as I slept, my Lord God spoke in a dream, and he asked me what I wanted him to give me." Zaria watched as Solomon's eyes wandered to a faraway place, remembering that night many years ago. "I thanked him for allowing me to be king in my father's palace, and then I told him that all I wanted was wisdom to rule and judge the people of Israel. I wanted to have clarity on the difference between right and wrong." Solomon turned to Zaria and smiled. "Without wisdom it is impossible to rule a great nation. You need God and the right person to support you."

Zaria nodded slowly. He was right, of course. She turned to Jaleel and smiled, taking one of his strong hands into hers. The action surprised him, and his eyes widened, unsure what to do. Zaria knew this was inappropriate, but she wanted to acknowledge that he was the only one who did not question her ruling or doubt her ability. She mouthed a little *thank-you* and hoped he understood why. Jaleel did not pull his hand away. Instead, he relaxed and gave her hand a gentle squeeze.

Zaria turned her attention back to Solomon. "Then God said to me that because I only asked for wisdom and not riches and greatness for myself, he was going to make me wise and intelligent but also shower me with riches and honour in my life. He said there would be no other king in the world as great as I." Solomon's voice broke. He cleared his throat and shrugged. "As you see, my lady, I am not wise on my own but by the grace of my God. He is the gift giver and the one who gives me success."

His story took her breath away, and the more she heard about his God, the more she wanted to know him. Would his God talk to her as well? Would she be able to get to know him like the king had? It sounded wonderful to her, and everything he said about his God, she locked in her heart.

The night ended on a joyous note, and Zaria looked forward to the next few days before she had to leave and return to Sheba. She wanted to make the most of her time with the king.

One morning, as she was in the garden attempting to talk to Solomon's God, the king sent a message inviting her to join him in the temple for a burnt-offering ceremony. She made haste and prepared herself with fine clothing. It intrigued her to know about this burnt offering he mentioned.

The king and his advisor escorted her to a section of the temple. The temple, Solomon explained, had not been finished, but he promised, when it was done, it was going to be the grandest monument ever built. Queen Zaria had absolutely no doubt that it would be as he said.

After a prayer and some melodious music, the king, along with the high priest of the temple, set on the altar an animal as a burnt offering to their Lord. As the smoke evaporated into the sky, Zaria listened to the king ask for forgiveness for him and his household. He thanked the Lord and concluded his praises until his sacrifice had disappeared from the altar. Zaria asked him many questions, and he patiently answered each one. Talking to this man made her feel that ruling a kingdom with God *was* possible. Solomon's God was becoming more appealing to her with each passing day.

After the ceremony, they escorted Zaria to eat a sumptuous breakfast of the finest fruit, nuts, and food she had ever seen. To her delight, Jaleel had been invited as well, and he was in the banquet room talking to other officials when she arrived. Her heart skipped a beat when he looked up from across the room, grinned, and inclined his head. She waved back timidly and headed toward him. She heard him excuse himself from the group and head her way. They stopped in the middle of the room, unaware of their surroundings.

"Good morning, Your Highness." He bowed.

"Good morning, Jaleel. Did you sleep well?" she asked.

"I did." He smiled with his eyes. "I presume you also slept well?"

She laughed. "Why are we talking about sleeping?" They chuckled. Of all the things they were allowed to talk about, this was not one of them. She felt very juvenile.

"I have just been to a burnt-offering ceremony held by the king." She felt excited to talk about it. "It was such a solemn moment, and I felt God."

"I have felt God multiple times for the last few days," Jaleel replied. "It is hard to explain the true feeling, but it is like nothing I have ever experienced."

Zaria nodded. "I agree with you, and it makes me want to know him better."

Jaleel's light brown eyes gleamed. "I must confess that I do too."

Their conversation was interrupted by a servant boy announcing breakfast was served. Never had she seen servants dressed in such finery, delicacies of foods filling the tables and elegant fine furniture adorning the room. As

Zaria looked around the room, she felt her heart swell with emotion and thankfulness for having made the trip to meet the mysterious King Solomon, who ended up being more than she imagined.

That night, after a dinner and more entertainment, she walked through the gardens that joined her bedchambers. She had invited Jaleel to join her on her walk, as she had many things to discuss with him. Her maids were in her room, and both doors were open for when she was ready to enter and retire for bed.

"Oh, Jaleel, I have been amazed at everything the king has spoken about. The wisdom he possesses is remarkable." She shook her head. Her long, dark hair cascaded past her waist. Yara had already brushed out the elaborate hairstyle, and she was ready for bed. She loved the feel of how light her hair felt with no jewels decorating it. "Did you see the food on his table? And the robes of the attending servants?" Zaria covered her mouth in awe.

Jaleel laughed. "And did you see the cupbearers in their robes imported from Macedonia and the elegant officials he invited?"

Zaria tilted her head to the side. "And the offering this morning was so reverent. I could feel his God." Zaria stopped walking and grabbed both of Jaleel's hands in hers. This time he didn't react. "Oh, Jaleel, I feel overwhelmed and scared."

"Why?" Jaleel frowned.

"How can I ever be a queen of Solomon's and my father's calibre? I will never reach their level." A little sob escaped her lips.

"You do not need to reach anyone's level, Zaria." Jaleel took one hand away from her grip and reached out to touch her cheek with the back of his hand. "You only have to rule the way God tells you. You cannot be Solomon or your father. You need to be you and rule according to your strengths and gifts."

She swallowed and nodded. "You are right, of course. At times I falter."

"It is okay to falter," he whispered.

Zaria watched his face, and because he didn't wear a turban, one of his curls fell over his eye. Timidly, she reached out and moved it away from his face.

"Thank you," he murmured, and ever so slowly, his lips touched hers.

Zaria gasped and stepped back as if someone had slapped her across the face.

"Forgive me, Queen Zaria! I broke the rule." His eyes filled with remorse.

"Do not apologise, Jaleel. I have wanted you to kiss me ... for a long time," she finished breathlessly.

He beamed and reached out and kissed the backs of her hands. Whether it was inappropriate or not, she leaned in and they embraced. Never had she felt so loved by a simple act. Why did Jaleel make her feel so secure and at peace?

By the time she went to bed, she could not fall asleep. Her heart danced with joy as she remembered Jaleel's tender kiss, but she worried about the outcome when she was back home. She knew she had to marry a prince. She flipped to the side and forgot the rules for now, trying to enjoy everything Jerusalem had brought her. She only had one day left before heading home, and already she felt convinced that the God of Solomon was the one true God.

Chapter Six

Queen Zaria made the most of her last day in Jerusalem, and during one of her walks around the palace with the king, she asked him about a few pressing matters that lay on her heart. Jaleel was preparing the camel caravan with the caravan master and could not join them on the afternoon walk.

"My lord, I have many questions for you, and it would honour me to get your advice on these matters." She halted and looked up into the king's kind brown eyes. The two young servant boys who walked with them holding a parasol over their heads came to a sudden stop as well.

"My lady, ask all the questions your heart desires. My God will give me the wisdom to answer them." King Solomon motioned for them to take a seat on the garden bench closest to them, which was shaded by one of the many leafy trees that adorned his extensive garden. She especially loved how the seats around the garden had been placed to overlook the cascading fountain.

The two servant boys moved away to one side and rested from holding the parasol while the king and the queen talked.

"What is on your mind, Queen Zaria?" The king cocked his head to one side with keen interest.

She took a deep breath and began. "I have a palace advisor who does not believe that I am capable of reign. He was my father's advisor and highly respected him. Our kingdom of Sheba flourished under my father's ruling. I do not have the same business mind he did, and Alim, the advisor, reminds me constantly. I cannot work under him. I would like to replace him with another advisor. However, I do not know how to go about such a task delicately." She ran a hand over her impeccable gown of yellow.

"Replace him with someone like . . . Jaleel?" The smile on the king's lips made Zaria suspicious that he knew about their secret love.

She nodded shyly.

"I believe you could ascend Alim to a higher-ranking position. It would be wise to move him into something where he shows strength." The king looked around the garden and then turned his attention back to her. "If he has the mind to run business, why not make him head of trade and imports? He could move closer to the trading town and work from there. He will then have to report to your advisor, who will report to you. The role is not only interesting, but he will feel extremely powerful in executing it. After all, the money coming into Sheba would depend highly on him."

Zaria gasped. "Oh, Your Majesty, that is the most exquisite plan I have ever heard. It is wonderful. Yes, I can see that working well. He is a brilliant man, and I absolutely believe he will take Sheba to even higher riches. Thank you!" She wanted to reach out and hug the king, but she knew that would be highly unsuitable. Her heart could rejoice silently.

"What else is on your heart?"
She inclined her head and debated whether she could confide in him about Jaleel.

"Let me guess." The king chuckled softly. "You are in love with Jaleel but feel that because he is not a prince, you cannot marry. Is that correct?"

Zaria's eyes widened. "Oh, King Solomon, I have never felt this way before." She placed her hand over her chest. "When I am with Jaleel, I feel understood and respected. Loved even." She glanced to check the quietness of her surroundings. The sound of birds chirping, along with the sound of water and rustling of leaves, filled the garden. "How can I marry below my station? It has never been done before."

"Queen Zaria, are you not going to promote Jaleel to become an advisor to the queen?"

"Hmm . . . yes."

"Since he will be your advisor, I see no reason you cannot marry and live a full, happy life. After all, you are the queen and can make new rules." He winked.

She laughed and nodded. "You are right, King Solomon."

Zaria continued with her many questions on trade, ruling wisely, and love, absorbing everything that came out of his mouth. She sat in awe at the brilliance of this man, and she felt even more convinced his God was *his* advisor. His God sounded fair and loving. He was someone she wanted to introduce to her country.

After their many hours of discussion, Zaria went back to her bedchamber and took a long bath to get ready for the last banquet at the palace. She was eager to go home but also saddened to leave Jerusalem.

The festivities cheered her heart at seeing the decadent food and fruits adorning the table. They ate until they could not eat anymore. The entertainers played music that made her feel serene inside, and a beautiful servant girl recited one of King David's many poems. Zaria could not help but smile through the whole evening. Unfortunately, Jaleel could not join them, as a problem had arisen with their departure and he needed to get it sorted. Although Zaria was disappointed, she knew she had him for a lifetime, where they would spend many hours together. That was sufficient.

The king, looking very elegant in his royal attire of purple and gold, stood to make an announcement. Silence descended upon the banquet hall.

"It has been an honour and my privilege to have had Zaria, the lovely queen of the South, grace us with her presence."

Zaria dipped her head in acknowledgement and smiled.

"I have gifts for Your Highness." Solomon clapped his hands, and many maidservants came laden with copper, weapons, precious stones, scrolls, and other artifacts of Israel. She accepted each gift in humble thankfulness. How kind the king was.

Before she retired for the night and left the festivities, King Solomon gave her one more personal gift. She unrolled the scroll.

"It's your father's poems!" she exclaimed as her eyes scanned the melodic words.

"These words can be taught to your children and to your children's children. Having the word of God resonate in your household is of utmost importance."

She clutched the scroll to her chest and bowed; her jewels jingled with each movement. "I am humbled, my king."

That night she slept lightly, with many thoughts that swirled in her mind. But they were thoughts of improvements she would make in Sheba. A new God was going to be introduced, new roles were going to be given to her loyal workers, and a new love would bloom. She felt elated.

Early the next morning, as the first rays of sunlight appeared over the horizon, Zaria sat on her camel, watching King Solomon disappear into the distance. When he was only a speck, she turned back and rested her head on her seat. She felt like a different person going back home. She felt blessed to have met the king of the North, and she knew that her country would embrace the new direction she would take them in.

A little clicking noise made her sit up. *What was that?* She heard the click sound again, and as she leaned over, she looked down and saw Jaleel clicking his heels against a smaller camel that wanted to settle down. She smiled and watched him a little longer. He must have sensed her eyes on him, because he looked up and grinned when he saw her face. She saw his eyes soften and spark. Oh, how she loved him.

She sat back and closed her little curtain to pray. She needed to talk to the God of Solomon, who was now *her* God, about this new love she had found.

Closing her eyes, Zaria prayed fervently.

<h1 style="text-align:center">Epilogue</h1>

964 BC, Sheba

Queen Zaria's stomach flipped with emotions as she walked into the garden of her palace. The statues that had once lived on the grounds no longer existed. When she had arrived home from Jerusalem two years ago, she had ordered for them to be removed and destroyed.

She stopped next to a pillar and smiled as she touched the inscriptions that had been carved all around it. She touched each word from the poems of King David. Poems of God and his greatness and love.

Her people had noticed the change and confidence she now possessed because of the wisdom she asked God to give her. Ruling a kingdom was serious business, and she wanted to perform the role to the best of her ability.

"Zaria?"

At the sound of her sister's voice, Zaria swirled around and touched the base of her stomach.

"Naja, I am so nervous. My stomach is twisted like a rope."

Her sister hurried to her side and grabbed both her hands. "It is natural to be nervous on the day of your wedding." Her sisters' eyes shone. "Especially when you are going to marry the love of your life."

Zaria beamed. "Oh yes! Jaleel *is* the love of my life. With him on my side and God's blessing and wisdom, we will rule well." She remembered when she had asked Solomon about marrying someone beneath her station and how it was forbidden in Sheba. He had advised, since she was the new queen, she could have a few rules changed. She had agreed and introduced new things soon after she arrived home. The first one was introducing people to the God of Solomon. Some embraced it; some did not. But she left it to everyone's discretion. She knew whom she believed in, and that was enough. She had also elevated Jaleel into the position of advisor of the palace and for the queen. With that new position, they could marry. There had been whispers for a few months; however, people admitted he was a wise young man and one who would complement the queen superbly. Many months later, they commented it was a good choice for Sheba and for Queen Zaria.

"Are you happy?" Naja let go of her hands, and the sisters walked back toward the palace doors.

"Blissfully." Zaria looked up at the bright sun illuminating the day. "My heart is as bright as the day!" She giggled.

Naja laughed and hooked arms with her sister as they entered the coolness of the room with its almost translucent marble floors. "Is Alim, your old advisor, going to make it to the wedding?" she asked.

Zaria beamed. "Alim said he would not miss it for anything. He is flourishing as our chief official of trade. He is content."

She remembered telling him about his new role and how his face had brightened. Soon after, he moved into the trading city with his wife. Zaria was pleased things had worked out so well. Solomon had been right about this move.

"You cannot see the bride!" The sudden yelling from her sister made Zaria jump, and she turned to see Jaleel descending the stairs. She drew in her breath at seeing him.

"Jaleel!" she breathed.

Behind her, Naja pushed her toward the open door, into the room where she was to dress and be out of sight. "It is not a good idea to see each other before your wedding tonight," she said.

Zaria could hear Jaleel chuckle, and when her sister wasn't looking, she quickly made a move from the door and rushed into his arms. Instantly, his arms went around her, and she drowned in them, her nerves disappearing.

"I love you, my beautiful Zaria," he whispered into her hair. "I cannot wait for God to unite us."

She leaned into his chest and sighed. "And I love you, Jaleel, my wonderful teacher, advisor, and friend. God sent you to me and I am pleased."

He kissed the top of her head, and she remained in his embrace a little longer.

In the distance, she heard Naja calling her.

Both of them laughed, and with one quick kiss, she hurried back to her sister's side, who had both arms on her hips and was tapping her foot. "Finally!" she exclaimed. "You two are like children."

Zaria laughed and followed her sister into the room. Her heart was full. She counted the hours before she and Jaleel would be husband and wife.

She felt at peace and knew that God would bless their union.

Three

Jezebel: Idolatrous Queen of Israel

Ahab son of Omri did more evil in the eyes of the Lord than any of those before him. He not only considered it trivial to commit the sins of Jeroboam son of Nebat, but he also married Jezebel daughter of Ethbaal king of the Sidonians, and began to serve Baal and worship him.

—1 Kings 16:30–31

Find the story in 1 Kings 16:29–34 and chapters 17–21, and 2 Kings 9:30–35.

874 BC, Israel

Running footsteps and rushed whispers echoed on the marble tiles of the grandiose palace. Elana and Ayelet were busy preparing the bedchamber for the new queen of Israel. They both looked up from folding the bedcovers as the golden door of the room swung opened.

Zethara, one of the eunuchs, burst in huffing and puffing.

"What is it, Zethara?" Elana asked, moving toward the tall, dark man as he mustered a few breaths to speak.

"The princess has arrived! She is here, Elana!" He let out one more puff and scarpered out of the room.

Elana felt the blood drain from her face and her stomach tighten into a knot. She turned to Ayelet, who was grinning from ear to ear.

"Oh, Elana, I cannot wait to meet our new queen. Do you think she will be beautiful?"

Elana chose not to reply to the younger girl's question; instead, she said, "Let us finish her room before she is brought in. We do not want to get in trouble and be punished for our lack of work."

Ayelet giggled nervously and continued talking about the Sidonian princess coming to marry King Ahab.

Elana tightened her lips and let the girl talk. She was not doing any harm by letting out her emotions. Elana knew a little more about Princess Jezebel, and her concern was that she would be a negative influence on King Ahab.

Sadly, he did not have a resilient character. He had moved away from God and was doing things his ancestors would recoil at. He was easily swayed and tended not to think before he acted. However, his strength lay in his obsession with ivory artifacts. The palace gleamed in white accents throughout.

"All done!" Ayelet said triumphantly.

Elana smiled. "Thank you. You have done a splendid job. Soon you will train other slaves . . ." Her voice trailed off, and she corrected herself before continuing, "Maidservants."

Before another word was spoken, both young women were interrupted by the voice of Obadiah, the overseer of the palace household, coming down the hallway. Sounds of other voices and footsteps joined his. Elana motioned with her hand for Ayelet to put her back against the wall and remain bowed. The girl nodded and followed instructions.

Elana stole a quick look at the new princess as her escorts of eunuchs carrying trunks and her personal maids entered the room. Quickly, she bent her head down again and remained as still as a statue. It was forbidden for slaves to do anything unless they were addressed first. No one was speaking, and all that was heard was the scurrying of feet and scraping of furniture. Elana guessed the eunuchs were placing the trunks in the room. Soon they left with the maids. When it was quiet again, Obadiah spoke.

"My lord, Ahab, will return later this afternoon in time for the banquet given in your honour."

Elana held her breath, waiting for the future queen to speak.
"I am not impressed he was not here to greet me. I will speak to him when he arrives. Let me know as soon as he returns to the palace." She sounded displeased.

"Of course, Princess Jezebel." Did Elana detect a dry tone in Obadiah's voice?

"Who are these slaves?"
"These, my lady, are household maids. Elana has been with us for a few years. Brought here from one of the finest families of Israel, she—"

"And the other one?" Jezebel interrupted.

"Ayelet has been here for four weeks, my lady. Both girls will be the maids to bring water for your bath, clean the room, arrange flowers, etcetera."

"Very well. They can leave my presence as I rest for the banquet."

Elana heard the jingling sound of jewels move with every movement.

"Elana, Ayelet, you may leave," Obadiah said.

Finally, Elana lifted her head and saw the future queen standing in the middle of the room, staring out the window at the view below. She wore her hair in an elaborate Phoenician hairstyle with golden jewels decorating the back and dangling long. An almost transparent veil covered her head, and her dress made Elana gape. It was gold, shimmering and sheer under the sunlight pouring in through the window—every curve and bump of her slim body was accentuated by the tightness of the dress. *She might as well not be wearing a gown,* Elana thought. Just then, the woman lifted her hand and ran it over her veil as it slightly moved with the soft breeze. Her nails were shaped thin and long and painted in the colour of blood, looking like weapons on her hands. Elana shuddered at the thought that those nails could extract a person's eye.

Before walking out of the room, she caught Obadiah's eyes and saw great sadness and disappointment in them as he studied the future queen of Israel. She quickly averted her eyes and left the room, followed closely by Ayelet.

Once outside, the younger maid whispered excitedly, "Is she not absolutely beautiful? Did you see her hair and her royal gown of gold? Oh, and those nails!" The girl clutched her chest and giggled. "If only I was a queen like her."

Elana grimaced and looked at the naive girl. She truly didn't know anything about the ways of the Phoenicians or the supernatural influence they had over people. She hoped that King Ahab would not succumb to his new wife's ways. She doubted he would stand up to her.

Elana shook her head and spoke. "We are to go to the kitchen and later help prepare the banquet hall."

The girl moaned. Her light brown curls bounced as she shook her head. "Aren't we Princess Jezebel's maids? Why must we work the banquet hall?"

"The princess is resting, and we will not be called to clean the room or fetch water until tonight. Remember, we are not her personal maids. She has her own. We are general maids and work where we are needed." Elana smiled. "Besides, imagine her face when she sees the banquet hall decorated so elaborately. And to know that *you* had something to do with it will bring happiness to her."

Ayelet grinned. "Oh yes! I want to make the princess happy." With a little skip, she hurried in front of Elana.

Elana laughed and followed the nine-year-old to the kitchen. To be young and innocent was a blessing indeed, and being unaware of the danger lurking in the background was even better. Evil that was masked by festivities. Sometimes she wished she was the young girl of seven instead of thirteen. She still remembered the day her father had sold her to pay a large debt he owed. Being the eldest sibling and a female made her the first choice to fix his problems. Not because she was valued but because she was beneath every man. Her brother would never be sold as a slave—being a male gave him privileges. She was now used to being a slave at the palace, and what kept her going was the thought that her sacrifice had saved her younger sisters from the same fate that had fallen on her.

"Elana! Cook is calling you. Hurry!"

Elana jumped at Ayelet's loud voice, bringing her back to the present.

"I'm coming, I'm coming." She hurried her pace and listened as her worn leather sandals made little screeching noises on the marble floor.

The days that followed were filled with festivities and celebrations for the new princess. Food, entertainment, wine, and drunk guests had filled the palace for days. Elana and Ayelet had been instructed to help with the festivities, and after the princess became the wife of the king, they would be summoned to serve and see to her needs. Not as personal maids but as water carriers for her baths and anything that involved hard labour.

Elana groaned as she rushed to get more wine to fill the golden pitchers on the tables. Another yawn escaped her lips as she poured wine from the water pots of stone and into pitchers. When would she have had time to sleep?

"Elana! The wine master says you must make haste! Guests are thirsty." Ayelet's voice broke through her sleepy stupor, and she nodded, working as fast as her tired body would allow.

Finally, after a week of celebrations, the wedding day had arrived. The day was elaborate and opulent. Ivory and gold precious stones decorated the palace corners. Tapestries enhanced with images of Baal and other gods adorned the hallways, and music played day and night. Elana could not wait for the day to be over. Kings, queens, princes, and nobles from all over the province graced the wedding of King Ahab and Princess Jezebel.

For the first time, Elana caught a clear view of Princess Jezebel's face, which she had kept veiled since her arrival. The princess wore a long white gown adorned with a gold border around the hem, sleeves, and collar. They piled half her dark hair high in a Grecian hairdo, and the rest cascaded to her waist in flowy curls. Her white dress flowed to the floor, covering her bejewelled feet that Elana had helped adorn earlier that morning. A sheer white veil rested behind her crown and trailed to the floor. Her nails had been painted the colour of the moon and decorated with little gems. Her eyes had been enhanced with kohl from Egypt, and her eyelids shimmered with silver, making her amber-coloured eyes stand out.

"She looks like a goddess," Ayelet whispered.

Elana nodded. She looked incredibly beautiful but also cold and stiff, like the statues in the garden.

The girls were looking from a back window that remained hidden from the guests and bridal party. They watched as King Ahab took hold of his bride, grinning like a fool and oblivious to her evil charm.

A foreigner. An idolater. A Baal worshipper. And a witch who was now their new queen of Israel.

Elana sighed and said a silent prayer to Jehovah to help them all.

Chapter One

870 BC, Israel

The sounds of drumming, humming, and chanting woke Elana from her deep sleep. She blinked and sat up, noticing that it was still dark outside. What was that noise? As quiet as she could so she would not waken Ayelet, she tiptoed barefoot across the floor and peeked out the window of the servants' quarters.

The noise sounded like it was coming from the north garden of the palace. Curiosity filled her mind, and she hurried quietly across the room, opened the door, and peered out. Silence greeted her as she stepped outside and quietly shut the door behind her. The soft flickering lights of the stars and brightness of the moon cascaded from the open windows in the slaves' area. She crossed the small hallway and ran up the back steps that led toward the gardens.

The cool night air rustled her tousled long dark brown hair. She wished to have brought a thick veil or head covering to keep herself hidden and warm. The rough coolness of the damp grass under her feet made her gasp. Why had she not thought about her clothing before leaving her room in a rush? She rolled her eyes, but despite being uncomfortable, she wanted to know what the noise was. She knew something was wrong. Elana tiptoed onto the slightly warmer stones of the path and walked faster. She turned right at the corner; then she went left and the rhythmic drumming got louder. Finally, she reached the northern garden where King Ahab and Queen Jezebel enjoyed bathing in the enormous water pond.

Silently, Elana hid behind one of the thick pillars and peeped out from behind it to see who was there.

She gasped. It was Jezebel and Ahab. They stood in front of their Baal god. They had erected another shrine for their worship. The golden half-oxen and half-man was not very big. However, they had placed him on a higher level and had built seven steps for them to climb and reach the image. On the sides of the statue were men with drums while women and men dressed in white danced as in a trance around the statue. Elana recognised them as Jezebel's priests and priestesses. She had seen them many times come to the palace, and each time the queen held a banquet for them.

The music and chanting continued for many minutes, and just as Elana was about to leave, she watched in horror as the priestesses and priests cut their flesh with sharp objects, causing blood to come out. They splattered their blood toward their god shrine, while wailing, growling, and reciting gibberish. Ahab stood to one side and watched Jezebel, who dressed in a dark translucent gown, walked toward Baal with her arms outstretched, holding what looked like an animal. Her voice rang loud as she called different names to her god, her head thrown back as if in ecstasy. Elana felt her body tremble. This must be the witchcraft ritual Jezebel performed on a weekly basis. She had heard others speak of it, but never had she witnessed it herself. Should she be surprised? Four years ago, Queen Jezebel had been brought to the northern kingdom to be King Ahab's bride in order to strengthen the military alliance between her kingdom of Phoenicia and the kingdom of Israel. Her father, King Ethbaal, was not only a king but also the high priest of Baal. This ritual had been seeped into her since childhood.

Fire spat out from the laps of the golden oxen where a gold giant bowl was laid. When Jezebel reached the top of the step and stood in front of her god, she threw her head back and shrieked the word *rain* over and over. Then suddenly she hurled the animal into the fire pit. She bowed low, did a distorted dance, and shouted words Elana had never heard before. Everyone cheered, and soon they broke out into unsuitable behaviour, making Elena shrink back in disgust and bolt from the obscene and disrespectful acts. Trembling, she continued running, leaving behind the smell of charred, burnt animal and smoke.

All of a sudden, she banged into a solid body. She opened her mouth to scream, but strong hands covered her mouth and dragged her to a corner of the wall. She closed her eyes and waited for the soldier to kill her.

"Elana! What are you doing out here?"

Elena's eyes popped opened at the voice of her dear friend Obadiah.

"Obadiah!" she cried as tears rolled down her face. "I thought you were a soldier ready to kill me."

In the moonlight's softness she saw his grim old face. "You should not be out here alone! You know it is forbidden. If Jezebel sees you, she will sacrifice *you* in the oxen fire pit."

Elana trembled. "I heard noises and had to see what was happening. It was disgusting," she whispered. "They even killed a little animal of some sort."

Obadiah shook his head. "Sometimes they sacrifice babies and people."

"Oh!" She covered her mouth and let her tears flow.

"Come, Elena, come inside." Obadiah gently guided her to the side door and into the area where a bench was, and both took a seat.

"Elana, you must keep away from Jezebel. There is evil in this palace, and it is growing. The king has turned his back on God and now worships as his wife does. The witchcraft, the sacrifice, the illicit acts are all an abomination to Jehovah."

Elana bit her bottom lip and shook as she remembered how King Ahab had also set up an altar for Baal in the temple! God, Jehovah, forbade idol worship. Ahab had degraded himself with each passing month, and he had made Jezebel his *only* god and turned his back on the only God of Israel. The palace and the entire city emanated with idols, shrines, and Asherah poles. Images of Baal were everywhere. The drunken cries of heathen priests who sacrificed children and animals were heard for miles away. A great darkness and heavy veil of evil had fallen over Israel. King Ahab encouraged the Israelites to worship and join his idolatrous ways. Many people did, but very few, like Elana, Obadiah, godly prophets, and Elijah, stayed faithful.

"The prophet Elijah was here yesterday afternoon." Obadiah broke through her thoughts. "He had a message for King Ahab, and I believe it was not a positive one." He ran his hand through his white-and-black hair.

Elana let out a scant breath. "Do you know what his message was?"

Obadiah looked away and nodded slowly. "I was present when Elijah delivered the message."

"Obadiah, I feel afraid when Elijah visits." Elana looked up at the man whom she loved like a father.

"Why afraid, dear Elana?"

"Whenever he speaks, something bad happens! I have a feeling nothing good will come from his visit." She shook her head. "Are you allowed to tell me what he said?"

Obadiah nodded, and Elana leaned in to listen.

Chapter Two

Elana held her breath, wondering what the prophet had prophesied. She had only seen Elijah a few times in her time at the palace, and it always fascinated her what a spiritual man he was. Chosen by God to help Israel turn back to Him. Whenever she had been in his presence, she could sense the Holy Spirit. He was intimidating, and he never buckled or bowed to anyone.

"He has declared that there will be neither dew or rain in the next few years. Until God speaks its time."

Elana gasped. A drought in the land? Her heart fluttered. "That is not good, Obadiah. How will we survive?"

"You, my dear, leave that to God. He always looks after his faithful children."

Now it made sense to her when she had heard Jezebel screech, "Rain"—they must be preparing and asking their god to send rain. Their god was dead. He would never listen to their cries.

She yawned and shivered slightly as the wind blew around her. "I must go back to my quarters." Elana stood and looked down at Obadiah, the overseer of King Ahab's household. Her only true friend and a fellow believer in God. How he worked with Ahab always intrigued her. He was just and faithful, yet he served a man who had degraded himself for too long.

He gave her a tight smile and patted her hand gently. "Go, dear child."

As she walked away, Obadiah called her name. "Elana?"

"Yes?"

"Do not be afraid. Our God is more powerful than anything. He will look after his children."

Elana nodded. She believed with all her heart, even as she heard the screeching and screams of the immoral priests and priestesses.

The days seemed to travel gradually, and soon after Elijah's predictions, Elana noticed how the trees broke under the burning of the sun. Leaves disintegrated under her touch, and the bottom of the surrounding rivers was visible. The drought had surely started. For the last few days, Elana and Obadiah had been discussing the disappearing of Elijah. After his prophecy, the prophet had gone away. No one knew where he was. Elana wondered why he had left at a time like this. However, she imagined God had given him another command, and he had to obey. There must be a reason for his withdrawal.

"Elana, do you think we will go thirsty and die?" Ayelet asked her as the girls carried water to the queen's quarters.

"I hope we do not." Elana glanced at the girl as sweat dripped from her face. "We can only hope it will not last long."

The younger girl let out a loud sigh. "I hope so. I would be so afraid to die thirsty."

Elana hid a smile as she listened to the maid speak. "Oh, Ayelet, do not fret. I will take care of you and make sure you always have water."

"Oh good! Thank you, Elana!" The girl turned her squinted eyes to look at her and grinned. "I feel safe with you."

Elana felt her heart give a little leap at the girl's words. "You're welcome," she whispered.

Without another word, they hurried to Queen Jezebel's room to fill her bathtub. She was overheated and wanted to cool her body. Elana shook her head, feeling anger simmer inside. How dare she use the water for something as frivolous as a bath! The palace needed every ounce of water available, yet Jezebel did not care about anyone else but herself.

The girls climbed up the ivory staircase and toward Jezebel's quarters, who seemed to be in a rage.

"Enough!" The high pitch screech made Elana jump, and before entering the room, she turned to Ayelet. "Go help the cook in the kitchen. It is not safe when the queen is in a rage."

Ayelet gulped and nodded slowly. She placed the pitcher on the ground and almost ran down the stairs.

Elana entered the room, holding her clay water jar. Trying to hold her composure and show no emotion, she walked toward the bath but gave a little yelp as a golden goblet filled with wine flew across the room before smashing against the wall and crumbling to the ground.

Zethara, one of the queen's eunuchs, rushed to clean up the mess. Trembling slightly, Elana tried not to look where the queen sat reclined. She did not want to get caught and flogged for staring.

"Jezebel, my love. There is no need for any fury—"

Elana's eyes widened. King Ahab was in the room? This did not sound good. Whenever they were together, they were worshipping idols or arguing about Elijah or whatever the godly prophets of God had said.

Pretending not to hear what was being spoken between them, Elana went behind the veiled section where the bathtub lay. Gently, she poured water from the heavy jar. The argument on the other side continued.

"You, Ahab, are a weak man! You let all those prophets cause havoc and ruin our lives. Look at Elijah, who disappeared. Where is he? Where did he go? One day he was here cursing us with drought, and the next he disappeared. Where to? No one knows!" She screamed again, and Elana covered her ears when something else flew across the room, shattering. "He needs to die!"

"Elijah is nothing to us, beloved. If he disappeared, he has probably left us for good. Who knows, maybe he is already dead," Ahab answered in a soothing tone.

"Is he dead? Did you see him die?"

Elana shuddered at the poison in Jezebel's voice. Another object thundered and shattered against the wall.

"All those prophets must die, Ahab. None must be kept alive." Jezebel seethed.

"They are yours to do as you please," Ahab replied with a tired tone to his voice.

Suddenly a low hysterical laughter echoed in the room. The hairs at the nape of Elana's neck prickled in fear.

"I don't need your permission, Ahab." More laughter. "I will do as I please. Today those prophets of God must be killed! Let it be done!" she screamed and threw yet another object against the wall.

Elana heard a few gasps from the servants. Then Ahab spoke again.

"Let it be done as my queen has commanded," he shouted. "I will alert Obadiah of the decree."

Elana heard footsteps leave the room. With a pounding heart she leaned against the wall to settle her nerves. Tears filled her eyes as she thought of all the prophets of God that were about to lose their lives. Why? For the whim of an evil woman who did not want to follow rules or be told what to do. Such a waste to have these good men die. Elana wiped her tears, took in a shaky breath, put her shoulders back, and went to the door. Before leaving the room, she stole a quick glance at Jezebel, who sat reclined in her seat with her eyes closed and a hand over her forehead.

"Hurry with my bath!" Suddenly she sat up and pointed her long, thin finger at Elana. "Do you want to die as well? Get my water now!" The room thundered under her shouts, and Elana, trembling, hurried to do as she was asked.

She hoped she would see another day—it was hard to tell how long a person had to live with a demonic person like Jezebel.

Closing her eyes briefly, she said a quick prayer and asked God for strength.

Chapter Three

The days that followed were sad and full of gloom. The death of the prophets had rocked the believers. Everyone trembled at the thought that Jezebel could have anyone killed if they angered or irritated her. She commanded, and it was done. Never had Israel felt so fragile and unsafe.

Elana's heart felt broken, and although she was a simple slave girl and could not do much, she still wanted to assist. One stifling afternoon, as she hurried with an empty jug to the almost dry pool, she saw someone in the distance coming toward her. She squinted and recognised it was her dear friend Obadiah. As he got closer, he said hello and whispered as he walked past, "Meet me near the north wall tonight as the moon rises." Then he continued walking to his destination. Her heart thumped in her chest. She was sure he had a secret to tell her. Evening could not come soon enough.

"Are you going to bed yet?" Ayelet asked when she saw Elana sitting outside near the servants' quarters.

"No. I cannot sleep tonight. I will get more fresh air." She lied.

The younger girl nodded and bid her good night before going in.

Elana exhaled, covered her head with a dark veil, and hurried to the north wall—the wall where Obadiah had scared her the evening she had seen the ritual. She had left her worn sandals in her room and walked barefoot on the hot, dusty ground. She was afraid they would make too much sound and she would be discovered before reaching her friend. As she got closer to the wall, she looked around, trying to see if she saw a figure in the shadows.

"Psst."

She turned around at the sound and saw a dark silhouette. Obadiah! She ran the last few steps to him.

"Obadiah!"

"I cannot stay long, my dear." His voice sounded anxious.

Elana felt her heart beating faster. "What has happened?" she whispered, leaning closer to the wall to avoid being seen by any guards or anyone roaming at night.

Obadiah cleared his throat and leaned closer to her. "I have saved one hundred prophets."

Elana's head came up with so much force her veil fell to her shoulders. "Obadiah, how?"

"With God's help, I have vowed to protect them. I could not get to all of them in time, but I did all I could." His voice shook.

"What if Jezebel finds them?" Her voice trembled with emotion.

"They are in two different caves." He exhaled. "I put fifty in one and fifty in the other."

"What can I do to help?"

"I need you to help me feed them. I know with the drought there is not much food in the land, but the palace has plenty. Please save me some every day if you are able to."

In the darkness, she nodded. "I will."

Without another word, Obadiah fled, and she watched the shadow disappear into the dark night. She did not even realise she was crying until she felt the corner of her eyes wet. She wiped them with her veil and looked up to heaven.

"Thank you, God," she whispered and hurried off to bed.

Elana worked hard and volunteered a lot of her time in the kitchen helping cook meals. She needed to gather food for the prophets. Every day, the palace cook gave Elana bags of food to discard. The waste was immense, even amid a famine.

"This bread is still good." She peeked inside the bag.

"The queen wants freshly made bread every day." The short, plump woman shrugged. "There is nothing to do but obey."

Feeling happy, Elana nodded and hurried out of the kitchen to place the bag with the other ones she had collected. She had fruits, nuts, breads, honey, and even dates stashed away.

Jezebel demanded that new food grace her banquet table daily. As night settled in, Elana hurried to the back door carrying a sack, opened the door, and saw Obadiah waiting for her.

"It's all here. More than usual," she whispered, looking around to make sure no prying eyes saw their exchange. "Now go!" Elana handed the sack filled with food.

The older man touched her cheek gently. "Thank you, dear Elana. The prophets will be grateful." Then, without another word, he covered himself with the cloak and ran into the silence of the night.

"May God protect you!" she called softly.

Elana bolted the door shut, ran up the few stairs that led to a higher area of the servants' quarters, and peered out the window to watch Obadiah go. She closed her eyes and said a silent prayer for his safety and for the safety of the one hundred prophets of God Obadiah had saved.

"What are you doing?"

Elana jumped and put her hands to her racing heart. "Ayelet! You frightened me!"

"Did you think it was Queen Jezebel coming to get you?" The girl laughed.

"No." Elana let her heart calm down before speaking again. "I could not sleep and was looking out the window at the . . . stars."

Ayelet frowned and pushed herself up on tiptoe. "I do not see any."

Elana laughed nervously. "I did not either. That is why I was going to bed. Come, Ayelet. We have a busy day tomorrow." Elana moved away from the window to head to their room.

The younger girl looked out the window one more time and sighed. "I thought you were watching something exciting happening out there." With hunched shoulders, she followed Elana.

Elana let out a breath of relief. The last thing she needed was for this guileless girl to tell someone what she and Obadiah were up to and have them both killed by Jezebel. The thought paralysed Elana. She did not want to die.

The day was hot and dry. The famine was severe in all the land, and every pond and lake had been swallowed by the burning sun. In Israel, rain and dew were life-giving. It was essential for the growth of grains and fruit trees and for watering the livestock. Wells were drying fast, and Elana feared they would soon have nothing to eat or drink.

The pools of the palace had no water for Jezebel to keep, and therefore, every day she demanded they take water from the wells to draw her bath. Besides the work being arduous and tedious, Elana felt more anger than fatigue at the selfish ways of Jezebel. She wondered when it would end. It had been several very long years of drought. The only hope she felt was that Elijah had come back. She did not know where he had been all these years, but he had returned.

Elana had heard whispers from the slaves before coming up to fill the queen's bath that a few days ago the king had been up at Mount Carmel with Elijah, 450 priests of Baal, and the prophets of Asherah. Elijah had challenged all of Israel that it was time to stop wavering between two opinions. They were to follow God or Baal.

They had placed an altar with the sacrifice of the meat of bull in the middle, ready for the ceremony. Elijah had said that they were to call on the name of their god, and he would call on the name of the Lord, and the god that answered by fire and consumed the sacrifice— he would be the one true God.

For hours, from morning until noon, the priests called on the name of Baal. They slashed themselves with swords and spears, as were their customs until their blood flowed. Midday passed, and no response came from Baal.

Then it was Elijah's turn. He took twelve stones for each of the tribe of Jacob and dug a large trench. He arranged the wood, cut the bull into pieces, and laid it on the wood. Then he asked for four large jars with water and poured the water on the offering and on the wood. The water ran down around the altar and even filled the trench. Then he prayed, "Lord, the God of Abraham, Isaac, and Israel, let it be known today that you are God in Israel. Show them you are God."

Suddenly the fire of the Lord fell and burned up the sacrifice, the wood, the stones, and the soil. It also licked up the water of the drain. When the people saw this, they prostrated themselves and acknowledged that God was indeed the only God! When Elana heard this, tears filled her eyes. Her God was alive!

As Elana rounded the corner and walked through the door, she saw Jezebel's painted face distort with fury. Her amber eyes slanted, and fire seemed to burn from within them. Four servant boys stood in different corners, circulating air with fans created with many ostrich feathers. They held the papyrus-umbel handle with both hands, and with their white knuckles, Elana knew they were trying desperately not to drop them.

"He did *what?*" Jezebel sat up from her reclining ivory-coloured seat and swung her legs over the side. Today she wore a luxurious dress made of purple, the colour worn only by royalty. On her head she wore a crown embellished with too many stones, a gold necklace adorned her neck, and multiple bracelets cascaded from both her arms. Her feet were clad in golden sandals. As she paced the room, her jewellery jolted along with her. Elana tried not to stare, but it was hard not to watch her. She looked like one of her many idols that filled the gardens. Her presence demanded attention, but it also brought fear and unrest. Elana could never relax when she was around. Jezebel turned back to the person she had spoken to, her husband, Ahab, who had obviously returned from Mount Carmel.

"Jezebel, it was . . . it was . . . astonishing to see." Ahab sat across from his wife dressed in a blue gown and red cape. Today no crown adorned his head, and he had groomed his dark beard.

"Astonishing?" she growled. "Do you hear yourself, Ahab? You sound impressed by Elijah."

"My dove, I am not impressed. I am merely . . . astonished . . . surprised." He reached out for her hand, and she pulled it back angrily.

"Why does his God listen to him, Ahab?"

Ahab shrugged.

"Oh, Elijah, how I loathe you." She fumed. "One day I will kill you."

Her husband chuckled.

"Ahab, are you laughing at me?" She stood and towered over him.

"No, I do not laugh at you, my beloved. I think your wish to kill him will become true."

She sank back in her seat. "Oh?"

Elana watched Ahab lean forward and take her hand. "I think you will need to take a deep breath and let me finish until the very end. I do not have pleasant news."

Elana felt her stomach flip as she waited to hear the unpleasant news.

Chapter Four

"Tell me!" Queen Jezebel demanded.

"Calm yourself, my love." Ahab took a deep breath and spoke words that stunned Elana.

"During the ceremony at Mount Carmel, Elijah had all of your priests . . . killed."

Elana gaped.

"No!" The thunderous screech from Jezebel trembled through every fibre of Elana's being, and in her shock, the jar fell from her shaky hands, shattering and splattering water and pottery all over the immaculate marble floor. She sucked in her breath and became like a statue. She was *dead*.

To her relief, both Ahab and Jezebel did not turn to glance her way. Instead, Ahab shot from his seat and stood against the wall, watching his lunatic wife go wild. Jezebel was maddened and threw everything she could reach for across the room. Her mouth spat profanities, and she tore at her purple gown. Her face was crimson, and smoke seemed to puff out from her ears. Furiously, she hit one of the servant boys and sent him flying across the room. With significant force, she upturned her reclining seat, and with a sharp object from her ivory desk, she tore at her delicate pale wrists, slashing her skin until blood trickled out. Her body trembled as she reached out and rang her bronze gong.

A soldier appeared and bowed low, waiting for her instruction.

"Find Elijah and eliminate him. He has destroyed my priests, so I will destroy him!"

The soldier saluted and was just out the door when Jezebel roared, "Give him a message: may the gods deal with me, be it ever so severely, if by this time tomorrow I do not send his life to Hades!" Another object was hurled against the wall as the soldier disappeared, and Elana heard him run down the long corridor.

In a panic, Elana ran out and did not pause until she was outside, sitting in a quiet corner of the garden. Dark forces controlled Jezebel! Poor Elijah, they would kill him. Elana cocked her head to one side, but then again, God Jehovah had protected him so far. She must rest assured that his protection was undeniable.

She glanced at the sky and for the first time noticed dark clouds forming above. Her eyes widened. Could it be rain? The darkness across the sky continued, and suddenly she heard the sweet sound of thunder. It was going to rain!

Elana's heart danced with joy—there was still hope for them, and the miracle of their God was still palpable.

She looked at her arms as refreshing water droplets tickled her skin. How could something so simple as water feel so incredibly perfect? Finally, the animals, the vegetation, and the wells and lakes would fill up and overflow once again with living water.

As the thunder got louder, she reluctantly headed indoors with a contented heart, trusting that the Lord would look after Elijah and he would live.

Even though the weeks were slow, the fresh rain that graced the fields made Elana not dread each day. The earth smelled of new life, and all around her, everything looked lovely and alive. A soft breeze blew as Elana and Ayelet hurried through the garden carrying silken wraps, ointments, and scented oils to hand over to Jezebel's personal maids. Earlier that day, while taking a stroll in the garden, Jezebel had felt the urge to bathe in the pool and demanded her scented oils and clothing be brought to her.

Ayelet reached the maids first and handed over the oils and ointment; then Elana also gave the maids the silken wraps from Persia and hurried to get away. She did not want to watch or be near Jezebel.

"Ayelet!" she called when the younger girl had stayed behind gossiping with the maids.

Reluctantly, Ayelet followed, dragging her sandaled feet. "Oh, Elana! I was just catching up on palace rumours."

Elana shook her head. "Sometimes it is better not to listen. I have learnt to keep quiet and keep working. I live a much happier life that way."

"It is true. But Bemnet, the queen's Ethiopian personal maid, said that the queen is angry because Elijah is missing. He ran away when she threatened to kill him, and they haven't seen him since that day."

Elana didn't say a word and let the girl talk. She had to ask Obadiah as soon as she could.

Later that day, as she made her way to the servants' quarters, she had the urge to look out the window. She ran up the little steps and peeked out the window. To her delight, she saw Obadiah coming with an empty food sack. She ran back down and opened the door before he knocked.

"Obadiah! Is it true!?" she puffed.

"Is what true, child?" His brow wrinkled.

"Is it true that Elijah is missing and not dead?"

Obadiah put his index finger over his lips, motioning for her to be quiet, and moved his head to one side for her to follow him.

Elana closed the door and followed him to the side of the building. She waited for him to speak.

He turned to her and beamed. He looked older today and a little weary. "It is true." He chuckled. "The day Ahab came to me to with the decree, I was horrified and sent word as fast as I could. I do not know if the news ever reached Elijah, but he disappeared soon after."

"I am so pleased." She clapped her hands softly.

"As am I. We cannot lose another prophet." He shook his head.

"I hope one day Jezebel and Ahab leave this place. I know it is wishful thinking, but it is my hope."

"I do not think that will happen, my dear Elana. Sadly, they have children, and they will follow in their parents' evil ways. Only God can save us."

She groaned. It was true.

Many weeks later, Elana found out through Obadiah that Elijah was finally out of hiding and safe. Jezebel's anger had subsided for the time being until she burst with another anger fit because something did not go according to *her* plans.

When Elana went to the kitchen to help, she was told she was not needed and was sent to the king's meeting room in the west wing of the palace. She was to water the endless plants he kept there. She was then to water Queen Jezebel's plants and those in another four rooms after that. The process was simple, but it did require for her to make many trips to the water hole they used for plant watering. Ayelet was sent to dust the ivory ornaments throughout all the palace. Guests were arriving in a few days, and everything needed to gleam spotless. Elana sighed and hurried to do her duty.

It would take her a while to gather water and carry it from place to place. She started with Jezebel's room since she wasn't there and would finish with the king's room. Two hours later, she hurried to the king's meeting room to water the plants. She heard voices coming from within. The door was slightly ajar. She glanced inside and to her horror saw that Jezebel was pacing the room and fanning herself with a delicate red fan. Her golden sandals made noise each time she walked. She was talking to the king, who was resting face down on his reclining seat. It sounded like he was crying. Elana frowned. Why would the king be crying? And why were there fresh fruits tossed on the floor?

She resisted the urge to run away and waited silently on the other side to gain confidence to knock on the door. She lifted her shaky hand to knock but stopped when she heard Jezebel speak.

"I do not understand why you are tearful and refuse to eat?"

Elana saw an enormous plant in a corner near the door, and she hid slightly behind it so as not to be seen. Then she silently watched the scene unfold before her through the opening.

Ahab sat up and crossed his arms across his chest. He wiped tears from his eyes. Elana covered her mouth with her hand to stop from laughing. He looked like a petulant child!

Ahab turned away.

Elana rolled her eyes at seeing Ahab's behaviour. What had caused such behaviour? Her curiosity was piqued, and she leaned in closer to listen.

Chapter Five

Jezebel paced the room and finally paused in front of her husband with both of her jeweled arms on her hips. "Ahab, you must tell me why you are so sullen!" she demanded, her voice losing its patience.

Ahab sighed, pouting, and said, "I feel angry and sad!"

"That part is obvious," she stated. "Look at the platter of fruits hurled on the ground like pigs' food. You cannot put any of that in your mouth."

"I won't!"

"Tell me what the matter is." She paced the room.

Ahab groaned and put his head down. "I went to see Naboth, that pestilence from Jezreel. We had words, and he refused the king!"

Jezebel stopped pacing and sat across from her husband. "What do you mean?"

"Naboth refused to sell me his vineyard!" Ahab slapped his leg. "How dare he!"

"You want his vineyard? Whatever for?"

"I want to grow a vegetable garden since his vineyard is so close to the palace. I think it's very convenient for me to use. I offered to give him a better one farther away, and I would pay whatever he asked for his vineyard."

"And?" Jezebel leaned and rested her elbows on her knees, her bangles moving noisily with her.

"He refused!" Ahab hurled a piece of fruit from his bed to the back wall.

"What exactly did he say that makes you think he refused your offer?"

"He said, 'The Lord forbids I should give you the inheritance of my ancestors.' Can you imagine such vulgar words?" Ahab folded his arms across his chest again and scowled.

Jezebel threw her head back and roared with laughter. By the look on Ahab's face, he was not amused by his wife's reaction.

She stood and sauntered to sit next to him. She rubbed his back and grinned. "My beloved, is this a way the king of Israel acts?"

He stared at her with a blank look and shook his head.

"Get up and eat! Rejoice." She smirked. "I will get you the vineyard of Naboth." She kissed him and walked over to the desk, sat down, and wrote on the open scroll.

"What are you planning?" He stretched his neck, trying to decipher from where he sat what she was writing.

She did not reply.

He did not ask again; instead, he rubbed his beard, deep in thought.

Jezebel folded the scroll, placed his seal over it, and rang the gong. Elana watched in fascination as a soldier entered from the side door and bowed.

Jezebel stretched her arm with the scroll. "Take this to the elders and nobles who live in Naboth's city, and tell them I command they do as this says."

The man took the scroll, bowed, and left the room.

Jezebel rubbed her hands together. A satisfied look registered on her face, her amber eyes slanted and malicious.

Ahab reached for her hand and pulled her with force onto his lap. "What did you write?"

She placed her hand around his neck and leaned her embellished head onto his. "I have proclaimed a day of fasting and have requested they seat Naboth in a prominent place amongst the people so—"

"Prominent?"

She placed her index finger on his lips. "Shh. Once he is seated, two vagabonds will accuse him in front of everyone that he has cursed both God and the king." An ominous smile crept over her red lips. "The town will be horrified to know Naboth has turned against you, and they will stone him to death—when that happens, you are to take possession of your vineyard!"

Ahab stared at his wife with his mouth agape. He blinked a few times, and a grin appeared on his lips. "My beloved! You are too ingenious!" He threw back his head and laughed. "I adore you," he whispered hoarsely.

Jezebel leaned into his kiss, and Elana recoiled in disgust. Without another glance she ran from her hiding area, covered her mouth with her hand, and cried.

A few seasons had passed since the awful incident with Naboth and his vineyard. The king had confided in Obadiah what was to happen, and Obadiah had confirmed with Elana that Naboth had indeed been stoned to death. Her heart constricted and anger bubbled inside thinking of Ahab roaming the stolen vineyard.

A few days later, as the sun settled for the night, Ayelet came running to where Elana stood washing the evening dishes.

"Elana! Elana!"

"What is wrong?" Elana dried her hands on a cloth and turned to the girl. Her brown eyes looked bigger than usual.

"The king has gone crazy!" the girl exclaimed. "No one can understand, especially the queen."

Elana frowned. Was this another wild imagination of Ayelet? "Well, let him be a lunatic if he desires. I cannot worry about his antics. I have work to do!"

Ayelet moaned and ran back out. "I will find out more."

Elana smiled and shook her head. That girl loved the palace scandals.

A soft knock on the back door startled her. She hurried to open it and was surprised to see her friend there. "Obadiah!" She opened the door wider and walked outside. In the shadows, no one would see them.

"What has happened?" she asked.

The old man put a finger over his lips and motioned for her to follow him to the east garden, the one with barely any idols. Elana followed his footsteps silently and wondered what this could be about. Finally, they stopped behind a grand pillar. Obadiah pointed, and she followed his finger. Soft light from the palace illuminated a figure sitting on the hard ground.

"It's King Ahab."

She gulped. That was not the king. All she could see was a bearded man with torn clothes, covered in a sack, looking dishevelled and very much like the beggars who invaded the streets of the city. Surely this could not be the king!

Obadiah must have sensed her hesitation and uncertainty, because when she looked at him, he nodded.

"What happened?" she said. Ayelet was correct. He had gone mad.

"Elijah went to see him while he was in the vineyard of Naboth."

"Oh?"

Obadiah continued, "The Lord sent Elijah to tell Ahab that the dogs will lick up his blood when he dies because he has sold himself to evil and has done great wrong in the Lord's eyes."

She gasped. "That sounds torturous."

"That's not all," Obadiah continued whispering. "He told him great disaster will be brought to him and his descendants would cease to exist."

Elana covered her mouth.

"God also had a message regarding Jezebel. He said dogs will devour Jezebel by the wall of Jezreel. Dogs will eat those belonging to Ahab who die in the city, and the birds will feed on those who die in the country."

Elana's stomach turned at the thought of the great disaster that awaited Ahab and his family.

She now understood why Ahab mourned. Her eyes travelled from Ahab, who sat whimpering, and noticed a shadow standing at the window. Jezebel stared at her husband below. She was too far for Elana to see her face, but her posture showed that she was angry. One of her children stood next to her, and she rested her hand on the child's shoulder.

Elana sighed as she contemplated the future of the house of Ahab.

Chapter Six

The years trickled by, and although Ahab had experienced a sorrowful moment, he resumed in his old ways as if nothing had been predicted. He continued to enjoy their pagan worship and his idolatrous ways. The queen continued being a major influence not only over Ahab but also over her children. They were growing as corrupt as their parents.

One early morning, as Elana made her way to Queen Jezebel's room with a pile of soft linen, she bumped into Zethara, the eunuch. His eyes were wild and crazed.

"The king has gone to war!" he cried.

"To war! Who has called a war?"

"The king of Aram."

Elana's brow creased. For a few years, there had been peace between Aram and Israel.

"I thought there was peace between—"

"Aram has called a war," he interrupted, "and the king has left. Pray for him, Elana!" Then, with those words, the big man ran down the long corridor and down the stairs behind the servants' quarters.

Elana had often wondered how long the peace would last between these two countries and was disheartened a war had arisen again. She shook her head sadly and had a feeling deep in her heart that Ahab would not come home alive. She remembered the prophecy Elijah had told Ahab a few years ago.

The dogs will lick up his blood when he dies because he has sold himself to evil and has done great wrong in the Lord's eyes. A great disaster will be brought to Ahab, and his descendants will cease.

She cringed at the thought and, taking a deep breath, hurried to the queen's bedchamber. Jezebel sat with her son and daughter, deep in quiet conversation. They did not look up when she entered and quietly placed the material in its rightful place.

She walked out again and was not seen once. Did they, too, sense the dreadful fate that awaited the king?

The next week seemed to drag, and news from the war front continued to arrive at the palace. Messengers came and went day in and day out, and each time Elana waited with dreaded anticipation when the awful news would come. Although King Ahab was a very flawed man, she wanted nothing fatal to happen to him. Death caused too much pain. Yet she knew the God Jehovah was in control and he would act accordingly.

One early morning, she woke up to loud cries in the servants' quarters. Elana sat up on her bed and blinked a few times, trying to adjust her blurry eyes to the soft light coming through the tiny window. Rain pelted outside and thick clouds roamed the sky. It was going to be raining all day, by the look of things.

She turned to look at the empty bed of Ayelet and wondered where she had gone. Covering her head with a veil, Elana stood and wandered out of her room to see what all the commotion was about. She saw Ayelet running toward her. The girl took her hand and with round eyes whispered, "The king is dead."

Elana grimaced. She feared that was the case. "How did he die?" She was almost afraid to ask.

"Someone drew their bow at random and hit the king of Israel," a male voice responded.

Elana looked up and saw Obadiah standing at the doorway with a grim look on his face. Although the king had been evil, she could understand how Obadiah would be feeling. He had been his overseer for many years.

"Ayelet, Queen Jezebel needs some essential oils for an oncoming headache. Please take them to her," Obadiah asked the girl.

Ayelet nodded and hurried away.

Once the girl left, Obadiah continued talking. "The king asked to be taken out of fighting because he was wounded. The battle raged all day long, and the king was propped up in his chariot facing the Arameans." Obadiah's eyes moistened. "The blood from his wound ran onto the floor and chariot, and that evening he died."

Elana's heart felt heavy. She patted Obadiah's arm, showing that she understood. "How is the queen?" she asked.

Obadiah shrugged. "It is hard to tell—she did not show emotion when I told her . . . she has been silent. I assume she is suffering in her own way."

"Hmm," was all Elana could say. Outside she heard the rain strengthen and the wind howl. She wrapped the veil a little tighter and looked up at her dear friend for many years. A father figure who had become her constant strength.

"Thank you, Obadiah, for all you do at the palace and for all you do for. . . me."

Obadiah smiled and touched her face with the back of his hand. "My child, you have been a great comfort to this old man. You truly have been like a daughter."

Elana sighed and threw her arms around his shoulders. "Thank you for being so kind to me." She knew this was not protocol, but she did not care. She was thankful for all his loving care. She was unsure of what the future held for the palace now that King Ahab was dead, but she knew that with God Jehovah, she had a secure future.

Epilogue

841 BC, Israel

Elana walked the long corridors of King Ahab's ivory palace and looked up at the tapestries covering the walls. The opulence of the place remained, but one thing had changed. Jehu, the new king appointed by the prophet Elijah a few years back, reigned as the new king of Israel.

Jehu had destroyed all the descendants of Ahab and Jezebel. He had also abolished Baal worship in Israel and had burnt the statues in the temple. All of Israel felt a sense of cleanliness and revival.

Elana walked past the room that had once belonged to Jezebel, and she stopped to take a quick look inside. Everything remained as it had once been. The new king had refused to use Jezebel's room, and she could understand why. Every time she had entered the room, an unpleasant presence seemed to fill it—unrest and tumult had been the constant occurrence in those quarters. Elana closed the door quietly and leaned her head against the door. So many unpleasant memories resurfaced—she had not been in Jezebel's room since her death.

Elana closed her eyes as her mind travelled to that unpleasant day.

News had come to Jezebel that Jehu had killed her beloved son, Joram. The news shattered her heart, and she mourned him deeply. Then one day a messenger announced Jehu was on his way to see the queen. Two of her eunuchs entered the room and helped the queen prepare.

Rising from her reclining seat, Jezebel washed herself, adorned her hair, put on heavy makeup, and looked out the window to see Jehu enter the gates. The eunuchs were going to leave, but she told them to stay in the room for further instructions. She had a plan for Jehu. She was prepared to eliminate the man who had caused the death of her son.

When Jehu entered the gates in his chariot, he looked up and met Jezebel's cold eyes. Leaning over the vast window, she screamed down to him. "You murderer. You killed my son. Now I will kill you!"

Jehu remained calm as he observed her enraged, distorted features. "God is the one who repays the wrong." He rode his warrior chariot closer to the window.

"Come up, Jehu, if you are not a coward," she hissed.

The warrior stayed quiet, and suddenly he lifted his arms in the air and shouted, "Who is on my side? Who?"

Jezebel's two eunuchs came to the window behind her, Zethara being one of them. Jehu motioned for the men with his head and cried, "Throw her down!"

Without hesitation, Zethara and Admathe pushed Jezebel from the window, and her blood splattered onto the palace walls, while the horses of Jehu chariots trampled her underfoot.

When the sickening news reached the entire palace, Elana, Ayelet, and the other servants were horrified at the horrific death she had endured. Although a great relief settled in the palace with the ending of a wicked monarch, there was also a heavy gloom that resided for weeks.

Later Jehu had ordered for Jezebel to be buried, but all they found was her skull, her feet and her hands. Dogs had devoured Jezebel's flesh just like the prophet had spoken.

The sound of running feet brought Elana back to the present. Ayelet, who had grown into a lovely woman and was married to a servant man, was coming toward her with a big grin.

"Obadiah is here, Elana. He is here to see you!"

Elana squealed like a little child and rushed down the long corridor, through the servant quarters, and out the back door. Her dear friend, who had left a few years back after the death of King Ahab, no longer worked for the palace, and she did not see him as often as she would like. A new overseer had taken over, and nothing was the same.

His back was toward the door, but he turned when she clicked the door shut. The man standing there looked older but in good health. His kind eyes and smile brought so much joy to Elana.

"Obadiah!" She reached for his hands and gave them a squeeze. "What are you doing here? It has been too many seasons."

He grinned. "I am here on official duties."

"Oh?" She hoped he was coming back to work for the new king.

"This is for you." He extended his hand and held out a scroll for her to unfold.

Elana looked down at the paper, then at Obadiah, and back at the paper, feeling perplexed.

"Go ahead, open it," he encouraged.

Frowning, Elana unrolled the piece of paper and read the heading: "DEED OF FREEDOM—PAID IN FULL."

Confused, she looked up at him. "What is this?"

"This, my dear, is your deed of freedom. You are no longer a slave to the palace or anyone. You are free!"

Elana's hands trembled, and tears filled her eyes. "How?" she said, although her throat was constricting.

"I paid for your freedom in full."

Elana felt her heart accelerate and twist with emotion.

"My wife and I want to see you liberated from slavery." He beamed.

Tears rolled down Elana's face, and she threw herself into Obadiah's arms and shouted with elation. Laughter and joy bubbled up. She was *free*? She was free!

"Obadiah, I would love nothing more than to be free. Thank you!" She hugged him one more time and cried joyful tears.

After all these years, she was finally going to be a free woman.

She looked up to heaven and shouted, "Thank you, God Jehovah!"

Four

Jehosheba: Fearless Princess of Judah

When Athaliah the mother of Ahaziah saw that her son was dead, she proceeded to destroy the whole royal family. But Jehosheba, the daughter of King Jehoram and sister of Ahaziah, took Joash son of Ahaziah and stole him away from among the royal princes, who were about to be murdered. She put him and his nurse in a bedroom to hide him from Athaliah; so he was not killed.

—2 KINGS 11:1–2

Find the story in 2 Kings 11:1–21.

Prologue

849 BC, Judah

"Sheba, Sheba, *stop*!" a voice shouted behind her. But she could not stop. Desperately, she ran along the dark corridors of the palace. Her feet were bare on the marble floor. In the distance, she heard the screech of a person or animal. She was unsure which.

The sounds of soldiers yelling, children shrieking, and women sobbing penetrated the very core of her soul. Involuntary shivers ran down her neck and spine, and a sob escaped from her lips. She hoped she was not too late. Jehosheba tightened the dark veil that wrapped around her hair and continued running.

Finally, she came to a door. Her heart pounded as a baby cried from within the closed room. Maybe she was not too late. She stretched out her hand and, with trembling fingers, turned the giant brass doorknob. It did not budge! She pushed again, but the door did not open.

Panic filled her soul, but she did not want to give up. She leaned her whole body against the door and pushed with all her might. She had to hurry. The voices and shouts in the background were getting louder, and soon she would be discovered. Just as she felt the door give way, a hand grabbed her arm. Long fingernails dug into her wrist and sunk their sharpness into her tender skin. Jehosheba winced in pain and looked up.

"Athaliah!" she gasped, and desperately tried to tear her hand away. "Let me go!"

The grip intensified, and an unpleasant smile formed on Athaliah's lips. "I know what you are doing, but I will *not* let you." Her eyes narrowed, and reaching under her cape, she retrieved an object.

The moonlight shifted, and with horror, Jehosheba watched the glistening blade make its way to her throat.

"Athaliah, no!"

Her eyes flew open, and she sat up on her bed. Jehosheba's hand encircled her throat as she rubbed the place the blade had touched in her nightmare. It had felt so real; she was sure Athaliah was going to kill her. Letting out a shaky breath, she rubbed her hands where the nails had sunk into her skin.

"Princess Jehosheba, all is well?" Hila, her personal maid, walked through her bedchambers with a concerned look on her face.

Jehosheba winced. "I'm sorry, Hila, I didn't mean to wake you. Please go back to sleep. All is well." She did not like to lie, but she could not tell her about the nightmare.

Hila frowned. "Very well. I will make you a hot spice drink to help you go back to sleep." With that, Hila left the room.

Jehosheba opened her mouth to protest, then closed it again. There was no use arguing with Hila, who had been her maid since birth.

"Psst."

Jehosheba smiled. She knew that sound as soon as she heard it. She turned her head toward the secret door, which was now ajar with Adina's smiling face peering out.

"All is clear." She motioned for Adina to come in.

Adina's curly long hair bounced as she scurried in. "I heard you scream!" she whispered and sat down on the bed.

Jehosheba exhaled. "I had *that* nightmare again." Her bottom lip trembled slightly as she rubbed her neck.

Adina's hazel eyes widened. "It sounds to me like it's a vision. Maybe something bad will happen and you will have to rescue the crying baby!" Her rushed whispering sent little shivers down the princess's spine.

Could it be a vision? Visions were only the privilege of prophets chosen by God. Not *her*. Jehosheba grabbed her thick, dark mane and plaited it quickly to get it out of her overheated face. She loved the hairstyle and had copied the look from a Roman princess, who had visited her father, King Jehoram, and Athaliah, her evil stepmother. At the thought of Athaliah, Jehosheba quivered.

"I think I am having these dreams because Athaliah is evil and I dislike her."

Adina exhaled and flicked her vast curls. "Hmm, maybe. But either way, just pray to God and let him know how you feel."

The princess gave a slight smile and reached for her friend's hand. "Thank you. I will. He is the only one that gives me peace."

The sound of soft footsteps announcing Hila's return made Adina scurry. Jehosheba shook her head as she watched Adina disappear swiftly. Being a servant in the palace since she was little made her know every secret passage and door that the palace kept hidden. A skill she was proud to hold and one she had readily shared with Jehosheba. Of course, as a princess, Jehosheba barely ever used secret passages, but it was convenient when she wanted to spy on Athaliah. The princess had found out a lot of secrets behind those hidden walls.

"Here you are, my princess, a spice drink to relax you." Hila smiled. Jesosheba reached for the hot drink and inhaled the aromas. She picked up the lovely scent of cinnamon and honey. She blew on the tea and took a little sip. Her eyes lit up. It was *delicious*. She licked her lips.

"Thank you. It's delicious."

A satisfied look crept over Hila's wrinkled face, and she beamed. "Now drink up and sleep."

After Hila left, Jehosheba's thoughts went to her nightmare. She did not appreciate losing sleep over something that scared and confused her. Taking the last sip of her drink, Jehosheba yawned and let her body relax. Putting the silver cup on a small table next to her, she leaned back and closed her eyes. But Athaliah's face intruded each time she closed her eyes. Frustrated, she got out of bed and stretched. Maybe a little night air would relax her. She walked to her balcony and took a deep breath. The night was calm and warm. The gentle flickering of the stars flashed in the darkened sky. She loved looking up to heaven and imagining that God was looking directly down at her and extending his hand.

A sudden scream broke through the night. Jehosheba jumped and held her breath. The scream came again, closer this time. Her skin prickled as she peered over the balcony to see if she could see whoever was in trouble. She waited. Then she saw them. Her heart hammered in her chest, and perspiration wet her forehead. Drops of sweat rolled down her face. *Athaliah!*

Her stepmother led a procession of about fifteen priests and priestesses dancing, chanting, and playing tambourines. Jehosheba leaned over the balcony, trying to get a better look at who was screaming. Then she saw her: a young girl about her age dressed in a thin white gown being dragged by two guards. The princess frowned. What wrong could the girl have committed to deserve to be a prisoner of Athaliah?

"Let me go! Let me go," the girl pleaded.

Suddenly Athaliah turned her head and looked up at her. Jehosheba drew in her breath and stepped back into the shadows. Her heart fluttered.

Another scream pierced the darkness of the night as they passed in front of the princess's balcony. Jehosheba expected them to walk down the pathway to the prison divisions, but instead of continuing, they turned right toward the temple of Baal, which rested on a hill overlooking the city.

Realisation hit Jehosheba, and her heart stopped. The girl was going to be sacrificed to Athaliah's god, Baal! She gripped the edge of the balcony, fighting a sudden dizzy spell and nausea. Hot tears fell from her face and onto the ground. What god demanded for people to be sacrificed as a gift to them? Jehosheba wiped her tears furiously. Another scream followed as the chanting got louder. Jehosheba buried her face in her hands and cried. She cried for the girl and for feeling helpless to save someone in need. Her heart hardened, and she glared at the pagan temple mocking her. How she loathed Baal.

Chapter One

849 BC, the palace of Judah

There was evil in the palace. Darkness loomed in every corner—it seeped through the decorated walls like honey oozing from a beehive. Jehosheba shuddered as she walked tentatively down the long hallway with its marble corridor floors. She wondered if she was overreacting, but she did not think so.

The spirit of unrest and doom seemed to grow with intensity the viler Athaliah became. Jehosheba's woven sandals click-clacked too loudly for her liking. Not wanting to get caught, she continued walking on tiptoe to avoid the sound of her shoes.

In the distance, she heard a door slam, followed by shouts. The princess shuddered; it was *her* yelling at her father again! Their shouts became louder as she got closer to her father's meeting room. She wondered what they were fighting about this time. Thinking quickly, she ran to the scroll room, which was next to her father's meeting room, and softly closed the door behind her. The dust in the room made her nose itch, and the desire to sneeze increased— she covered her mouth and nose with the sleeve of her soft, light blue linen gown and sneezed. She sighed with relief when the voices continued arguing.

Jehosheba went over to the silver sword that hung on the wall, grabbed the handle, and turned it to the right. Instantly, a small part of the wall opened, and she slipped inside. Then she turned the handle of the second sword in the secret room and watched as the piece of wall screeched softly into place. Feeling safe, Jehosheba walked a few steps down the slight, dark secret passage. She let her eyes adjust to the darkness and padded to her father's meeting room, which was a few steps away.

"She is too young, Athaliah. I will not have it!" her father shouted.

The princess pressed her chest against the wall and peeked through the tiny hole.

Athaliah's dark hair was piled high, covered with jewels and glimmering with precious stones. Today she wore a white-and-golden dress that accentuated her slim body. Her crimson lips pursed angrily.

"What do you mean you will not have it?" she scowled, spitting like a cobra. "It is not your decision to make." She hissed.

"Jehosheba is *my* daughter!" the king hollered, slamming his fist on a nearby table. "I decide!"

Jehosheba gasped and covered her mouth. They were discussing *her*! But why were they so angry? She listened with intent and waited to see why she was causing problems between them.

Athaliah rubbed her temples. "Jehoram, it is normal for girls her age to be ready for marriage. I believe Prince Aziel will be a wonderful match and bring political alliance between our kingdom of Judah and the kingdom of Edom."

Marriage? Jehosheba felt herself almost choke. She was not ready for marriage at fifteen years old—and certainly not to Prince Aziel who was in his thirties and made her uncomfortable every time he came to see Athaliah. The realisation that they must have been discussing her each time he visited made her cringe.

"I do not want my daughter to marry anyone from another kingdom." Her father slumped in a nearby seat. "Her mother and I decided, from Jehosheba's birth, that she would marry into the Levi tribe."

Jehosheba's eyes rounded. Levi tribe? Did he mean a priest? The Levites served in the temple. She did not object to marrying a godly man. She knew in her heart that she would not marry an idolater.

"A Levite? A Levite?" Athaliah's hand flew to her throat, and her face distorted in horror. "You jest!"

Her father turned his head, stood, and stared at his wife. "I speak in truth. Jehosheba is to marry Jehoiada in due time. He is a direct descendant of the lineage of David. The match is exceptional."

Suddenly Jehosheba felt lightheaded. *No!* Not waiting to hear anymore, she left the secret passage and ran all the way to find Adina. Her heart thundered in her chest at the thought of her arranged marriage. She was not ready to become a wife today or ever!

Hours later, she lay on the cool grass staring at the pictures the clouds made above. Her friend Adina sat next to her, making wreaths with grass shots and tiny flowers.

"I think you would make a wonderful wife for a high priest. You love the God of our fathers, and you are very kind."

Jehosheba smiled. "You are the sweetest friend a girl could have."

"Just think, Sheba, you will no longer witness any of the Baal worshipping. You will be gone from the evilness of this place." Adina tucked a loose curl behind her ear. "Your father is *not* a godly man. He walked away from God many years ago, yet he admits he wants you to marry a godly man. Something that your mother and he decided long ago. That is only from God, Sheba. Take the step and do not be afraid to serve God in the temple with your future husband."

Jehosheba closed her eyes. Adina spoke wisely beyond her years, and everything she said resonated in her heart. She was right, of course. God was arranging her marriage to a good person. The thought of not being part of the palace and witnessing Baal worshipping or seeing Athaliah daily made her heart flutter with anticipation. Maybe getting married would be a good thing for her soul.

"Princess Jehosheba!" The panicked cry from Hila, her maid, echoed in the field. Adina stood, waved good-bye, and ran off, heading toward a back section of the palace where she claimed a secret passageway existed. Jehosheba shook her head but smiled.

"Jehosheba!"

At the sound of Hila's voice closer than before, she blinked, stood, and looked around. There she was, hurrying up the little hill. The princess waved. "Hila, I am here. What is wrong?"

Hila stopped and exhaled. Relief on her face. "Oh, child." She shook her head and pointed to Jehosheba's gown. "Your dress is absolutely dirty. Now you need to change again before the Baal worship ceremony and dinner." The maid wiped her brow with one hand and motioned for the princess to follow.

"Oh no! I forgot about the ceremony." Jehosheba groaned and pouted as they walked back inside and to her room.

"I will also arrange your hair. I do not want Queen Athaliah to be upset at your tardiness and state of clothes." Hila's round face frowned as she continued talking nonstop. She helped her change and arranged her hair in an elaborate Greek style.

Princess Jehosheba grumbled. She did not want to go to the Baal worship room or see Athaliah again. She was afraid of both! Once dressed in her soft white linen tunic and a gold sash around her waist, Hila told her it was time to make her way to the ceremony. Reluctantly, she walked out of the safety of her room and went down to the worship room. Before even seeing the room, she heard its soft drumming coming from inside. She shivered as she entered through the doors. The room was dark and smoky, and the heavy anise and spice scents burnt her nostrils. Instantly, she sneezed.

"Jehosheba!"

The sharp voice startled her, and she jumped, not realising anyone was there. Slowly, her eyes adjusted to the darkness, and she saw her father in one corner talking with two of his concubines, and then she saw her stepmother. Athaliah stood at the foot of the grand Baal altar, dressed in a dress the colour of fire—her golden cobra headdress glimmering under the softness of the candles scattered around the room. The bells on her ankles jingled with each step her bare feet took.

"You are late!" She walked around the princess and looked her up and down. "Your dress is too simple. When you come to worship Baal, you come adorned in your best gown." Her eyes narrowed. "Is that clear?"

Jehosheba gulped, nodded, and stepped slightly back—the woman smelled of incense and wine. The urge to rub her nose was intense, but Jehosheba was aware she could not do that in front of the queen.

"Mother!"

Jehosheba and Athaliah swirled around at the sound of her half brother Ahaziah's voice. The princess smiled at seeing her brother. He had an air about him that commanded attention. Although he was the youngest son and would not be king, he always acted with superiority and claimed he would one day reign. Everything he did was so regal. Jehosheba suppressed a smile at seeing him with his hands on his hips, staring down at them. Sadly, Athaliah had complete control over him, and Jehosheba noticed how she manipulated his every action.

Athaliah's thin red lips broke into a smile, and she extended her arms as she walked toward her son. "Oh, my Ahaziah, it pleases Mother you are here to worship today."

Ahaziah's boyishly attractive face grinned. "I have some requests to make to Baal, Mother, and I know he will answer my prayers."

She took his hands in hers. "He will indeed, my son. He will indeed."

Jehosheba watched the exchange and cringed. He had come late as well, yet Athaliah did not yell at him. Neither did she criticise his simple yellow tunic or the gold sash around his waist. Jehosheba turned her head away and made her way to the back of the room to avoid being seen. She was forced to attend the worship services; however, for Ahaziah it was optional. She shrugged and hid in the darkest corner she could find.

"Jehosheba, why do you insist on hiding when you come to these ceremonies?"

A smile crept on her lips as she turned around and saw her father standing close to her with a smile on his bearded face. He was tall and his arms strong from being in battle.

"Father, I feel shy in these ceremonies. Please allow me to hide." She inclined her head and waited for his response.

"I will not force you to move from your secret spot." He reached for her hand and gave it a pat. "It is good to see you, Daughter."

"It is good to see you too, Father," she whispered, suddenly feeling sad inside for lying. Her father had changed so much throughout the years. The influence of Athaliah had been great. He had become wicked like the queen and even killed his six brothers in order to secure his position in the kingdom. Jehosheba shook her head, trying to get the memory out of her mind. The death of her uncles still felt raw. How she missed her *old* father, but she did not miss the one who stood in front of her.

King Jehoram patted her arm and moved away to the front of the room, where Athaliah would begin the ritual.

It was going to be a long ceremony.

Two hours later, at the conclusion of the service and feeling sick and exhausted, Jehosheba asked her father if she could be excused from dinner and head to her room. He consented, and she was allowed to have dinner in her room. She hurried upstairs while Athaliah remained distracted with her son. The drumming music, the putrid smell of a charred animal that had been sacrificed, the indecent acts, and the cries and gashing of flesh had been nauseating.

During most of the ceremony, she had looked away or covered her face. At one time, she had even covered her ears. Thoughts of the young woman she had seen being taken to be sacrificed in the main temple resurfaced, and she covered her mouth and cried. She ran up the last few steps, flung the door open, and fell on her bed to cry. She was tired of all of this. She could not wait to leave the palace. The idea of marrying the high priest appealed to her more and more. For now, though, she would have to wait at least another few years to marry when she was eighteen. Or at least until her father spoke to her about it and made it official. With an exhausted breath, she closed her eyes and fell asleep.

Chapter Two

The end of the week arrived with much anticipation for Jehosheba. After having been at the ceremony of Baal the other day, she had been feeling quite unsettled. She had anxiously and joyously been waiting for today to arrive. Even though her father no longer practiced going to the temple on the Sabbath day, he allowed the princess to attend, accompanied by two of her maids. Jehosheba always attended with Hila and Adina, as they were also believers and could worship with no one from the palace witnessing.

Once they were seated at the front of the temple, Jehosheba closed her eyes and the soft, melodious music went into her soul. The peace she felt was so very different from the loud ordinary worship she attended at home. When the music was finished and the singing of the choir ended, Jehosheba leaned forward as the high priest made his way to the front and addressed the congregation.

The thought of marrying a high priest entered her mind, and she felt a tremor run down her spine. She turned her gaze back to the priest, who wore an impeccable priestly gown and an ephod which was tied with a linen girdle around his waist. A mitre rested on his head, but what Jehosheba admired was the priest's breastplate, covered in precious stones. The high priest spoke words of inspiration, and there was no chanting or cutting and bruising of skin. He then lifted his hands over the attendants and blessed them.

He read from the Torah: "The Lord bless you and keep you; the Lord make his face shine on you and be gracious to you; the Lord, turn his face toward you and give you peace."

The words settled in her heart, and she lifted her face to welcome the blessing her God would pour out over her. When the service was over, the princess and her maids returned home. Hila remained silent and walked behind the girls as they talked about God and everything they had seen. Jehosheba felt so light as she walked, almost as if she was not touching the ground. How was it possible to go to two worship services yet walk away burdened by one and so peaceful from the other?

Her heart confirmed that everything sinister she felt with worshipping Baal was correct! Feeling content, she burst into a psalm of King David, and seeing her enthusiasm, Adina joined, and both girls sang all the way to the door of the palace. There was no reason to continue singing out loud in the palace—she would only be hushed by those who heard her. She sang in her heart instead.

Jehosheba ran her eyes over the grandeur of her home, with its ivory pillars adorned with an intricate design. The architecture shouted royalty. The vast courtyard was decorated with potted plants and exotic trees. Fountains of waters with statues graced the grounds. However, as her eyes turned to look at the west side of the garden, her eyes rested on the menacing statues of Baal. She wriggled her nose and silenced the song in her heart for the time being.

One afternoon, three weeks after having seen her brother Ahaziah at the Baal ceremony, she bumped into him in the garden.

"Ahaziah!" she grinned, happy to see him.

"Jehosheba, my dear sister." He smiled big, and his light brown eyes twinkled. "You are looking more beautiful by the day."

She inclined her head. "Thank you. But may I comment on how handsome you look?" She pointed to his deep blue tunic elaborately decorated with designs on the collar, sleeves, and hem. He also wore a gold-coloured cape clasped with heads of Baal on each side.

He laughed. "I must confess, there is a reason for my attire." He wiggled his eyebrows up and down.

Jehosheba giggled.

"They have introduced me to my betrothed."

"You are to marry?" She was intrigued. "Who is she?"

"Her name is Zibiah of Beersheba." He rubbed his chin, deep in thought. "We will marry in the next two years. We are making an alliance between our countries." He sighed. "She will make a fine queen one day."

Jehosheba winced. Will he ever get the idea of being king out of his head? His brothers would ascend to the throne, not him. She pursed her lips and instead said, "Congratulations." Jehosheba felt happy for him—hopefully with a wife in the picture Athaliah might loosen the reins she had on him and let him think for himself.

However, he also had influence from his grandmother and his grandfather. His uncles were also close to Ahaziah and had significant influence over him. She sighed deeply, and after talking a little longer, they each parted ways. Jehosheba turned around and watched her younger brother walk away.

"Princess Jehosheba." At the sound of her name, she jumped and swirled around. Hila, her maid, stood there.

"Yes, Hila?"

"Your father would like to see you in the meeting room."

Jehosheba frowned, nodded, and followed the maid to her father's meeting room. She wondered what he wanted to speak to her about. A sudden thought crept into her mind as she knocked on the door. Did he want to discuss her marriage?

"Come in."

She opened the door and went inside. Her father stood from his seat and went to greet her.

"Jehosheba, my child. Take a seat."

The subtle rustle of material made her turn her head to the right, and she almost gasped when she saw Athaliah sitting on a gold chair.

Athaliah watched her with icy eyes. Her thin lips were grim. Today she wore a blue dress elaborated with a lovely design of gold leaves around the waist, bodice, and hem. Her hair was done in the same Grecian style she usually wore. Gold pieces of jewellery completed her flawless look.

Jehosheba looked away and turned her attention back to her father and sat on the chair he pointed to.

"What did you want to see me about, Father?" She tried not to look at her stepmother, who made her uneasy.

"Athaliah and I have been discussing your future," he began, gesturing with his hand toward his wife. "We believe it is time for you to create your own path and future."

Jehosheba nodded, her suspicions of the marriage topic growing. "How?" she asked.

"When you were a little girl, your mother and I had wonderful plans for you. We—"

"Cease flowering the topic, Jehoram." Athaliah's sharp voice interrupted their conversation. "Tell her she is to marry!"

"Athaliah, let me do this my way. She is my daughter, after all." Her father's jaw tightened.

"Who am I to marry?" Jehosheba tilted her head, trying to keep her composure calm.

"I wanted you to marry the wonderful Prince Aziel from the kingdom of Edom. However, your father has another suitor in mind."

"Athaliah! You are not to interrupt!" He pointed his index finger at her. "Remember, you are here against *my* will."

A chuckle escaped Athaliah's lips. "Oh, my dear husband. Although you are the king, you know it is my brains that run the kingdom."

Jehosheba's bit her bottom lip. She spoke the truth. Her father did everything Athaliah commanded. There was nothing he would refuse her.

The king grunted and turned his attention back to his daughter. "As Athaliah mentioned, I have decided for you to marry in the next twenty-four months. Your mother's desire was for you to marry a man from the tribe of Levi."

"Who am I to marry, Father?" She felt her voice tremble slightly.

"Jehoiada, the temple's high priest." Her father stood and paced the room.

Jehosheba covered her mouth. *Jehoiada!* Her father had not changed his mind, and she was to marry a man older than herself. She had seen him at the temple a few times, and although he was years ahead of her, he looked kind and spiritual and was attractive.

"How could your father marry you beneath your station? You are a princess!" Athaliah shifted in her seat and crossed her leg, revealing a long split on the skirt of her gown. Her thin leg was exposed.

Jehosheba averted her eyes, feeling disgusted.

"And how could he make an alliance with a priest? With someone who shuns my god, Baal? I am mortified and offended." Athaliah gave an exaggerated sigh and uncrossed her leg again.

"It was *her* mother's wish!" her father declared.

Jehosheba let them argue while her thoughts travelled to the high priest. He might be a lot older than she was, but she knew she would be happy and away from Athaliah and her nightmares. She wanted to leave and make her life elsewhere. Her mother was a wise woman for having so much forethought.

"Father?" Her voice broke through the argument, ringing loud and clear.

Silence descended upon the room as both distorted angry faces turned her way.

"I will be honoured to marry Jehoiada, the temple's high priest. The man my mother had chosen for me. I thankfully accept." She inclined her head.

"Jehosheba! Do you know what you are saying?" Athaliah jumped up from her chair and stormed toward her. "A high priest in the family? A man who rejects my Baal? I will *not* allow it!" Her nostrils flared, making her look like a wild boar from the Judaean desert.

"Enough, Athaliah!" her father commanded. "Leave my presence now!"

With a screech and cursing under her breath, Athaliah flounced out of the room, leaving behind the scent of frankincense that Jehosheba found repulsive.

When she was gone, her father turned back to her. "Are you sure you are consenting to marrying the high priest?"

Jehosheba nodded. "I have never felt more convinced of anything before." She knew in her heart that if she refused to marry Jehoiada, Athaliah would marry her to the prince she had chosen. The brainless Aziel who was manipulated by her stepmother. No, she would marry the priest and live a content life away from Athaliah. It was a good choice for her.

Her father walked to her and patted her hand. "My fearless Princess Jehosheba. Your mother would be ever so proud."

Jehosheba smiled at the mention of her mother. How she missed her and especially now, as she would soon prepare to become a wife.

Chapter Three

"Oh, Sheba! He is too old!" Adina cried.

The girls were sitting in the garden in a secluded area behind the west wing of the palace. Adina had shown her a secret entry so she could escape into and out of the palace whenever she wanted to remain unseen.

Jehosheba laughed. "It is not too bad, really."

"What about love? I would like to see you marry for love, Sheba. You deserve that." Adina twisted a curl in her hand.

"You forget, Adina, that I am a princess and we do not marry for love. Our marriages are arranged and we obey." The princess's eyes travelled to the birds flying above. "Just imagine, Adina, how free I would be from now on. No more Baal, no more Athaliah. I would be a free woman serving with my husband in the temple. I *am* content with this plan."

Adina reached out for Jehosheba's hand and gave it a squeeze. "I will miss you." Tears filled her eyes.

"I am not getting married yet. Father is waiting until I am seventeen." Jehosheba exhaled. She would miss her dear friend as well. "I will miss you too, dear friend, but I will visit."

"You could also sneak in to visit only me," Adina grinned. "I have taught you all the secret entrances, so you will be safe to come and go."

The princess laughed. "Yes, that is true. But I doubt I will ever need to sneak in. I do like knowing that little secret of ours, though."

The friends looked at each other and laughed wholeheartedly. Statuses forgotten. Only two friends enjoying each other's company and making the most of their short time together.

The two years of preparation for her wedding seemed to fly. From the day she found out she would marry Jehoiada, she began preparing herself spiritually and learning more about the scrolls. Her father planned for the high priest to visit on a weekly basis so they could both get used to each other. They usually met in the garden under the watchful eye of Hila. Jehosheba did not mind. She was used to being watched and looked after. Slowly, she got used to talking to him and her shyness dissipated. She loved talking to him about the God of Abraham and the future of Israel, which did not seem bright.

They talked about Baal and the people who followed him. Jehoiada always said to pray for those people so they could turn away from their confused ways. Jehosheba looked forward to discussing topics she never got to speak with anyone. Although Jehoiada was years older, she never felt he saw her as a child. He respected and treated her like a woman of worth. She liked that.

When they strolled the gardens, she would sense someone watching. Her eyes would turn to the top windows of the palace and know that Athaliah was spying on her. She could not wait to leave the palace grounds. Twenty-four months could not come soon enough.

The day of her wedding was simple. She and Jehoiada asked for nothing opulent and few guests. They wanted something quiet and sweet. Although her father was present at the temple, Athaliah was not. Jehosheba had invited her out of courtesy, but she knew Athaliah would never appear at the temple. Even her father looked uncomfortable and was ready to flee from the wedding scene. The ceremony was beautiful, and Jehosheba beamed with happiness when it was over. Her heart rejoiced knowing she had left the palace for good.

Chapter Four

Jehosheba walked out of the palace, covered her head with the veil, and hurried to the temple—her home. She had been married to Jehoiada for over seven years and had developed a deep affection toward him.

They understood each other well and respected one another. He served at the temple and would come home in the evenings—their home was on the same property as the temple but further toward the back, hidden from the visiting audience. Jehoiada was a zealous man of God and kept the temple and the worship pure. Jehosheba loved being in proximity to her God of Abraham—her mother's God.

She had found serenity away from the palace, and whenever she went back for a visit, her heart felt heavy. The palace had changed even more throughout the years. Jehosheba had witnessed the painful death of her father of an incurable bowel disease—judgement from God, predicted by the prophet Elijah. She also had witnessed the ascent of Ahaziah becoming king after the Arabs attacked the palace carrying off the goods and murdering the sons of her father.

Ahaziah, being the youngest, had not been touched, and he became king chosen by the people. Jehosheba shook her head, remembering those trying days—now she visited the palace to see the children and visit Ahaziah, especially baby Joash, who brought her so much joy.

However, today as she left, she was not feeling cheerful. Hearing Ahaziah planning a visit to his uncle who lived in Israel had bothered her. She instructed him to be careful. But Ahaziah had brushed her off, as he did with almost everyone who tried to advise him. His mother still had full control over his life, and he had become so wicked. As much as Jehosheba loved him, she could not deny and turn a blind eye to his evil ways. Ways so much like Athaliah's. How could one woman have so much influence over a man?

Jehosheba hurried home and was relieved when her feet touched the temple grounds. She was surprised when she exhaled and realised she had been holding her breath. She went inside her home and smiled when she saw her husband sitting at the table reading a scroll.

He looked up when she entered and grinned. "My dear wife, it is good to have you home."

Jehosheba removed her veil and placed it on the table before going over to give him a kiss hello. She took a seat opposite him.

"There is sadness in your eyes. Ahaziah again?" Jehoiada moved the scroll to the side and took hold of her hands.

"Yes. I do not understand why I feel so sad when leaving the palace." She rolled her eyes. "I mean, I can guess why. But I do not want to feel bothered or heavy burdened each time I visit . . . not even baby Joash could cheer my heart today."

"When your love is great for your family, you suffer because of their ways. Ahaziah is your brother, and you dislike seeing him become the victim of his mother." Jehoiada released her hands and leaned back.

"You are right, of course, my dear." She rubbed her sore head with the tips of her icy fingers. "I am also concerned that Ahaziah is going to Israel to visit his uncle." Jehosheba shrugged. "It is weighing heavily on my soul. I had hoped he would not go. He is only a boy of twenty-three."

"Jehosheba, sometimes we make our own path. Young Ahaziah has made his." He stood and went over to a table where a warmed pot of cinnamon tea rested. One that Hila always made for them. He poured a cup and took it to her.

"Thank you," she whispered and, blowing gently, took a sip. The liquid warmed her whole body. "You, my love, are a kind man, and I love you."

He laughed, and his light blue eyes twinkled. "God blessed me with you and for that I am thankful. I love you, my Jehosheba." He kissed the top of her head before taking a seat again.

Her heart bubbled up with happiness. She was blessed too.

The months crept on slowly, and she received word from Adina that King Ahaziah, her brother, had indeed left for Israel. Jehosheba had hoped that he had lost interest in seeing his uncle, but he had gone ahead with his plans. Jehosheba finished reading the letter and burned it as she usually did when she received Adina's letters. Not because she did not want her husband to read it, but more because it was "rumours," as Hila called it, from the palace, and Jehosheba was afraid someone would find it and show Athaliah. She did not want her dear friend Adina to get in trouble and be flogged.

"More palace rumours?" Hila harrumphed as she hobbled around, putting dinner on the table.

Jehosheba laughed. "Oh, Hila, it is not rumours. It's information about my family members. I love reading and knowing how they are doing. Sadly, Ahaziah has decided to go to Israel." She shook her head. "More influence from his uncle."

"Sometimes you need to let them learn hard lessons so they can mature." Hila placed the freshly baked bread on the table and slowly made her way to Jehosheba. She placed her hand on her shoulder. "Princess, do not fret. He will be back soon enough."

And if he's not? she wondered. Jehosheba watched the last remnant of the paper disintegrate in the fire and, without another look, went to her quarters to change for dinner.

Tonight Jehoiada would not join her as he was on duty with his division of priests. Priestly custom chose him to go into the Lord's temple to burn incense. When the days of his service were over, he was to return home.

The pounding of the door woke the princess with a start, and she sat up on her bed with eyes wide. She heard voices and quickly put on her outer robe and went to see what had happened.

A soldier from the palace stood at the door with Hila, who had opened the door. The princess tensed. Something was wrong. The soldier saw her coming over Hila's shoulder and moved to one side and bowed to her.

"Princess Jehosheba, I bring news from the palace." He remained bowed, waiting for Hila to leave.

"Thank you, Hila." She pursed her lips and waited until Hila had left.

"Please." She motioned for the soldier to take a seat, but he refused.

"My visit is short."

"What news do you bring?" She tilted her head to one side.

"King Ahaziah is dead."

The words penetrated Jehosheba's soul, and she froze. Had she heard correctly? She shook her head. "Please repeat what you just said?"

The soldier inclined his head and repeated the dreaded words she thought she had heard wrong. "Your brother King Ahaziah is dead." The man remained with his head inclined, waiting for her to respond.

"How?" she asked.

The soldier lifted his head. "Jehu, the son of Jehoshaphat, gave the orders for him to be killed." The soldier paused, then continued. "He was wounded on the way to Gur near Ibleam. But he guided his chariot to Megiddo, where he died."

Jehosheba covered her mouth. "Have they brought his body home?"

"He will be brought to Jerusalem and will be buried with his ancestors in his tomb in the city of David."

"Has Athaliah been told?"

"She has." With another inclination of his head, he gave her his condolences and left.

Tears welled in her eyes and slowly dripped down her cheeks and onto her nightdress. She sat down and reclined in her chair. How she wished Jehoiada were home to talk and pray together.

"Poor Ahaziah," she whispered. Her heart ached for him. Jehosheba's heart melted at the thought of how kind her brother had been at one stage.

She also remembered him as proud as a peacock, with his chest exploding from pride, when he had become king one year back. Jehosheba did not even remember if he had mourned the death of his brothers when the Arabs had invaded and killed them all.

She groaned. If only he had not visited his uncle frequently. Her heart went out to his wife, Zibiah, and his baby.

At the thought of baby Joash, Sheba drew in her breath. *Joash will grow up without a father, and no child deserves that.*

With an aching heart, she went over and made herself a hot drink to calm her nerves. She wondered what Athaliah would do now that her beloved boy was dead. Jehosheba shuddered and was relieved that she could not become queen after his death. One of her older nephews, the heir to the throne, would reign in Ahaziah's place.

"Would you like something to eat, Princess?" Hila's voice interrupted her thoughts.

"Thank you, Hila, but I am not hungry. The hot drink is sufficient." Jehosheba watched the tired old maid's saddened face. "Please rest, Hila. It will do me good to be alone and pray."

Hila nodded and bid her good night.

Chapter Five

The days trickled slowly, and Jehosheba could not wait for her husband to arrive. He always had the right thing to say and do. She had eaten little the past few days, and Hila was concerned.

"Do not worry, Hila. I am using my lack of appetite as fasting and communion with God." She smiled at the maid.

"Very well, Princess." Hila gathered some clothes and took them to the back rooms to fold.

The loud banging on the back door alerted Jehosheba something was amiss. Usually, no one, besides Adina and the occasional nephew, went through the back door when they visited her. She stood and hurried to open. She unlatched the heavy door and opened it slightly, peering out.

"Adina!" Jehosheba gasped when she saw her dear friend standing outside the door. Her face was pale, her curls barely visible under a black veil, and her body trembled uncontrollably. The princess opened the door wide.

"There's evil in the palace!" Adina choked out as tears streamed down her face and neck.

Jehosheba ushered her friend indoors and closed the door, latching it securely in its place.

"What happened?"

Adina cried harder and buried her face in her hands. Sobs tore through her body. Jehosheba felt panic rise within her. Something terrible had happened, but Adina could barely speak. Jehosheba guided her to a seat near the door and sat with her.

"Adina, please calm yourself. Tell me what's happened!" She rubbed her friend's hands to warm them. She spoke soothing words until Adina settled.

"She killed them all."

Jehosheba frowned. "Killed?"

Adina nodded.

The princess shook her head. "Adina, I do not understand. Who killed whom?"

Adina tightened her grip. "Athaliah . . ." She took a deep, shaky breath. "Athaliah . . . has killed . . ." Her voice trailed off as tears rolled down her cheeks again.

Jehosheba froze. *Killed whom?!*

"When news of your brother's death came to the palace, Athaliah went crazy. Wild like a lion about to attack its prey." Adina paused, closing her eyes. "She tore her clothes and cut herself. She chanted to Baal and asked him to bring her son back."

"Oh, Adina," Jehosheba whispered.

Adina took another deep, unsteady breath. "She vowed no one would ascend to the throne but *her*."

Jehosheba shook her head but did not comment, waiting for her friend to speak.

"Sheba, then she . . . she . . ." Sobs tore through her body once again.

The princess's heart suffered with her friend, and she rubbed her back.

"She then commanded that every royal family member who would ascend to the throne was to be killed!"

Jehosheba's hand went to her throat. "Oh, Adina." She felt the blood drain from her body. *Her family members were dead?*

Her heart thundered like a trapped bird trying to escape. "Has she . . . has she killed them all?" she stammered.

Adina shrugged. "Maybe." She closed her eyes briefly, opened them, then grabbed Jehosheba's hand. "There's evil in the palace, Sheba. It penetrates every room and every dark corner. We hear screams of the victims and shouts from the bloodthirsty soldiers who are more afraid of disobeying Athaliah than killing innocent children." Her voice broke, and she burst into tears again.

Jehosheba felt her body start to shake, but she could not lose her mind right now.

With a great effort, the princess spoke. "Adina, you need to rest now. Come and sleep in one of the extra bedchambers we have. Hila will bring a spiced hot drink for you."

Adina's red, swollen eyes turned to Jehosheba. "I'm so glad she can't get close to you. I'm grateful to God for keeping you alive and away from that possessed woman!"

Jehosheba leaned over and gave her friend a hug. "I'm grateful to my God too."

All these years she had known that God had given her Jehoiada, her husband, the high priest of the temple.

With her mind twirling with thoughts, she walked Adina to the extra bedroom and put her on the bed. She rang the bell and asked Hila to bring Adina a hot, calming drink.

Seeing her friend's fluttering eyelids, Jehosheba walked out of the room and took a deep breath.

The royal family was no more. Her dear nephews were gone? Leaning her forehead against the wall, Jehosheba cried. She took the long sleeve of her tunic and stuffed it in her mouth to muffle her cries. Her heart hurt. Her family. The children were gone. Had Athaliah killed the wives and concubines as well? Had she killed Ahaziah's wife, Zibiah? Then, like a lightning bolt, a name came into her mind. *Baby Joash!*

Has Athaliah killed baby Joash? She gasped for breath. Her mind raced. *What if the soldiers haven't gotten there yet? What if there is a chance?* She had to do something! Her heart trembled at the thought of facing Athaliah. She wiped the little wet droplets on her forehead and her wet face. *Why must she be afraid?* She was no longer a young girl hidden in the shadows, watching helplessly from her bedroom balcony as young girls were taken to be sacrificed to Baal. She was a woman now, and she had *her* God. The God her mother had revealed to her when she was a young girl. The last time she and her mother had been together was while her mother was quite unwell. Taking her daughter's hand into hers, she had prayed over her:

> Lord of Abraham, Isaac, and Moses, bless my daughter, Jehosheba. May she be brave, courageous, faithful, and kind. May she remember whom she belongs to and always depend on you. Bless her with a God-fearing husband and anoint her with your spirit. Protect her from the claws of evil and keep her safe under your wings.

After opening her eyes, Jehosheba saw tears roll down her mother's cheeks. "Remember, Sheba, you are a daughter of a God who protects you from evil."

Jehosheba had nodded and embraced her mother for the last time. That prayer was buried deep in her heart with strength and conviction.

Jehosheba straightened and knelt on the cold floor. She closed her eyes and whispered a prayer:

> God of Abraham, listen to my humble prayer. My heart is breaking at the death of the royal family. *My* family. My God, please give me the bravery to see if someone is still alive. Protect me from evil and cover me with your wings; give me courage and strength.

Her voice trailed off. She opened her eyes as a sudden wave of serenity washed over her heart and a determined spirit filled her soul. She knew what she had to do.

She hurried to her room and looked for a dark gown and veil. She must not be recognised and would take the posture of a servant woman. Feeling frustrated, she found nothing. She might have nothing appropriate, but Hila would! She hurried to Hila's room and knocked gently on the door. No reply.

She must still be tending to Adina! Jehosheba ran down the corridor to the extra bedchamber.

The door to Adina's room was open. Jehosheba stood outside and watched Hila give the hot drink to a trembling Adina.

"Hila." When Hila turned around and looked at her, Jehosheba motioned with her head to come outside.

"Rest a while, Adina. I will give you more spiced tea a little later. Sleep now, dear girl."

Adina didn't complain. She lay back on the bed and closed her eyes.

"Princess?" Hila closed Adina's door halfway.

"I need to borrow one of your dark gowns and a head covering. Please do not ask questions." Jehosheba lifted her head as she did when she meant she was serious and nothing would convince her otherwise.

"Princess Sheba!" Hila's dark, wrinkling eyes widened, and her mouth opened. "Adina told me what has happened. You cannot go to the palace. There's evil there."

Jehosheba grabbed the old woman's hand and gave it a little squeeze. "My God *will* protect me. I need to do something! This is my blood."

Hila's eyes flickered with emotion. Jehosheba could see the turmoil in them. Finally, she took a deep breath and nodded.

Jehosheba leaned over and gave her a squeeze. "Thank you, Hila!"

Jehosheba followed Hila to the room and waited while Hila rummaged through her trunk. Finally, she pulled out a long black gown and matching head veil.

"I wore this when I mourned the loss of my beloved Eitan." Hila held the clothing close to her heart.

"I will not destroy your memory, Hila, I promise." Jehosheba waited for her to give her the clothes.

She knew what it felt like to lose a loved one. She missed her beloved mother dearly. Sadly, she didn't miss her father, King Jehoram.

"Be careful, Princess," Hila whispered as she stretched out her hands and handed her the gown.

"I will."

Without another word, Jehosheba grabbed the gown and hurried to her bedchamber to change. Her heart thumped as she thought about what she was about to do. Was she being impulsive? She shook her head. *No!* She had to see if she could rescue baby Joash. She had to preserve the last seed of David. If baby Joash died, so would the linage of David. She could not allow that to happen.

Chapter Six

The night was dense and silent. The screech of an animal made Jehosheba jump as she stood hidden outside the palace walls.

She had arrived covered under the thickness of the night and hidden with dark clothing and a black veil that reached past her waist. She desperately hoped no one would recognise her.

Jehosheba took a deep breath and ran her eyes all the way up the menacing wall. She could never climb that! She had to enter the palace courtyard through the gates to reach the secret passage—the passage Adina had shown her when they were young girls so many years ago.

She stood outside a little longer, trying to come up with a plan. In her haste, she hadn't planned the next step.

Suddenly her head snapped up when she heard voices approaching. She couldn't understand what they were saying, but they sounded gruff, like soldiers. She took a deep breath and walked through the massive, ornate gates of the palace. It was now or never.

"Who goes there?" A soldier watched her as he drew his sword, ready to strike.

"It is I, Princess Jehosheba!" she shouted, taking the veil off her head, an act forbidden, but she had to save her life.

"Princess Jehosheba! I beg your pardon." The man bowed his head and hid the weapon behind his back. The soldier behind him also inclined his head in reverence.

"I came to pay my condolences to the queen for the death of my dear brother." Her voice quivered.

"Please, Your Highness, enter." They moved aside.

She dipped her head in a thank-you, covered it again with the veil, and hurried to the front door, her heart thundering in her chest. She turned around, but the soldiers had walked away, making another round of the courtyard.

When they were not looking, she dashed toward the side of the palace where the secret passage remained hidden. She could not risk entering the front door where she would be seen and Athaliah alerted. Suddenly the nightmare she had when she was younger resurfaced. She had not had the dream for many, many years.

The shouts of the soldiers and the cries of children echoed in her mind. She stopped walking and leaned against the cold, dark corner of the wall. Maybe this was the dream—a revelation of things that would happen. Suddenly she felt afraid to face Athaliah—in her dream, Athaliah caught her and held a knife to her throat. She covered her neck protectively and took short little breaths. *Calm down, calm down,* she told herself. God would protect her. Without another thought, she ran the last few steps almost blindly. The moon on this side of the palace did not shine well.

She ran her hands over the spot she remembered and felt the tiny lump of unevenness under her hand. She'd found it! Slowly, she pushed the wall and watched it screech open. It was not a big opening; she could barely fit through. It was a lot easier to get inside when she was a young girl. Jehosheba took off the veil and tied it around her waist and got down on all fours, ready to crawl through. She squeezed in and continued crawling in the darkness. Her eyes adjusted slowly to her surroundings, and shadows became visible. Finally, after a minute or two, she came to a section where she could stand.

Cobwebs tangled in her hair, and she heard the squeak of a mouse as it scurried past, rubbing its warm body against her sandals and toes. Repulsed, she paused and waited for the creature to disappear. She tilted her head to one side, listening for any sounds she could make out. Running footsteps and voices echoed above her. She continued walking and looked at the walls and the long passageway ahead.

"If I go this way, it will take me to the maids' quarters." She rubbed her sore temples. "If I go north, it will take me to my old room. Yes!" Feeling excited, she followed her instincts and walked all the way until she reached the place that Adina would use to access her room. She ran her hand along the rough wall until she came to an uneven part.

"Yes! This is it." She pushed the wall and light penetrated the secret passage as the wall opened wider. Light greeted her, and she hurried inside. She paused and looked at her old room. A wave of sadness washed over. How could a place hold so many unpleasant memories? As her eyes roamed the room, she noticed nothing had changed. The tapestries still hung on the walls, rugs covered the floor, her bed and corner seat were still the same, and her writing desk remained intact. It looked like it had not been in use. The princess had not been back to her room since she married Jehoiada so many years ago. Seeing how intact and clean her room was, she was sure the maids maintained it that way. Adina, maybe?

A scream in the distance made her jump and swirl around. She had little time. She had to grab Joash. She prayed she was not too late. Slowly, she opened the big brass handle and peeked out the door. More cries and shouts echoed around her. Closing the door quickly, she took a deep breath, opened the door, and tiptoed into the dark hallway—it seemed the maids had not lit up the passageways with the oil lanterns. She was relieved and dashed toward the children's wing. Her heart thumped as her sandals made little clicking sounds on the marble floor—except in certain areas where thick plush rugs covered the flooring.

All she needed was to get to the stairs and turn left to find the other secret passage Adina had shown her. In the distance, she heard someone cry, then a shriek. She shut her eyes—it agonized her to hear her family suffering. Finally, the staircase came into view, and lifting her tunic dress, she ran the last few steps. She stopped at the tiny room where the maids kept oil lantern artifacts. She shut the door and in the darkness ran her hand along the wall until she felt the unevenness, then slowly pushed the secret door open. Fumbling in the darkness, she reached out for a lantern and opened the door further to get a bit of light coming in. She wiped the tip of the small candle wick from any dust and turned it on.

A soft light glowed in the darkness, and she sighed—now it would be easier to see. She shut the door, walked into the darkened passageway, and slowly made her way to Joash's room. She stopped and looked around, pointing and envisioning in her mind the layout of the palace. Yes, this was the correct area. She walked a little further and stopped when she saw a set of swords decorating the wall of the secret passage. *Excellent,* she thought. Taking hold of the handle with her free hand, she turned it to the right and stood back, waiting for the door to appear. *Nothing. Hmm.* She cocked her head to one side. She tried again, turning the handle to the left. *Nothing.* Feeling panicked, she closed her eyes to think. Aha, maybe if she pushed the sword . . . When she did so, she heard a scraping sound as a small section of the wall moved. She exhaled with relief and, hunching over, went inside the very dim room. She stood in the corner and looked around at all the baby furniture, several soft rugs, and a tiny candle burning out. The room was empty.

How? She was sure this was baby Joash's quarters. How did she get it wrong? Maybe she took a wrong turn? She stood quietly, holding the lantern high to illuminate every area. Suddenly she heard soft breathing. There *was* someone in the room!

"Hello? I come in peace," she whispered.

No sound.

She tiptoed around the room, looking behind the tapestry and anything big enough to hide behind.

Her eyes travelled the room until they came to a stop on the bed. Gradually she made her way toward it, placed the lantern on the rug, and got down on her knees and peeked underneath.

A woman dressed in black hid with a bundle in one corner under the bed. The woman trembled, and the little bundle next to her had a steady snore coming from it.

"Elisheva?"

The woman lifted her eyes. Tears streamed down her cheeks.

"Elisheva! It is *you.* We need to leave immediately before baby Joash is killed." The princess took a deep breath. "Please." She watched the petrified face of the baby's nurse.

Jehosheba reached out and pulled the baby toward her with care. "You will be safe with me. I know a secret passage out of here."

The nurse nodded and crawled out. Jehosheba grabbed her sleeping nephew in her arms and held him tight while Elisheva crawled out.

"Let us strap the baby to you and leave immediately. Soldiers are near."

The maid nodded as Jehosheba took off her veil and made a strong pouch for Joash to sleep in and strapped it to Elisheva's back. It would be better for both to have free hands. The baby stirred slightly but continued sleeping. His rosy cheeks and pink mouth were full of life. Jehosheba resisted the urge to kiss his little face.

Once they were ready, she picked up the lantern and motioned with her lips to be quiet and to follow her. Jehosheba retraced her steps—stopping now and then to check that both baby and nurse were fine. She almost cried when she got outside the palace. Her joy was short-lived when she remembered that she still needed to get past the soldiers at the front.

"Elisheva, we need to distract the soldiers before Joash awakens." Jehosheba touched the nurse's arm. "Are you still doing well?"

She nodded and gulped.

Jehosheba bent down and put some dirt in the lantern to put out the flame. Then, with both hands, she opened a small hole in the ground and buried the lantern. "We cannot leave any evidence," she whispered, wiping her hands on her dress as she stood. "I will talk to the soldiers if I see them, and you will scurry by. Be fast and go undetected. Ready?"

"Yes." The young woman's frightened eyes glistened.

The princess walked to the front corner of the palace and waited to see if there were soldiers. To her great relief, there was no one in sight.

"Let us run!" She ran down the long courtyard and out the front gates. When they both made it unscathed outside the palace walls, they continued rushing to the temple courtyard for safety—a place Athaliah detested and would never think of coming. Jehosheba banged on the door and waited for Hila to answer.

The door opened slowly, and she almost pushed Elisheva and the baby through the front door.

"We need a hiding place!" she shouted, closing and latching the door behind her. Her hands were trembling.

"Oh, Princess, we do not have any secret passages." Hila rushed to Elisheva and Joash's side. The baby was stirring. He would wake soon.

Jehosheba rushed through the house. "There must be a place we can hide them." She wrung her hands.

"There is a place." Hila's eyes rounded. "The bedchamber where I store bedding!"

Jehosheba gasped. "That is perfect. Make haste before soldiers come this way." Jehosheba and Hila ushered Elisheva and the baby down the small hallway and came to a stop at a room that served as a storage area. Hila unlocked the door and used the lantern she carried to brighten the chamber.

The room was small—when guests and other priests came to stay, the bedding was taken out and used in the spare rooms of the smaller living dwellings on the temple grounds.

Jehosheba nodded. At least it was clean.

"This is where you will be hidden. We will take care of you both." The princess gave Elisheva a little smile and squeezed her arm. Then she leaned over her nephew and kissed his little forehead. Only the Lord had kept the baby asleep, she was sure of that.

"Thank you, Princess." A tiny smile appeared on the nurse's relieved face.

"I will get you clothes to change into, and then you can eat and feed the baby." Hila fumbled with a few cushions and bedding and made some room for them to be comfortable.

"Let me unstrap Joash." Jehosheba gently untied the straps of the veil and grabbed the baby in her arms. Joash stirred as his eyes fluttered open.

He blinked a few times, and when he saw his aunt, his little face broke into a smile.

"You are safe now, my love," Jehosheba soothed, touching his small, round face.

The baby wriggled and squirmed and cried.

"I will feed him, Princess, so he can sleep again and rest for the night." His nurse reached for him and took him in her arms. Soon he was feeding.

Jehosheba smiled, ran her hand over his curls, and walked out of the room.

"I will return when he is resting," she whispered.

"Thank you, Princess, for rescuing us both. You are a fearless woman of the God of Abraham."

Jehosheba inclined her head. God had given her the strength and wisdom to get them out. Her only regret was not letting Joash's mother know he lived. But she knew that no one outside their house must know the truth. The secret must remain between Hila, herself, the baby's nurse, Adina, and her husband.

She closed the door and leaned her head against the door with a full heart.

Epilogue

836 BC, the temple of God

"Auntie Sheba! Auntie Sheba, where are you?"

At the sound of feet running, Jehosheba dropped the dough she was kneading and grinned. "I am making bread for your breakfast."

A little curly head peeked through the door where she stood and ran to hug her around the legs.

"Good morning, Joash." She leaned down and gave him a kiss on his cheek.

In return, he encircled his arms around her neck and hung there, kissing her all over the face. Jehosheba laughed and finally detangled herself from her seven-year-old nephew.

"What is all this noise?" Jehoiada appeared, trying to look stern, but it did not work as his face melted into a big smile. "Joash, my son." The young boy ran into his arms and gave him a hug.

Princess Jehosheba's heart leaped with joy as she watched her handsome little nephew talking with her husband. Joash loved to discuss the temple—Jehoiada had also told him the story of how she had saved him and how one day he would be the rightful heir to the throne of Judah. He would always grow solemn and promise that he would not be like his grandmother queen, Athaliah. Jehosheba shuddered thinking about her. The people of Judah were terrified of her, and sadly, with her reigning, the kingdom was in ruin and Baal worship was in full swing.

After talking to his uncle, Joash went off in search of his nurse, Elisheva, who had become more like his second mother, tending to his every need.

When he was gone, Jehoiada kissed Jehosheba good morning—she noticed his face was solemn.

"Is something the matter?" she asked, wiping her hands on a kitchen cloth.

He shook his head. "Nothing is wrong, dear, but God has spoken to my heart and it is time." He walked to the side window that had the view of the palace.

"Time for what?" Jehosheba frowned and went to stand next to him.

"It is time for Joash to become king."

The princess gasped. "He's only seven! How can he be king?"

He nodded. "He will be guided until he is old enough to run the kingdom on his own."

Jehosheba let out a shaky breath, and her stomach trembled. "What if Athaliah tries to kill him when she finds out she has been tricked all these years?"

Jehoiada smiled softly. "God has preserved the line of David, and he gave you courage to rescue Joash from the claws of Athaliah. God will continue to look after Joash." Her husband patted her hand. "Do not fret, my dear. God is in control."

Yes, God was in control. She must trust him.

The next few days were busy, as Jehoiada planned how the child king would be revealed. Jehosheba stood with him as he had asked her to be present during the big reveal meeting. Her stomach turned, and her hands shook.

Her husband called the commanders and the guards and had them brought to the temple. He made a covenant with them and put them under oath at the temple of the Lord.

"All you see today must remain locked in your heart until the Sabbath, when the plan God has impressed me with will occur." Jehoiada looked at the men's faces as they vowed.

When Jehosheba, having been instructed beforehand, moved the curtain to one side, and out walked Joash with Elisheva, a murmur went around the room.

Jehoiada lifted his hand for quiet. "Your future king, the rightful heir to the kingdom of Judah. Joash the son of King Ahaziah and Zibiah of Beersheba."

Loud gasps erupted throughout the building as the burly soldiers and commanders gaped, looking at each other, unsure what had happened to bring Joash into their presence in this moment. Questions sprung around the room.

"How is that possible, Jehoiada? Were not all the heirs to the throne killed by Athaliah six years ago?" A commanding officer stood.

Another one jumped up. "No one lived!"

Loud talking flew across the room as the soldiers' faces showed confusion.

Jehosheba stepped forward and grabbed her nephew's small hand in hers. She lifted her hand for silence.

Finally, the room settled down.

She looked at each one's face as she spoke. "Joash has remained hidden in the temple grounds, rescued by me from the death decree Athaliah had commanded. The Lord has preserved his life, and together with Jehoiada, we have raised him. Elisheva, his nurse, has also been here." The young boy looked shyly at his aunt, unsure of what to do. She squeezed his hand reassuringly and gave him a playful wink.

Questions went on for a little while as the officials wanted to know many things. Jehoiada and Jehosheba answered each question carefully and patiently. When the soldiers were convinced of what they were hearing, the entire room of men stood and bowed low, shouting, "Our king lives!"

Goosebumps prickled Jehosheba's skin, and tears filled her eyes. Young Joash stared at the soldiers and then at his aunt. He frowned and whispered, "Now I am king?"

"Soon," she whispered.

Jehoiada then discussed the plans for when the child would be crowned and all of Israel would be informed.

"On the Sabbath a third of you will guard the royal palace, the other third will be at the Sur Gate, and the remaining third will be at the gate behind the soldier who guards the temple." Jehoiada had taken out the map and pointed to each location. "Station yourself around the king, each of you with weapons, and stay close to Joash wherever he goes."

Jehosheba watched as the men agreed and prepared to follow instructions. Her heart beat with anticipation, knowing that it was going to be a significant day.

The whole week, they prepared the young king for the happenings to come, and he captured every detail. Finally, the day arrived. Jehosheba dressed Joash in his best clothes and gave him a quick kiss on his cheek. "Be brave today—you will be introduced as king!"

The little boy nodded but did not say a word. He looked pensive. "Will I ever see you again?" he murmured.

Jehosheba sat down and took him in her arms. "You will always see me and your uncle Jehoiada, but you will live in the palace." She felt her heart tear. "And you know what the most exciting thing is?"

He shook his head.

"You will live with your mother."

"Is she kind and not mean like Grandmother Athaliah?"

Jehosheba laughed. "Your mother is lovely. You will love living with her in the enormous palace." She touched the tip of his nose with her finger. "She will be thrilled to see you today."

The young boy smiled. "If she is kind like you, then I will be happy to see her too."

After everyone was ready, Jehosheba took Joash by the hand and walked to the temple grounds. Soldiers were everywhere—their eyes sharp like hawks.

Once at the temple, she handed him over to her husband, who took the young child and put him on a stage near a pillar. People from the city watched with interest at what was happening and why things looked different today at the temple. Trumpeters were ready to play once the crown was placed on his head.

With a signal, Jehoiada lifted his arm for silence, and with a loud voice he shouted, "Behold the rightful king of Judah! Joash the son of King Ahaziah."

The place erupted in shock as people looked around in disbelief.

"Long live the king!" Jehoiada cried as he placed the kingly crown on the boy's head, presented him with a copy of the covenant, and proclaimed him king again. Joash was then anointed, and the crowd and soldiers clapped their hands and shouted, "Long live the king!"

The trumpets followed in song and celebration.

Jehosheba wiped the tears off her eyes, seeing her nephew in his rightful place grinning from ear to ear.

She watched her husband lift his hands for quiet so he could speak. Silence resided; then suddenly a terror-stricken screech broke the solemnity of the ceremony.

"Treason! Treason!"

Jehosheba and everyone in the temple courtyard turned around at the voice of none other than Athaliah. Her face was distorted with anger, and her hands balled into fists.

"This is treason! I killed *all* of them!" She threw her head back and screamed, tearing the jewels off her ears and the precious stone necklace from her neck. She pulled her hair in rage. Watching her made Jehosheba tremble—this woman was indeed possessed.

Jehoiada looked directly at her and then at the soldiers. "Take her out of the temple, and put to sword anyone who follows her."

Four guards rushed to her side and took her by the arms—she screamed, cursing and calling to Baal.

She screamed until she was no more.

Jehosheba hung her head—her reign had finally ended.

With the celebrations finished, Joash moved into the palace and was reunited with his mother. Jehosheba cried as she witnessed their sweet reunion, and as Zibiah held her son, she sobbed.

"Mother, why do you cry?" He tilted his little curly head. "I am here now." He lifted his hand and wiped her tears with his small thumb.

Zibiah laughed. "I do not cry because I am sad, my son, but because I rejoice. I thought I had lost you, but you are mine once again."

He nodded and gave her one big long hug.

Jehosheba grinned and wiped her tears. Her heart could finally rejoice.

Five

Esther: Courageous Queen of Persia

Then Esther sent this reply to Mordecai: "Go, gather together all the Jews who are in Susa, and fast for me. Do not eat or drink for three days, night or day. I and my attendants will fast as you do. When this is done, I will go to the king, even though it is against the law. And if I perish, I perish."

—ESTHER 4:15–16

Find the story in the book of Esther.

Prologue

493 BC, home of Hadassah in Susa

Hadassah leaned her little head against the table and cried silent tears. Loneliness and sadness enveloped her heart. She looked up from the ground where she sat as she heard someone mention her name.

"Then who will take care of little Hadassah?" a woman in a blue tunic asked another woman, who was wearing grey.

The tall woman in grey shrugged her shoulders. "All I know is that once you're an orphan, you are destitute. Such a shame, really. She would have been a beauty when she was all grown up and would have married well."

"Oh yes, I agree. With beauty like hers, I'm sure one of the unreputable places in the hidden districts of Susa will capture her and turn her into a lady of the night."

The woman in grey covered her mouth. "That is absolutely ludicrous!"

As they spoke, Hadassah noticed another woman join the conversation. She didn't recognise her either. Ever since her parents had been killed in the carriage accident as they were heading to Jerusalem, strangers who obviously knew her parents had been gathering in her house for days.

"Are you two gossiping about young Hadassah?" the tall lady with the elegant veil turned to look down at her and winked.

The women cackled. "Daria! We were not gossiping. We only worry about the outcome of the little girl."

Daria continued talking. "She will have a wonderful life. Her cousin Mordecai has said he will adopt her as his own and give her a home."

The women gasped, and all three turned and looked down at where she sat on the ground.

"Well, isn't she blessed?" the woman in the blue dress exclaimed, staring down at her.

Hadassah stared back. Something about that woman didn't feel sincere. She was only seven, but she could tell when someone was kind and nice and when they were not. This lady looked to be the latter. Maybe it was the way her dark snake-shaped eyes narrowed and bore into her. A shiver ran down Hadassah's spine and glanced away.

"I am delighted for the child. Not all family members would take in an orphan and add another burden to their family." The tall woman with the grey dress straightened her head covering.

"She will not be a burden!" Daria exclaimed.

Hadassah stared at the kind lady, and Daria smiled. Her pretty brown eyes twinkled.

Despite her tears, Hadassah smiled back. She felt the stranger's warm kindness.

As Hadassah watched the women move away to another section of her house, Daria's words made her heart jump with joy. This was the only ray of hope she had experienced in the four long days since her parents' passing.

Her cousin Mordecai was going to adopt her? She wasn't sure what *adopt* meant, but from what she gathered from Daria's words, she was going to have a home with him. She liked that very much! She loved her big cousin with all her heart. Hadassah let out a shaky breath and closed her eyes. For the first time in days, she fell asleep.

Slowly, she woke up from her deep slumber. She opened her eyes and tried to focus on the unfamiliar surroundings. Where was she? Sitting up, Hadassah rubbed her eyes and stared at the furniture she could see. Instantly, the death of her parents came pouring into her mind, and she cried. She felt scared, sad, and alone. Just then, a figure appeared in the doorway. Through her tears, she watched the shadow approach her. Hadassah shrunk back and covered her face.

"Please don't hurt me!" she sobbed.

"Hadassah, I would never hurt you, my darling. I heard you cry and realised you were awake." The strong and soothing voice of her cousin Mordecai washed over her, and she stretched out her hands for him to pick her up. In seconds, he scooped her into his arms and held her while she cried on his shoulder.

"There, darling, you are safe now. I will take care of you. You do not need to feel frightened."

His words calmed her heart, and she eventually stopped crying. She wiped her tears and looked into his eyes.

In the shadows of the evening, she saw him smile, and she smiled back. She was so happy to be safe with cousin Mordecai.

"Sleep now, my little stāra. Tomorrow morning will be a brand-new day."

Hadassah smiled at the name her cousin called her. Her parents called her stāra too. They said she was their little star. It was why they usually used her Persian name, Esther, that meant star. Hadassah snuggled into her cousin's arms and felt the fear and sadness slowly drift away while she fell asleep in his arms.

Chapter One

483 BC, Susa: a city of Persia, east of Babylon

"Cousin Mordecai! Cousin Mordecai! Where are you?" Esther burst through the front doors and almost slipped on the marble floors of her cousin's house. Her leather sandals gave way, and she felt herself sprawling to the ground. Firm hands grabbed her arms and steadied her.

"Esther! What is the rush, child?"

The stern voice of her cousin made her smile sheepishly. "I'm sorry, Mordecai, I know you work at the palace gate, and I wanted to know if the rumours are true!" Her light brown eyes were wide with expectation.

Her cousin laughed and shook his head. "I see news travels fast in Susa." He walked toward the back of the house to their favourite place, the garden. "Come, Esther."

Esther followed Mordecai outside, who she felt was more like an uncle to her than a cousin. He was years older, with his slight ash-coloured hair and well-built physique, which reminded her of her father. Her heart gave a little leap when she thought of her beloved parents. Even though they had been gone for many years, she remembered them fondly often.

When they stepped outside, Esther closed her eyes and breathed in the cool afternoon breeze. Her long, dark hair cascaded all the way around her waist and swayed with the wind. She opened her eyes and admired the surroundings. She loved this garden.

As a little girl after her parents' passing, she would sit outside for hours playing with her friend Alya and their little fabric dolls. As she got older, she loved sitting in the garden reading from the scrolls or talking to the God of her parents and Mordecai. She especially loved the afternoon breeze that ran throughout the house—the garden wasn't large, but they had a few garden seats under trees and a small pool of water in the middle, surrounded by greenery that served as a refreshing haven. Esther loved dipping her toes in the water on hot summer days.

"What is it you want to know, Esther?" Her cousin's voice brought her back to the present.

She twirled around and almost skipped to where he sat.

"You are, after all, a member of the king's court, so I presume you know *everything*!" Esther collapsed next to him and gave an exaggerated sigh.

Mordecai laughed. "Esther, my dear, you are very melodramatic. I think I should have sent you to Jaleh's school of manners."

"Mordecai!" Esther frowned at her cousin. "Am I not well mannered and a lady?"

Mordecai shook his head. "No, it's not that. You are always a lady. However, at times you can be a little . . ."

Esther gasped. "A little what?" She crossed her arms and waited to hear what he had to say.

"Spirited."

She laughed. "Ha, you told me last week you admired my spirited character trait."

He chuckled and patted her hand. "True. But I especially like the kindness you show to everyone. How you dedicate your time to helping the poor in town. The countless hours in the marketplace feeding the orphans who beg for food. God has given you a gift, my little stāra."

Esther beamed and squeezed her cousin's hand. She loved helping the poor. Nothing gave her more satisfaction than seeing their faces light up when she arrived with food and clean clothes for them. Besides, he was the kind one to have taken in a lost and orphaned little girl into his home.

Everything she was today was because of Mordecai's guidance, spirituality, and wisdom.

"Now, what is it you want to know?"

Esther drew back her attention to him. "Is it true King Xerxes has banished Queen Vashti from the kingdom?"

Mordecai sighed and nodded sadly. "It is true."

"Oh, I was hoping it was only palace rumor picked up by the girls in the marketplace." Esther took a deep breath. "Is it true the king demanded she show her beauty to his male guests during a banquet?"

"As you might remember, King Xerxes has been celebrating the third year of his reign, and for seven days he gave a banquet for his male guests."

Esther nodded. It had been the talk of the city of Susa.

"It so happens that his thinking was clouded from too much wine." Mordecai paused. "That is why our God forbids us from drinking wine, Esther. It clouds our mind and makes us act irrationally."

Esther had seen too many drunk men at the marketplace when she went with her friend Alya to buy grain. They rudely howled and called out lustful names. They shouted for her to sway her hips so they could admire her beauty. Esther shuddered in disgust. She could only imagine how insulted Queen Vashti would have felt when asked to parade herself in front of the men.

Mordecai continued talking. "Queen Vashti was a brave queen."

"Do you think he will make one of his many concubines his newest queen?" she wondered.

Mordecai shrugged. "No one knows. We will have to wait and see."

"Can I ask one more question?"

He dipped his head.

"Was the king furious?"

"He was enraged and burned with anger. I have never seen him so incensed. But . . ." Mordecai's voice softened, and his brow wrinkled. "It infuriated him that his queen did not obey the defamatory request he demanded of her."

Esther leaned back in the seat, deep in thought. She had heard so much talk today that her ears were hurting. Cousin Mordecai had taught her not to pick up nonsense from town, so she never stopped or engaged. Today she had heard vendors talking, and the thing she had picked up was that Memukan, one of the king's wise men and confidants, advised him to remove the queen. Apparently, he had claimed that if she was not reprimanded severely for disobeying him, other women would follow her example and would only disrespect their own husbands.

Esther exhaled. It sounded utterly ridiculous to her. She was glad she did not have to live a segregated life in the palace.

Chapter Two

One morning, a few weeks after the scandal, Esther and her friend Alya visited the marketplace, looking for precious jewels for Alya's wedding. The girls giggled as they left another vendor's display of unattractive gems.

"Alya, you are going to make a lovely bride, and you need jewels to match." Esther wrapped her light blue head veil a little tighter so it wouldn't fly off. The wind was a little strong today.

"I'm so nervous about the wedding, Esther." Alya's light brown plait peeked from under her head wrap.

"Javad is a good man. Even if he was chosen by your parents." Esther touched her friend's shoulder. "You should not feel nervous. Besides, you love him."

Alya beamed. "I do!" she exclaimed. "I'm nervous, but I still want to be his wife."

Esther grinned and gave her friend a quick squeeze of her shoulders. "I'm glad. You deserve all the happiness."

Alya had been Esther's best friend since her cousin Mordecai had adopted her. Her father and Mordecai were friends, and the girls had connected immediately. Both were Jewish and believed in the same God. Esther had spent many hours playing with Alya, and she had filled a lot of the first few lonely months with joy.

"I want to see *you* marry too!" Alya exclaimed. "You are beyond beautiful, and I cannot understand why men do not propose."

Esther threw her head back and laughed. "Oh, Alya, thank you for the compliment, but you know very well why men will not marry me." She sighed.

Alya frowned. Her hazel eyes showed surprise. "Why?"

"Women in town have told Mordecai that I'm too spontaneous, spirited, and melodramatic. Apparently, those are qualities men dislike. They want an acquiescent wife."

"That is just absurd! Those women are jealous of your looks. They have always been, so you should not listen to them at all." Alya linked her arm with Esther's. "Who knows, your husband could be just around the corner."

Alya's words were drowned out by the loud sound of a trumpet and the galloping of horses.

Esther looked up as at least ten palace officers came to a halt in the market square, dust twirling around them and onto everyone else. She covered her nose with her veil and waited for the dust to subside.

"Hear, oh hear, people of Susa. A proclamation from King Xerxes."

The trumpet blew again.

Another officer unrolled a scroll and read: "King Xerxes has made a proclamation for all of Susa. In accordance with the law of the Medes and Persians, this decree has been put in writing and cannot be altered or revoked. It stands sealed."

Esther turned to her friend with a furrowed brow. It sounded important. She drew her attention back to the officer.

"Our reigning king has appointed officials in every province of his kingdom to bring every attractive young virgin to the palace complex of Susa, to the house of the women, unto the custody of Hegai, the king's chamberlain, keeper of the women."

Gasps and murmur erupted amongst the sellers and purchasers. Esther felt her friend stiffen and saw her cover her mouth. "No!" she whispered.

Esther reached over and grabbed her friend's hand for support. This *was* serious!

"Under Hegai's care, purification and beauty treatments will be given to the virgins, and the maiden who pleases the king will be queen instead of Vashti."

Loud murmurs erupted around them. People shouted. Some were opposed to the new decree, while others shouted their daughter would make a magnificent queen.

Esther gaped. They were choosing a new queen from ordinary girls from Susa? Weren't there princesses from Egypt or other exotic lands that could be chosen?

She winced when she felt Alya's fingernail dip into her soft hand. Esther drew back her hand and stared at her friend, who was now as pale as the veil she would wear on her wedding day.

The trumpet interrupted anything Esther wanted to tell her friend.

"This decree is final. All virgins will be brought to the palace. King Xerxes has spoken."

With those last words, the trumpet and galloping horses faded into the cloak of the dust.

The town had gone crazy, and everyone started to shout and curse. Some at each other and some at their daughters for not having been blessed with beauty since birth. A mother grabbed her daughter by the ear and pulled her all the way home, berating her for being so plain. Esther winced and felt tears fill her eyes. The girl did not deserve such treatment. She *was* beautiful. How could her mother not see it?

Esther shook her head and grabbed her statue-like friend and pulled her out of the marketplace before it got dangerous. She didn't stop until she reached their favourite tree near Alya's house.

They sat on a rock, and suddenly Alya burst into tears.

"Alya, what is wrong?"

"Oh, Esther. Don't you know what this means?" She sobbed harder.

Esther nodded slowly. "What I understand is that every unmarried young woman needs to go to the palace to be chosen as queen . . ." Esther's voice trailed off as the realisation hit her.

"Alya, oh no. No!"

Her best friend leaned on her shoulder and cried. "I cannot not marry my beloved Javad. That is not possible. We are betrothed and are to become husband and wife soon. I cannot go to the palace!"

Esther rubbed Alya's veiled head. Her friend should marry Javad. She was in love. God has united them. "Alya, marry him. Marry Javad sooner than planned."

Alya lifted her wet face. Her veil had fallen off, revealing lush light brown hair that matched her hazel eyes.

"But it's impossible," Alya moaned. "We are to marry in a few months' time. I don't know if marrying sooner will be possible."

Esther opened her mouth to speak but was interrupted by running footsteps. The girls turned to look. It was Javad.

"Alya, I heard about the proclamation!"

Alya stood and ran toward him. "Oh, Javad." Tears streamed down her cheeks.

"Let us marry this week with only our closest friends and family. We cannot waste another day."

Esther sighed with relief. She was so glad that Javad thought the same as she did and wanted to marry his beloved sooner. She stood, covered her unveiled head, and headed for home. She needed to leave them alone to discuss the finer details. She was sure to hear all about it later.

Chapter Three

As the days went by and the seriousness of recent events increased, Esther thought about the decree that had surfaced. Her mind knotted with worry. She did not want to go to the palace as a future wife to the king. Besides, she reasoned to herself, she didn't know if she was going to have to go. She had a choice, didn't she?

When she arrived home, Mordecai signalled for her to come outside to the garden. She placed the veil on a table near the window, patted her hair, and hurried outside. The look of concern on his face told her that trouble was ahead.

"What is it?" she whispered as she took a seat next to him.

Mordecai sighed. "Do you remember the decree?"

Esther nodded.

"Esther, you will be taken to the palace." His voice was hoarse with emotion.

"By force?" Her brow wrinkled. She held her breath, waiting for his reply.

"Every unmarried young woman *will* be taken."

An *O* formed on her lips.

"If only I could hide you instead of sending you to be the wife of a pagan king!" Mordecai stood from the bench and paced back and forth in front of Esther. "What would my uncle think if he knew you were going to be part of a harem?"

Esther cringed and looked away as heat rose to her face. She hadn't thought of that part!

"There must be something we can do." Mordecai slapped his fist into his other palm. "I've got it!" He rushed to Esther's side. "I still have family in Jerusalem—what if I send you there?" he stated, not asking Esther her opinion but merely saying it out loud as if to soothe his own anxious soul. "I will take you myself."

"Mordecai, that will never work. Authorities will apprehend us and throw us in prison for escaping from a command of King Xerxes. You know we cannot run away."

Esther watched Mordecai's face pale. "Then what will you do?"

"I will stay here with you and wait it out. I might not even be chosen." She shrugged.

Mordecai let out an unexpected sarcastic laugh. Esther's eyes widened. He was acting so strange since this whole decree started.

"Not chosen? Not chosen?" Mordecai shook his head. "Do you know how many men have come asking for your hand in marriage? Do you know how many I have to turn away on a weekly basis?"

Esther gasped. He had never told her that before.

"You, my dear, will be chosen because you are one of the most beautiful women in all of Susa. Not only on the outside, but in here." Mordecai tapped his index finger on his chest. "The kindness and love you show to everyone is admirable. People all over Susa love your sweetness. You, my little stāra are more than just looks." Mordecai hung his head. "I just wished you would have married a good Hebrew man from the tribe of Benjamin, instead of being exposed to the idolatrous life of Persia. Scandalous and corrupt!" He spat the last words.

Esther sighed. "Mordecai, please don't be distressed. You have taught me that the God of Abraham is always in control of our lives. You have showed me He is the one who guides our steps. Let us trust He is still working in my life. I feel God close to my heart every day. I know He is with me. We should not fear."

Mordecai sighed and went over to sit next to her. "Oh, Esther, I am a fool of an old man." He shook his head. "For a minute, I forgot God is in control. Thank you for reminding me. By the way, since when did you get so wise?"

Esther chuckled and grabbed his big, strong hands into her small, slender ones. "These past few days have made my heart heavy, but it has also made me put my trust in God." She sighed. "Remember, no matter what happens to me, you must stay strong in our God."

He patted her hand. "I will. You must stay faithful in the palace. Temptations will arise, but you, my little star, must shine bright and differ from any other woman, because God lives in you." He lifted her hands and gave them a little squeeze. "One more thing," he added. "Do not tell anyone you are Jewish. Keep it hidden."

Esther frowned. "Why not? Should I be ashamed?"

"It is no shame, Esther. It is caution. Remember, we have been a persecuted race and have been enslaved for many years. I do not want them to know of your heritage. It could be dangerous."

Esther tilted her head to one side, deep in thought. She understood his request, but it weighed on her heart. However, Mordecai, being part of the palace staff, knew what he spoke about.

"I will obey."

She withdrew her hands from his and wrapped him in a hug. She was going to miss him immensely. He was the only father she had known almost all her life. His was the face that came into her mind whenever she thought of a father. She was afraid to be taken to the palace, but she did not want to tell him. He would worry, and she did not want to add to his worry. Ever since she was a little girl, he had told her to be brave, to be strong, to be kind, to love others, and to love God. Today she would choose to be strong and brave and face the situation like a soldier. She didn't know what would happen in the next few days, but she knew God stood next to her.

Chapter Four

The next few days were a blur. Esther heard throughout town that soldiers had taken different girls from her childhood to the palace. She did not know when her turn would come or how she would react when they took her. She hoped to act with strength and dignity.

Esther also attended the wedding of her dear friends Alya and Javad. Alya was radiant as a new bride, and she looked as happy as a bride should be. The new bride and groom were moving out of the city of Susa and into the rural outskirts to raise sheep and have children. Alya did not like the way Persia was heading into a more immoral, uncivilised political place. The best friends hugged for a long time before Esther and Mordecai left to go home. Her heart ached, for she did not know when they would see each other again.

When they arrived home, there was a mob of people standing at Mordecai's door, banging. They carried oil lamps to light the way and a palanquin; the portable seat they used to transport royalty or important officials.

Esther gaped and held on to Mordecai's arm. Immediately, they knew what the officials were there for.

"What do you seek?" Mordecai's voice boomed in the evening's darkness. The mob silenced and turned to face him and Esther.

"We seek the young woman to come with us to the palace. You, Mordecai, should know the decree," a burly man with a hard face said.

"I know the decree."

"Then you will not resist when we take the girl with us."

Esther stiffened.

"Now?" Mordecai asked.

"Now."

Esther gasped, and her heart fluttered like a trapped bird trying to break free. Her hands trembled as she dug her fingers into Mordecai's arm. A deep fear took over. She did not want to go.

Mordecai turned to face Esther, and in the soft glow of the night, she saw tears in his eyes. "It's time," he muttered.

Esther felt panic rise in her throat. She was being taken captive and away from the only home and father she remembered. She shook her head. "Please. Choose another," she whispered.

The hard-faced man threw back his head and laughed. He moved closer to Esther, and Mordecai moved in front to shield her.

"Your daughter has no choice but to come with us. Now we depart to the palace!" He lifted his oil lamp into the air, and everyone roared with him.

"Let her take her belongings," Mordecai cried.

"The king has provided everything she needs. She does not need any of her rags."

Esther felt her eyes fill with tears, and silently each one fell to the ground. She took hold of Mordecai's arm, and he turned to face her.

"It's time." Her voice cracked.

Mordecai let out a cry and encircled her in his arms. "Be brave and strong, my little stāra. Shine bright!"

Without another word, they lifted her into the royal litter and carried her off. She stuck her head out of the opening, watching her dear beloved cousin waving. She watched until all she could see was a slight dot fading into the darkness of the night.

The bumpy ride of her litter moving side to side made her feel unsettled. Were they truly taking her to the palace, or were they Arab raiders taking her to merchants who would sell her in Egypt as a slave? She had heard stories all over the marketplace about such happenings. She sighed, remembering that only a few days ago she had told Mordecai that God was with her. Then why was she afraid now?

Finally, a long while later, as she dozed off, she felt the palanquin come to a stop. Her eyes flew open. She moved the little curtain aside and peered outside. She gasped as her eyes travelled up to the endless height of the grand palace with its many floors. Lanterns and lights made of fires illuminated the grounds, the gardens, and the palace. She closed the curtain again and leaned against the seat—she wiped her sweaty palms and took a few soft breaths to calm her beating heart. She could hear voices outside telling the men to proceed.

Her litter continued moving until it came to a stop, and she felt it being placed on the ground. They pulled the curtain back, and a man with a beard and head covering looked her up and down. Esther pulled her veil closer to her face.

"We have arrived. Follow me." The man opened the door, and she stepped out. They were inside a grand hall—empty aside from draperies. Soft light cascaded through the windows.

Cautiously, she followed the man through the grand room, out the door, and down a long hallway.

A slim, older woman stood at the end of the corridor, waiting.

"This is Esther. Daughter of Mordecai of Susa." The man inclined his head, looked at Esther one more time, and left.

Esther did not bother to correct him—after all, Mordecai *had* adopted her.

"Follow me, child." The woman motioned with her veiled, covered head for Esther to follow. She lifted the oil lamp she was carrying and lit the way—more long corridors and dark rooms met her gaze as her eyes moved from side to side, taking in her surroundings. They walked by some pillars that were elaborately decorated with intricate designs of blues, reds, yellows, and golds. Esther felt overwhelmed at the thought of being the queen of something this grand. However, it was not guaranteed the king would choose her, so for now she could just relax and not think too far ahead.

"This will be your quarters for tonight." The women came to a stop at a large brown door with a giant golden-coloured handle. She turned the doorknob, and they walked in.

The room had a bed in the middle, a few plush seats, multicoloured rugs on the floor, thick curtains, and soft candlelight.

"Thank you." Esther moved the veil away from her face and took in the details of the room. It was lovely.

"Tomorrow morning, they will assign a eunuch to look after you. More instructions will follow." The woman lifted the lantern closer to Esther's face. "Hmm, although you are beautiful, your skin needs a lot of attention and care. Your suntanned skin will need to be lightened, and your hair desperately needs treatments of oils."

"Oh." Esther touched her face and hair self-consciously.

"You need not concern yourself right now." The woman walked toward the big windows and closed the curtains. "You can make yourself comfortable. If there is anything you need during the night, pull this cord. It will alert the maids to assist you."

Esther nodded and gulped.

After the woman closed all the drapes, she walked to the door. "Sleep well, child. All will be well." She walked through the door and stopped halfway. "No servants have been assigned to you yet. That is why you do not have anyone assisting you. But tomorrow you will be welcomed into the harem and have your own maid. If you get two maids, you will be so fortunate." The woman chuckled and walked out, closing the door behind her.

Esther exhaled and looked at her surroundings one more time—her new home.

Chapter Five

Esther could hear someone in the distance calling her name. Mordecai? She opened her eyes and tried to focus. She blinked a few times. Where was she? The sudden realisation of last night made her sit up in bed. Her heart raced and tears threatened to erupt. She took a deep breath and said a tiny silent prayer.

"You are awake."

She turned her head to the sound of the voice and noticed a tall, bearded man with frizzed hair. He was standing to one side, watching her. He wore a simple yet elegant long yellow tunic with a blue tasselled sash around his waist and a rolled yellow fabric headband around his head. Earrings completed the look. Although Esther could tell he was a servant, there was something elegant about his poise.

"Was your sleep satisfactory?" he asked as he walked toward her and looked her up and down.

Esther nodded and shyly ran her hand over her unveiled hair. The man stopped next to her bed and introduced himself.

"I'm Hegai, in charge of King's Xerxes harem. Welcome, Esther." He inclined his head of curly hair.

Esther smiled. "Thank you, Hegai."

He stared at her face. "You are one exquisite woman—I am sure many will envy you."

Esther felt heat rush to her face.

"Please wash yourself, have breakfast, and then I will return to give you a tour of the palace. This afternoon I will take you to the harem, where you will live for the next twelve months."

Esther froze. Twelve months sounded like an eternity.

Hegai gave her a few more instructions, showed her where the clothes were, and directed her to a basin with water so she could wash. Soon he left, and she was alone. Esther ate a light breakfast of fruit and dates, bathed, and dressed in a soft gown of blue she found on her bed. She wrapped the dress with a white tasselled sash. Now she was ready for Hegai.

The servant returned, regal and serious, and asked Esther to follow him. They spent over a few hours walking every room and courtyard of the palace, and she gushed in awe at all the splendour the palace offered. Never had she imagined a place could be so exquisite.

When they came to another division of the palace closed off with golden doors, Hegai did not show her in. "This door takes you to the inner court of the king's house. You are not permitted past this wing. The king will only allow you in with invitation directly from him."

Esther made a mental note never to trespass the grand golden doors. They continued the rest of the tour, and Hegai informed her of many things. He encouraged Esther to ask many questions, and she did. One question burned in her heart.

"Are family members allowed to visit?" she asked.

Hegai shook his head. "No outside visitors are ever allowed in the harem. You are the property of the king and are not to leave the palace grounds."

Esther sighed but did not say a word. Her heart ached, knowing she would not see Mordecai again. Maybe she should have left Persia when he had suggested it. However, she could not tolerate running away from every little trial. She had to face things as they were.

Hegai continued talking and asking Esther questions about her life in Susa. She mentioned the help she gave to the orphans and widows and how her heart rejoiced with everything she used to do in Susa. She mentioned she would miss it very much. Hegai seemed impressed as she spoke. The hours went by faster than she thought, and soon it was almost time for lunch.

"You will have lunch in the harem. The time has come for you to settle in your new home," Hegai informed her.

The thought of living with dozens of women all hoping to win the king's affection filled her with dread. Silently, she followed the eunuch's regal posture.

"The harem is on the northeast end of the palace. There will be more than one hundred and fifty virgins there."

Esther drew in her breath. *One hundred and fifty women!* The thought overwhelmed her.

Hegai continued talking, then stopped walking and turned to Esther. "There is a difference in your countenance, Esther. I feel you are one special woman."

Esther's eyes softened. "Thank you, Hegai," she whispered.

"I have splendid plans for you." He rubbed his beard and tilted his head to the side. "You have found grace in my eyes."

Esther was not exactly sure what he meant by "grace," but his compliment made her feel a little timid. She smiled and whispered another thank-you.

Before even entering the harem, Esther knew they had arrived—she could hear the female voices and laughter all the way down the corridor. Music and merriment filled the air. The residence sounded lively.

They entered a large columned hall with a portico facing an ample courtyard. In the courtyard were women sprawled on chairs, on cushions on the ground—they were dressed in different clothing depending on what they were doing. Some were having their faces painted, others were being taught how to dance, while others were walking regally up and down with a goblet sitting on their heads. Others played instruments. Servant girls stood in the corners holding parasols to cover them and shield the women from the heat of the sun.

Esther's eyes wandered around the room. She noticed the hall had six arched doorways that led to different areas. Each door depicted King Xerxes. In one, he was fighting a lion with a javelin. On another he was facing a triple-headed monster, and on another door he was dressed in armour with hundreds of soldiers bowing behind him. The magnificent details of all her surroundings took her breath away.

"It is exquisite," she said under her breath.

Hegai clapped his hands, and all the women turned their eyes in their direction. The music died down, and the laughter and talking ceased.

"We have Esther of Susa who will join the harem. Please make her feel welcome."

Every eye in the room watched her with interest. Some smiled at her, while others scowled and looked away. Two women in the corner whispered secrets to each other and looked her up and down, laughing behind their hands. Esther looked away quickly, uneasy about the whole situation.

"Follow me, Esther." Hegai continued through the door to another area that had rooms, smaller courtyards, seats, cushions, and an array of food on a banquet table. More women stood talking, laughing, and eating. The aroma of the food drifted into her nose, and her stomach rumbled. It had been a long time since breakfast.

"You will eat soon, but first I will organise your maids and room." Hegai motioned with his hand for her to stop while he went in search of someone.

Esther took a few steps back and hid amongst the potted plants that adorned the room. Breathing again, she relaxed. No one would see her behind the plants.

It wasn't long before she heard Hegai's voice again—quickly she moved out from behind the plants and saw him coming toward her with a young woman.

"Esther, this is Shirin. She will be your personal maid."

Esther smiled at the woman, who had her long dark hair in a thick plait, then coiled at the back of her neck. She wore a blue tunic with a fringed belt and leather sandals. She had a kind smile and beautiful, bright eyes. Esther liked her instantly.

"Hello, Shirin." She inclined her head a little.

"Shirin will be the head maid, but you will also have six other attendants to take care of your needs."

Esther gasped. Seven maids? Did not the lady from last night tell her she would be so fortunate if she had two? She was surprised but secretly pleased.

Hegai continued talking. "The eastern section of the harem will belong only to you, and you can roam the place as you like."

Esther felt her mouth fall open. An entire section was hers?

"Shirin, anything Esther needs should be given to her. Feed her the best meals in the privacy of her own courtyard, start her beautifying treatments by the end of the week, and find her the most luxurious clothes and jewellery available."

"Yes, Hegai. I will do as you say." Shirin dipped her head.

The serious eunuch smiled and took hold of her hands. "Esther, you will be well taken care of. You have pleased me and won my favour. You will be exalted amongst all women."

Esther's eyes filled with tears at his kind words, and her mouth gaped. She had no words, but her heart burst with joy. Her God *was* taking care of her, after all.

Chapter Six

The mornings and evenings were busy times at the harem. There were music lessons to attend to. Instruments to learn to play. Beautifying treatments to enhance the skin and hair. Nails to be painted. Drawing lessons to go to. Oils of myrrh, perfumes, and sweet scents imported from Egypt were lathered into her hair and rubbed onto her skin. The food she ate was the finest. Luscious fruits, nuts, legumes, and delicacies of meats adorned her table for breakfast, lunch, and dinner. Her maids tended to her every need and made sure she was comfortable at all times.

Everything she did was done to enhance herself for the king. They taught her to speak like a queen, walk tall, sit with grace, stand poised, bow delicately, and meet important guests such as nobles and dignitaries. As the months progressed, Esther noticed how she had changed—she was no longer the free-spirited girl Mordecai adored. At the thought of her cousin, her heart constricted. She wondered how he was. She knew he was still working at the gates of the palace, for she often enquired about him, but besides that detail, she knew nothing else.

Gradually, Esther fell into a daily routine she came to enjoy and made friends with a few women. Life at the harem was not as dire as she expected. However, her heart always ached for Mordecai. She had also obeyed him and not whispered to anyone that she was a Jew. That remained buried in her heart and soul. One day she hoped to be reunited with him and live a happy life back in Susa. Would that day ever come?

The months rolled from one into the other until the tenth month, the month of Tebeth, arrived. She had two months left before she had to see the king, and then she hoped she would be freed and she could go back home.

One early morning, as Esther woke up, she felt something was amiss. Her maids were frantically rushing around the room. Her bath had been drawn; petals and scented oils wafted through the air. Over thirty pieces of jewellery were scattered on a long table; the finest gowns were out of the closet and on display. Yes, something was not right.

"Shirin," Esther called as she got out of bed barefoot to find her maid.

As soon as she peeked out the door of her room, she saw Shirin, Hegai, and Shaashgaz, one of the king's eunuchs who was in charge of the concubines, coming her way.

"Esther!" Shirin reached her first, followed by Hegai, a solemn look on his face.

"News has reached us. You are to see the king today!" He took hold of her hands as he usually did when he wanted to get an important message across. "We have prepared you for ten months for this occasion. We have faith that you will also find grace with the king."

Esther gaped. Suddenly she did not feel ready to face the king. Everything they had taught her left her mind, and she did not know where to start. No, she could not see the king yet. It had not been twelve months!

"Hegai, I do not think I am ready. I have only been here for ten months. Surely, there is a mistake." Her mouth felt dry.

Hegai eyes softened. "You are ready, Esther. You are ready to see the king."

Esther turned her head to Shirin, who smiled with encouragement and nodded.

"It's time to get ready, Esther." Hegai opened the door wider so they could all walk back into her room. "Shaashgaz will escort you and your seven maids. He will then show you where to go after seeing the king."

Esther nodded slowly, and the frantic morning began.

By the time Esther was ready to meet the king, she had been prepared with scented oils, luxurious gowns of soft materials, the finest jewellery, and her hair was adorned with an elaborate hairstyle. When she was ready, her maids placed her in front of the mirror for her to admire herself. Everyone stood back and watched.

Esther drew in her breath as she touched the softness of the material of her green dress, adorned with ravishing designs all over. The dress glimmered under the day's light with hundreds of delicate precious stones that had been hand stitched. The train of the dress was long, and the intricate design continued all the way down. Her sheer veil was draped from her head and around her shoulders until it reached the floor. The delicate material had a few designs on the border. They had left her hair long, cascading to the waist, and Shirin had softly twisted the sides and clasped them with a green jewel. Her face had been painted so delicately and tastefully that Esther felt she was not wearing any colour at all.

"You are ready," Shirin whispered, looking very proud of her hours of work.

A few more words were exchanged between Shirin and Hegai. The ten long months of laborious preparation had finally ended. With a quick prayer in her mind, Esther was ready to see Xerxes. She followed Hegai and Shaashgaz to the northern part of the main wing of the harem and stood at the base of the two stairways that connected the harem to the palace of Xerxes. The doors were opened, and she walked in—her body trembled. Hegai stayed but wished her well.

"If you become queen, Esther, then I will no longer have the pleasure of having you under my care. I will miss you, my dear girl. Your kindness and spirit have brought me joy." The eunuch's eyes glistened before she leaned in and gave him a hug.

"Thank you for having been wonderful to me." Her voice broke, and she was quickly ushered out of the room by her maids.

"We cannot have any tears." Shirin lifted the long train of Esther's dress and assisted her as she walked out of the room.

Esther looked around at her surroundings and this part of the palace—it was magnificent. The walls, rugs, and pillars all spoke their own stories with their decorations of past wars and past kings. Giant statues made of gold and silver adorned the corners. Plants also stood tall and regal in front of grand, heavy doors depicting griffins in an array of colours.

They finally arrived at the king's council hall, which was where he was meeting the potential future queens. Esther took a deep breath as the doors opened. Tentatively she walked in, following the eunuch. She did not turn her gaze anywhere else but kept her eyes fixated on the man who sat on the throne. She ignored the music and entertainment being played. She did not see the soldiers and the nobles stare at her in awe, their gaze following every step she took. All she was aware of was the feeling of dread that took over. If she did not impress him, she might become a concubine. She did not want to be used only for pleasure. She wanted to be a wife.

"Xerxes, my noble king of Persia, I present you Esther, daughter of Mordecai from Susa." Shaashgaz bowed low.

The room suddenly went quiet.

The music stopped.

The entertainment froze.

Esther bowed and kept her head inclined, along with her maid, waiting to receive further instructions.

"Esther of Susa, daughter of Mordecai, arise."

Esther lifted her head and looked up at the king, who had spoken and given her an order. She gasped silently, realising that he was not old as she had envisioned. The king was tall and well built. His short, trim beard was mainly on his chin, leaving his face uncovered. His dark hair was adorned with a short golden crown, and he wore a deep blue tasselled tunic and a flowing red cape decorated with a golden sphinx. Light brown eyes twinkled as they roamed over Esther's attire, and his lips parted into a pleased smile. Without taking his eyes off her, he descended to meet her.

"Esther . . . stāra," he whispered.

Esther drew in her breath at the sound of the name her dear family called her. How did he know? Her brow wrinkled as she bowed reverently. "Your Highness. It is my pleasure to be in your presence."

"The pleasure belongs to me, oh one star of great beauty." The king grabbed her hand and took it to his lips. "Never have I seen such beauty on one woman. Yet your outer beauty does not outshine the radiance you evoke from within."

She gaped at the eloquence of his words. "Thank you," she replied.

The king kept her hand and walked her up to his throne, where another smaller golden chair rested. He motioned for her to take a seat, and as soon as she sat, the music and entertainment resumed.

Esther and the king ate and spoke for many hours. Everything she said fascinated him. He asked her questions, and she answered each one. She wanted to mention Mordecai but remembered her oath to keep her Jewish identity a secret.

When it was time for her to leave, he kissed her hand one more time and said he would call on her later that day.

For the next few weeks, Esther remained in the concubine quarters, under the care of Shaashgaz and close to the king. Esther and Xerxes spent many hours together getting to know each other. Although Esther was not in love with the king, she enjoyed talking with him.

She liked their discussion on politics and how to help the poor. She liked his smile and how kind he seemed and how he was concerned for his people. He was a good man. Each time he looked at her, her stomach dropped with an unknown emotion—he made her feel valued.

"Esther," he said one evening as they walked the garden under the soft light of the moon and lanterns. "I have fallen in love with you."

Esther's hand went to her throat. "King Xerxes!"

The king stopped and turned to look at her. He took both of her hands in his. "I want you to become my queen. Marry me, my lovely stāra."

Tears welled in her eyes, and she nodded. "It will be my pleasure to be your queen, my dear king."

The laughter of the king filled the night. "I am the happiest man in all of Persia!"

He took Esther into his arms and placed a soft kiss on her forehead. Esther closed her eyes and leaned her head on his chest. What would Mordecai say if he knew she would be queen? If only she could see his face.

The kingdom of Persia rejoiced when the king announced he had found his queen. Soon news would reach Susa, and everyone, including her dearest cousin, would know. The days that followed were filled with preparations for the upcoming wedding. Esther underwent more beauty treatments and training. She had met with nobles' wives who wanted to meet the upcoming queen. She got measured in her gown of blue. She would wear veils of ivory and no crown, only an elaborate hairstyle. The king would place the crown on her after the ceremony. King Xerxes was to give a grand banquet in honour of his wife and invite all the nobles and officials. He would proclaim a holiday throughout the provinces and distribute gifts with royal liberality. The king was rejoicing, and nothing would dampen his mood.

The day of the wedding arrived with pomp and splendour—Esther was informed that guests from all over the province were arriving. There was a great buzz in the palace, and although Esther wanted to feel the joy, there was one thing missing: Mordecai. She wanted to see him and wrap her arms around him. Her only family and adoptive father. Feeling inspired, she wrote a brief letter and asked Shirin to give it to a eunuch to deliver immediately.

"This must only fall in the hands of Mordecai of Susa. No one must know." She handed over the small scroll and entrusted the errand to her maid.

"Yes, Esther." She quickly went out the door.

Shirin returned with a grin on her face. "All has been set. Your note is on its way."

"Thank you, Shirin." Esther breathed a sigh of relief.

After a rosewater bath, the dressing and arranging of clothing began for Esther. In less than half an hour, she would become queen and the wife of King Xerxes. Shirin had just finished placing the last jewel on her head when a new young servant boy entered the quarters.

"Esther, my lady," he puffed. "I have been instructed that you are to look out the balcony."

Esther frowned. Out of the balcony? Suddenly her heart thumped. Could it be? She fled from her chair, lifted her heavy dress, and hurried to the balcony. Her breath caught when she looked below.

"Mordecai," she breathed, and tears fell from her eyes—he had aged in the last few months. He was slimmer, and his hair had many more streaks of white.

"My little stāra." He clutched his heart. "You are a vision of loveliness. My beloved child. May God grant you peace as you reign in this kingdom."

Esther blew him a kiss. "I may not go outside to see you, but I just wanted a glimpse of your face. I love you, Mordecai."

"And I love you, my little one." Through his tears, he smiled with joy.

Esther's heart soared, and after waving good-bye, he was gone. Her heart was full—she was now ready to get married.

The ceremony was long and elaborate. There was entertainment, music, poems, singers, dancers, papers to sign, speeches to make. Finally, sonorous trumpets blew, and Esther began her walk toward the king, who stood at the foot of their thrones. She watched his reaction and noticed how his eyes softened at her appearance. The trumpets silenced as she inclined her head, and he placed the crown on her head. He took her right hand and presented her to the audience. "Behold, your queen."

A roar and applause erupted around them as people celebrated their new queen. Great rejoicing entered the palace and kingdom of Persia. Finally, the kingdom had a queen.

Chapter Seven

Almost eighteen months after the wedding, Esther sat on the bench outside in her favourite garden area reading the letter Mordecai had sent her. She laughed at some parts and sighed at others. She gasped when she read about Mordecai infuriating Haman, the highest-ranking official in the palace, and reread his words.

> All the officials at the king's gate kneel and pay Haman honour, but I cannot. He is not my God, and I cannot bow down to a mere mortal. The royal officials at the gate have asked me why I dare disobey the king's command and threatened to tell Haman that I am a Jew and that he should not tolerate my behaviour. My little stāra, I have angered Haman, and he loathes me. I do not worry about what they will do to me. I remain faithful to my Lord. I tell you this not to distress you but to alert you in case you hear of this occurrence; you know where I stand.

Esther sighed and ran a finger along the paragraph. "Oh, Mordecai," she whispered. "I love your faithfulness, but please do not get into any trouble. I could not endure anything happening to you."

She shuddered as she envisioned Haman. She did not like being in his company and always felt he carried an evil spirit within. He frightened her. There was something about him that unsettled her whenever he entered the king's presence and she was there. Of course, Haman respected her because she was the queen, yet his respect never seemed sincere to her.

"My lady?"

Esther blinked and turned her head at the voice of her personal maid. "Yes, Shirin?"

"The wives of the nobles of Cush have arrived."

Esther rolled the scroll with her cousin's private words, replaced the seal, and handed it over to Shirin. "Please burn this."

Without a single question, Shirin took the paper, tucked it into her tunic's pocket, and followed Esther inside. Esther knew she would do as she was told. She trusted her maid with her life.

For the rest of the afternoon and evening, Esther met and dined with the wives of the noblemen of Cush. They discussed and planned a better way their city could support the orphans, the widows, and the poor. Esther's heart ached to think that in a country where royals reigned, there could be so much poverty. She longed to see a better future and educational opportunity for the children.

That night before bed, she knelt and prayed to God to protect Mordecai. She also talked to God about the plans she had made with the ladies of Cush to flourish under His guidance.

She felt satisfied with all the wonderful plans that were coming together and would tell her husband how things had fared. At the thought of Xerxes, her stomach did a little flip-flop. She froze. When had she developed strong feelings for him? She respected him and enjoyed his company, but she had not realised her heart would flutter as her thoughts travelled to him. She smiled and went into bed, feeling a surge of joy run through her. Things at the palace were going very well indeed.

Early the next morning, before the sun was yet to rise, Esther stood on her balcony welcoming the soft and fresh morning breeze. The peacefulness of dawn lightened her heart. How she loved hearing the palace asleep, so different from the hurried and busy pace of the day. She closed her eyes and basked in the silence.

Suddenly the sound of hurried footsteps made her open her eyes. She frowned. Below in the dim light of the garden courtyard, she watched Haman talking to three men. Haman? It was strange to see him in this part of the palace. What was he up to? She studied the men as they whispered in rushed tones. Haman looked around to make sure no one was watching and leaned closer into the circle. He said something that made them gasp. Esther leaned back into the shadows of the balcony so she wasn't watched. They talked a little more before the group dispersed and each one went their own way.

Esther stayed outside longer than necessary, feeling confused and a little uneasy about the whole situation she had witnessed. Why did it bother her so much? Was it because Haman hated her beloved Mordecai, or was it because Haman had always made her feel uneasy? What was Haman doing in this part of the palace? Not finding the answers, she sighed and headed back indoors. She had a long day ahead of her.

By midday, when the noon meal was served, Esther felt fatigued. She rang for Shirin and gave orders she was not to be disturbed and not to bring her meal until later. Once her lady's maid left, she closed her eyes and went to sleep.

The sound of agitated voices woke Esther up from her deep slumber—she blinked a few times and sluggishly sat up. Where were those voices coming from? She could hear two females talking loud enough for her to hear clearly. She stood and walked to the balcony. Underneath stood two young maids talking in rushed, eager voices. Their heads were close together whispering, but they were doing a poor job of remaining quiet.

"That does not seem like the truth," the girl wearing the blue-and-gold gown said. Esther recognised them. They belonged to one of the king's concubines, Tara. They were loyal workers and tended not to get involved in palace rumours. It surprised Esther to see them doing so. Esther shrugged and started back indoors. As she turned, Haman's name was mentioned; intrigued, she paused.

She listened intently.

"It is truth, Farah. I heard them talking. I tell you, Haman has really plotted something big this time." Dana paused, then continued talking. "Messengers have carried letters to the king's provinces written in their own languages. It also has King Xerxes's seal, which cannot be revoked!"

Farah drew in her breath. "Oh, Dana, that is tragic."

"My mother says that the entire city of Susa is in confusion and in mourning. No one understands why this decree has been issued. Yet the king and Haman celebrate!" The anger in the girl's voice was clear.

After the girls left, Esther stood outside a while, deep in thought. Something was happening in the city, and both Haman and her husband knew about it. The news did not sit well with her, and she felt restless inside. She was determined to find out what it was.

Two days later, as Esther hurried along the long, marbled corridor of the palace looking for her maids and eunuchs, she saw Mehuman, one of the king's eunuchs, as he walked along with a silver platter in his hands. He bowed when he saw her and waited respectfully for her to speak.

"Mehuman, I am seeking Hathach, Shirin, and my maids. Do you know where they are?"

"My queen, they have just arrived from the markets, and Hathach is seeking you as well. He claims it's on important matters."

Esther's face registered relief. "Please take me to him."

Mehuman, tall and dark with an imposing figure, bowed again and walked in front of Esther so she could follow him.

He balanced the heavy platter with fruits in one hand and opened the door to the room with the other.

"Queen Esther," he announced and bowed as she walked through the door.

"Thank you, Mehuman." Esther waited for him to leave and turned her attention to the people in the room. Her eyes widened when she saw her seven maids and Hathach all bowed low, waiting for her to address them. They seemed to have been deep in conversation. Their faces registered concern.

"Hathach? Shirin? What has occurred?"

Hathach spoke first. "My queen, I bring unpleasant news. It's Mordecai."

Esther drew in her breath and stepped forward. "What has happened?"

Her personal maid, Shirin, moved close to her. "He is in mourning, it seems," she said.

"Mourning?" Esther felt confused. Her cousin did not have any family close by. Did someone from Jerusalem die? Or had something else happened?

"Haman!" The name was out of her mouth before she could stop herself. Something in her soul irked.

A quick flicker of confusion appeared in Shirin's eyes. "Haman, my queen?"

Esther brushed the question aside and continued talking. "Tell me what happened to my beloved Mordecai."

"Many people, including us, have seen him in sackcloth and covered in ashes, wailing loudly and crying bitterly—his soul is in anguish. He has not been allowed in through the king's gates and is only permitted outside. He is not well, my queen."

Esther felt as if someone were squeezing her heart. "Why is he so distressed?"

"We do not know," Hathach replied.

Esther felt tears prickle the corners of her eyes. It hurt her that Mordecai was suffering from something she did not know. For him to tear his clothes, put on ash, and wail loudly, it could only mean that he was in agony. But why? *Haman!* The name jumped into Esther's mind again, but she shook her head.

"Hathach, please take the very best clothes to Mordecai. Tell him they are gifts from me to replace the sackcloth he is wearing."

Hathach inclined his head. "Let it be done as you ask."

"Please, make haste!"

Hathach bowed and hurried out of the door. Esther felt her heart go with him.

Chapter Eight

Esther was glad her day was busy, as she was in long meetings for many hours. Her busy mind was a pleasant distraction and prevented her from thinking of her cousin's dire situation. It wasn't until late afternoon, after the last meeting with the ladies of Cush, when she could finally retire to her room and write a long letter to Mordecai. She had just begun writing when someone knocked on her door.

"Enter."

The door opened, and Shirin entered. She carried a mountain of elegant clothing in many colours. Intrigued, Esther stood and walked toward her.

"Shirin, what is this?"

"Mordecai has declined the gifts you have sent him. He has returned them." She placed the pile of sophisticated fashion on an ornate table.

"Returned them?" Esther ran a hand over the pile of soft material. "Did he say why?"

Shirin shook her head. "He did not."

"Thank you, Shirin. Leave them here for now, and I will try again later."

After her maid left, Esther sat down but could not finish the letter she was writing. Something was very wrong, and she needed to know what it was. Maybe she could help, or maybe her husband could.

She stood and rang the bell. One of the younger maids came in, and Esther asked her to please bring Hathach to her. It was urgent.

The young girl dashed and disappeared through the doors. Esther sat on one of her golden chairs and rubbed her throbbing temples. Her heart was heavy.

It didn't take long for Hathach to come, and as soon as Esther saw him, she ushered him to close and bolt the door. He did as instructed and waited for her to speak.

"Mordecai has rejected my gifts, and I am more concerned than ever. Hathach, I need your help."

"At your service, my queen." He bowed.

Esther took a deep breath and continued. "I need you to go to Susa to talk to Mordecai and find out what is happening to him. I need to know why he is distressed. Mention this to no one."

After the eunuch left, Esther opened the back doors of her room that retreated to a private sitting area of her sunroom. She sat on the plush gold couch and stared at her surroundings. The white and red hangings fastened with cords of white linen onto marble pillars, the mosaic pavement of porphyry, mother-of-pearl, and other costly stones, did nothing to distract her. Frustrated, she put on her veil and headed outside to clear her head.

That night she added an extra prayer to God for her dear Mordecai. She hoped things would settle and he would be okay. Her sleep was filled with nightmares of beasts and Haman hunting down Mordecai. She tossed and turned, unable to rest peacefully.

Before the sun came up, Esther got out of bed and went for a walk in her private garden at the back of her quarters. The softness of the morning filled her with calm as she prayed to God. She was hoping Hathach would have some news for her today.

The bustle of the palace was soon in full swing as Esther finished signing the papers for the new program she and the wives of the noblemen of Cush were implementing. She was excited at the possibility of everything that was going to take place in the next few weeks.

Being queen had its restrictions, but it also opened many doors that otherwise she would not enjoy if she was still the Jewish girl living in Susa.

After many more hours of discussing the program and filling out paperwork, Esther and her female guests enjoyed a sumptuous meal. Musical entertainment and laughter filled the room as they rejoiced in their splendid alliance. However, through their time together, Esther experienced moments of apprehension. She constantly glanced at the door behind the sheer silk material swaying with the breeze. No Hathach.

The festivities concluded by late afternoon, and after farewells and well wishes, she watched her guests depart. Her mind was so preoccupied with Mordecai, she did not hear the footsteps approaching.

"Queen Esther."

Esther swirled at the sound of Hathach. The look on his face told the story that something was amiss.

Esther excused herself from the bustling as servants scurried around her. She motioned for Hathach to follow her into her meeting room. Once inside, she bolted the door.

"What is wrong with Mordecai?" she blurted out.

"My queen, I suggest you take a seat. The news is dire."

Esther's heart pounded in her throat as she took a seat on one of the Egyptian chairs that had been gifted to her by a pharaoh from Egypt on her wedding day.

"Please tell me everything."

Hathach exhaled. "Mordecai has been distressed because he is going to be killed."

A cry escaped Esther's lips, and she covered her mouth to suppress the sound. "Why? Is it Haman?" She dreaded the answer.

The eunuch nodded. "A decree has been issued and sent to all the provinces and to Susa stating that every Jew—child, young, old—is to be annihilated on the thirteenth day of the twelfth month. The month of Adar."

Suddenly Esther felt as if she had been thrown into the depth of a well and was drowning, unable to breathe. She felt like the tapestries on the walls were suffocating her. She needed air. She ran toward the door to her private garden and gulped a few breaths of fresh air once outside.

This seemed impossible. Who would allow this?

The soft clearing of the throat told her that Hathach had followed her. Without turning around, she asked, "Does the king know about this?"

"Yes, my lady. The decree has his seal. Final and irrevocable."

Esther turned to face the servant. "How is that possible? Xerxes would never allow such a criminal act. And how is Haman involved in all of this?"

Hathach continued talking. "Haman spoke to the king and told him that there was a group of certain people who separated themselves from the customs and disobeyed the king's laws and—"

"That is a lie!" Esther interrupted. "How dare he make such an accusation?" Unable to stand still, she paced around a section of her garden. "Please continue."

"In exchange for the decree to be issued to destroy the Jews, Haman offered the king ten thousand talents of silver to be placed in the royal treasury."

Esther stopped pacing and gasped.

"King Xerxes gave him his signet ring and told him to keep the money and to do with the people as he pleased. Once the script was written and sealed with the king's own ring, dispatches were sent by couriers to all the king's provinces with the order . . ." Hathach paused, then continued. "Mordecai has sent a copy of the king's command for you to see."

Esther stopped pacing and walked to Hathach to retrieve the paper he held out to her. *This must be what the two maids were talking about the other day, and Haman's meeting in secret with those men was definitely about the decree.* Anger boiled inside her. With trembling fingers, she unrolled the paper and read every word.

Tears filled her eyes and they silently rolled down her cheeks and neck. "Oh, Mordecai," she whispered. "What can I do to help you?"

"My lady?"

Esther turned her wet face to her servant.

"Mordecai also sends a personal message for you."

"What is it?"

"He is begging you to go to King Xerxes and plea for mercy for him and for all the Jewish people, so the decree can be eliminated."

Esther gulped. Mordecai did not know what he asked. It was forbidden for her to see the king without being summoned by him. If she went to see him uninvited, he would have her killed!

"Hathach, that is impossible. Unless the king calls for me, I cannot see him. I would be put to death immediately. It has been thirty days since I last visited him."

Hathach nodded. "I explained that to Mordecai."

"What was his reply?" Esther wiped her eyes with the edge of her long, transparent veil.

"He said that you should not think that because you are in the king's house, you alone of all the Jews will escape. For if you remain silent, deliverance will arise from another place. However, you and your father's house will perish. And who knows but that you have come to a royal position for such a time as this?"

Esther's head spun around at the words of Mordecai. She felt like she had just been gently slapped across the face. Her lips trembled and her heart hammered. He spoke the truth. Everything he said was correct. God had sent her to save her people.

She turned her back to Hathach and tried to make sense of her swirling thoughts. Was she able to save her people? Had she been sent for such a time as this, as Mordecai stated? What could she do? She knew she couldn't do this alone. She needed help. She knew what she had to do. Taking a deep breath, she walked to the eunuch and stepped closer to him. Her jewels jingled with each movement.

"Tell Mordecai to gather all the Jews who are in Susa and to fast and pray for me. Tell him not to drink or eat for three days, night or day. My maids and I will fast as well. When this is done, I will go to the king even if it is against the law."

Fear flashed in Hathach's eyes. "My queen! That means death!"

Esther rubbed her hands together, trying hard to keep her composure. Tears filled her eyes and silently spilled down her face and onto her elaborate afternoon gown covered in gold and jewellery. "If I perish, I perish!"

Seeing the queen's determination, Hathach bowed and left the room to deliver the message.

Unable to hold her composure any longer, Esther crumbled onto the nearest garden bench and sobbed.

The next day, Esther spoke to her maids and instructed them regarding her fasting commitment for the next three days. No one asked questions, but the fear everyone felt was evident. Their queen could die if she made an uninvited appearance to see King Xerxes.

That night, as Esther looked out the window at the flickering lights of the stars, her heart ached. The heaviness she carried was intense, but she could not let that consume her thoughts. She had to hold every thought captive, with God's help. She closed her eyes and prayed—nothing else mattered for the next three days but to be in silent communion with the God of Abraham.

Her life was in His hands.

Chapter Nine

Fasting and praying began immediately when Esther woke up from her sleep. She cleansed herself with oil of frankincense and rosewater and put on a simple white gown. She asked not to be disturbed, as she would spend the days in prayer. Everyone felt the pending doom.

On the first day, Esther and her maids began their fasting and praying.

On day two, Esther and her maids continued their solemn communion with God.

On the third day, Esther prayed one last time and entrusted her life to the God of Abraham.

Esther stood still as her seven maids fussed over every detail of her gown and jewels. She had a gown of ivory with gold and precious stones delicately embroidered on the bodice and hem. A sheer gold material was sewn from the shoulders and back, flowing toward the ground and forming a train. With each movement she made, her cape shimmered gracefully. To finish the look, Shirin placed a dainty golden crown on her elegant updo hairstyle that complimented every ornate jewellery piece she wore. When she was ready, Esther took Shirin's hands into her own and bowed her head to pray. The other maids followed suit.

There were tears in the eyes of her servants when she left the room, but Esther felt an indescribable peace within her. Hathach waited outside her bedchamber door, ready to escort her to see the king.

"My lady." He inclined his head. "The king is in the royal house."

Esther gave him a little smile. "Thank you, Hathach. I am ready."

Without another word, she followed him. Esther looked at her surroundings. The palace was renowned for its splendour and magnificence. With every corner she turned, she admired the hallways and rooms richly decorated with expensive silver, gold, and precious stones.

Hathach opened the grand, heavy golden doors to the inner court of the king's house, and they entered the viewing room, which was decorated with glazed bricks depicting winged bulls, sphinxes, and griffins. Esther's heart beat fast. She knew that at the end of that corridor, there would be another room with the door open, and the king would be seated on his throne. The time had arrived. Hathach slowed his pace as they approached the gold door decorated with sphinxes. He turned to look at her with deeply sad eyes.

"Queen Esther." He moved out of the way so she could proceed.

Esther touched his arm briefly and walked past him to her impending doom.

As she walked the last few steps, all she could hear was the sound of her jewellery rattling at her every pace. She came to a stop at the open door and saw the king sitting upon his royal throne facing the entrance. It looked like he was in a meeting with those around him.

Suddenly the king leaned forward with eyes wide. "Esther?"

At the mention of her name, the soldiers lining the entrance all the way to the throne rushed with spears toward her and blocked her from going inside.

A little moan escaped her lips, and she eagerly waited for God to act. Even though she felt afraid, she trusted Him.

She watched the king stand, frowning, and then his stoney expression melted away, and a smile illuminated his lips.

"Esther." He stood and stretched out his golden sceptre. "Let her pass!" he commanded.

The soldiers melted back and let her walk in. Her heart rejoiced with her thankfulness to God.

King Xerxes met her halfway and took her hands into his strong ones.

Esther's stomach flipped with pleasure. She looked into his eyes and saw genuine love and kindness toward her.

"Esther, my love. What is it?" he whispered and touched her cheek with the back of his hand. "Ask for anything you want."

She smiled.

"I will give you half my kingdom, if that is what you request." His gaze told her so many unspoken messages. "You are breathtaking." He lowered his voice and grinned.

"Thank you, King Xerxes," she whispered, feeling a little shy about being the centre of attention with officials, servants, eunuchs, and soldiers witnessing the scene.

"King Xerxes?" He threw his head back and laughed. "Why so formal, my love? I am Xerxes your beloved husband." He paused and studied her face. "Esther? Why the forlorn look? What is it, my beloved?"

Esther cleared her throat. "If it pleases the king, let the king, together with Haman, come today to a banquet I have prepared." She inclined her head.

At King Xerxes's silence, Esther lifted her eyes to see him. The emotions that flickered in his eyes told her he did not believe she wanted him for only a banquet.

"I would be honoured to have you," she added softly. She did not want him to change his mind.

He took her hands into his again and kissed them. "We will be there," he assured her.

Without letting go of her hands, he shouted, "Mehuman, bring Haman at once so that we may do what my queen has asked."

Esther felt every part of her body relax like a rope being untied. Her lungs opened up, and she could breathe again. When she finally walked out of the throne room, she was beaming from ear to ear. Her heart rejoiced at God's magnificence. She could not wait to tell Mordecai all that had happened. But first the evening banquet preparations!

Subtle aromas of food wafted through the air as Esther admired the banquet table filled with delicacies: oohs and aahs escaped both King Xerxes's and

Haman's lips. Each time Haman spoke or directed his eyes at her, Esther felt her insides revolt. How could this villain enjoy himself as if he had done nothing wrong?

"My beautiful wife, Zeresh, will be fascinated to know of all the delectable food served tonight. She has quite a passion for cooking." Haman grinned, then devoured another stuffed pigeon with pistachio nuts and candied capers.

Esther looked away and motioned for a servant to bring more food. Soon the table was filled again with succulent grapes, candied turnips, stuffed pigeons with pistachio nuts, goat marinated in Ethiopian oils, saffron, pomegranates, and candied capers.

For dessert, they served sweetened seed, almond cakes, and exotic sweet waters flavoured with garden herbs or fruits.

The king leaned over next to Esther and whispered, "My love, what is your petition? I know it's more than just the banquet."

Esther inhaled. What could she tell him? She looked over at Haman, who was busy flirting with the young maid and taking more food from the platter she carried. Esther turned back to her husband and smiled. "If it pleases the king, come back tomorrow with Haman for another banquet. Then I will tell you my request."

Her husband touched her face again. He was deep in thought. But he nodded. "Let it be as you say. Tomorrow Haman and I will be here."

The evening ended in high spirits for both men, although Esther felt a little weary and emotionally drained when she thought of entertaining Haman another night. She could not have exposed him tonight. It would have to wait until tomorrow.

The next evening, Esther clapped politely after another entertainment of dancers left the marbled floor in front of her. She felt restless and eager to talk to the king. When would he ask her? She could not bring up the subject unless she was invited to do so.

She watched her husband and Haman enjoy more food and cheer after the music ended. King Xerxes was in high spirits, and she hoped he would ask her soon. A young woman came to the floor to dance, and this time, losing interest in the dancer, the king turned to his wife.

"Esther, my queen, you have outdone yourself yet again with another delicious banquet." King Xerxes took her hand and held it in his while they continued talking.

"Thank you for gracing me with your presence. I have thoroughly enjoyed being with you." She leaned over and gave him a little kiss on the cheek. She had never done that before, but she hoped it was not forbidden.

Xerxes chuckled. "I think we need to do more banquets together."

Esther nodded and melted in his light brown eyes. His handsome face was strong, but he always looked at her with great fondness.

"I also thank you, my queen."

At the sound of Haman's voice, Esther was repelled and slowly turned to face him. She pasted a smile on her face and inclined her veiled head. She could not speak at the moment. It surprised her that he'd spoken, as he had been unusually quiet.

"Esther . . . what is your request? Surely it's not another banquet?" King Xerxes said.

Esther sat up on her reclining couch, and an overwhelming feeling took over. She watched the dancing girl with her many veils of colour; then she looked away, feeling dizzy. She clapped a few times and motioned for the girl to leave.

"It is a beautiful dance." Esther assured the shocked girl. "However, the king and I need a little privacy." The girl smiled with understanding and left the room quickly. In the night's silence, Esther felt more vulnerable than ever. She reached out to her husband and took hold of his hands while she kept her head inclined.

"My king, if I have found favour in your eyes, please grant me my life and the life of my dear people!" A sob escaped from her lips.

Esther heard the king draw in his breath. But she did not look up.

"Grant you your life and your people's?" His voiced echoed confusion.

"My people and I have been sold for destruction and annihilation. We are to be killed! . . . If we were merely being sold as slaves, I would not be pleading for our lives, my lord, and disturbing you with my distress. However, the death of my people torments me."

"Who has dared to threaten your life and your people's?" Esther could hear the wrath in his voice.

She gradually straightened from her bowed position, and with trembling fingers, she turned and pointed to Haman. "Haman is the enemy of the queen and her people!" Esther's heart thundered in her chest, and her legs weakened. She leaned back against her seat. Would the king believe her?

"Haman?!" The sudden furious outburst of the king reverberated in the banquet hall, and everyone came to a halt. He got up and towered over Haman.

Esther watched Haman, whose face was the colour of the lifeless statues in her garden, his eyes protruding and wild and his white lips parted. He shook his head but remained mute.

"Is that true, Haman? You have sentenced the queen to death?" The king clenched and unclenched his fists.

Haman trembled.

King Xerxes's face burned with rage, and without another word, he hastened outside to the garden.

Esther closed her eyes and rubbed her temples as head pain threatened to come.

"Esther, my queen!"

Esther's eyes flew open at the sound of Haman's petrified tone.

"I beg you, my queen, plea to the king to spare my life. I beg you." A cry escaped from deep within his throat. Suddenly he got up and lunged toward Esther and fell prostate on her couch. He grabbed her arms with tears streaming down his face. "Save me, my queen! Only you can save me. I beg of you!"

"Move away, Haman!" Esther tried to pull her hands away, but he was a lot stronger than she was.

Just then, Esther saw Xerxes return from the palace garden, his face reddened. "Will you also assault my queen with me in the house?" He signalled with his head, and strong men appeared from behind the king. They rushed to Haman and tore him from Esther's side. Haman struggled and screamed, but it was in vain.

"Get rid of him," the king ordered.

"What should we do with him, my lord?" the soldier asked.

The king thought for a second before Harbona, the eunuch attending the king, spoke up. "I do not know if this is common knowledge, my lord, but the gallows seventy-five feet high stands by Haman's house. He had it made for. . . Mordecai." Harbona glanced at Esther.

She gasped.

"Hang him on it!" The king motioned for them to leave.

Esther watched as they dragged Haman out of the banquet hall and took him to the place he had prepared for another. Esther shuddered, feeling utterly drained from the crisis of the last few days.

She turned to the king when everyone had left, and he opened his arms wide. She ran into his embrace and buried her face in his chest. Her trembling body began to calm down.

"No one will ever hurt you, my love." He kissed the top of her veiled head.

With her eyes closed, she said a quick prayer to God, thanking Him for saving her and her people. Although the decree could not be revoked, she knew God had a plan.

"By the way," the king said, "how do you know Mordecai?"

Esther lifted her head and gave him a little sheepish smile. "He's my cousin. He raised me when I was a little girl because I was an orphan. He's been like a father to me."

"Hmm . . . then he's family." He smiled and gave her a kiss.

Esther sighed as she placed her head on her husband's chest—it felt so good to have everything out in the open. No more secrets. She was a Jew, and she would be free to worship her God as her heart pleased. Her God of Abraham was a good, good God.

Epilogue

473 BC, the kingdom of Persia

Esther laughed as she watched her beloved Mordecai almost running from room to room, seeing his new house. After the ordeal they had experienced, and after the death of Haman, King Xerxes had given Esther the estate of Haman. Then the king, knowing that Mordecai was Esther's family, took off his signet ring, which he had reclaimed from Haman, and presented it to Mordecai and made him the prime minister. Esther had rejoiced to know that there were no more lies and she did not have to pretend to be anything other than a Jew.

"My little stāra, I am the happiest man in all of Persia!" Mordecai grabbed her by the waist and twirled her. Suddenly Esther felt like a little girl again. She giggled.

"I'm feeling unsteady," Esther said as he put her down.

Mordecai looked at her and hugged her. "Thank you for being so brave and saving an entire nation. You *were* called for such a time as this."

Esther nodded. "God helped me because I could not have done it on my own." It had not been easy.

She looked at Mordecai one last time, and her heart leaped with joy. He looked so handsome in his royal garments of blue and white. A gold laurel wreath adorned his head, and a purple robe of fine linen finished his elegant look.

Both of them went up to the new home's balcony and watched all the Jews in Susa in joyous celebration. For the Jews, it was a time of happiness, joy, and gladness. In every province and in every city to which the edict of the king came, there was celebration and feasting. Oh, how Esther rejoiced.

Her cousin gave her one last squeeze, and she leaned her head against his shoulder, rejoicing for a God who had chosen her to be queen for such a time as this.

Six

Salome: Seductress Princess of Jerusalem

On his birthday Herod gave a banquet for his high officials and military
commanders and the leading men of Galilee. When the daughter of Herodias
came in and danced, she pleased Herod and his dinner guests. The king said
to the girl, "Ask me for anything you want, and I'll give it to you."
And he promised her with an oath, "Whatever you ask I will give you,
up to half my kingdom."

—Mark 6:21–23

Find the story in Matthew 14:1–12 and Mark 6:14–29.

Prologue

15 AD, Rome

Princess Salome swirled and twirled around the luscious green garden—she giggled as she played hide-and-seek behind statues that her stepfather, Phillip, had erected around the villa. She peered from behind an enormous statue of Jupiter, who held a sceptre in his left hand and an eagle in his right. Salome stared up at the monument and shivered. It looked like he was watching her. Again, she peeked to see if Floriana, her personal maid, was coming to find her. She saw the back villa doors wide open and Floriana shielding her face with her hand from the rays of the sun. The slave girl put her hands on her hips, looked a little longer, then throwing her arms in the air, went back inside.

Salome chuckled. She leaned over and whispered in her little clay doll's ear, "We tricked her well, Lucia. We are very good at hiding." She tucked the doll under her arm and continued dancing and swirling around the gardens. She went past the pool surrounded with its mosaic walls, then ran further down the garden with trees that lined the garden path. She hopped down the steps and continued running under the canopy of greenery. Round ceramic white pots sitting on pillars adorned the rest of the garden.

Feeling tired and a tad puffed, Salome stopped and leaned against one pillar.

"I need to rest, Lucia. Do you need to rest?" She put the doll to her ear and pretended to have a conversation. She looked around and realised she had gone too far into the garden. Her mother had forbidden her to go past a certain point. She did not trust slaves and was afraid something bad would happen to Salome.

"Promise me you will stay close by?" her mother had told her when they first moved here after she wedded Phillip. That was a few years ago already, and she had been a lot younger.

"Maybe it does not apply to me anymore, Lucia. I am seven years old. A lot older than when I first arrived in Rome."

The doll remained motionless in her arms. Shrugging, Salome found a bench to sit for a while. She was thirsty, and the midday sun was prickling her skin.

"Hmm, maybe we should go back, Lucia. I don't think it's safe to go further." She stood and noticed this part of the garden was darker and secluded. Maybe it was the abundance of trees surrounding the area. She did not like the eerie feeling.

"Let's go back," she whispered into Lucia's ear and walked back home.

Suddenly she heard soft laughter. She looked down at her doll with widened eyes. No, it wasn't Lucia. Her hand reached for her gold bulla locket given to her by Phillip. He had told her that if she was ever in danger, she could just give it a little rub, and the bulla had the power to protect her from any evil forces. Somehow, rubbing it did not make her feel any better. She heard the laughter again, followed by soft voices.

"We should head back," the man said.

"In due time, my love. No one knows. No one is missing us." The woman's voice made Salome's ears perk up. *Mother?*

"Besides, everyone thinks I'm out for the day."

Salome grinned and placed her hand on her chest, relieved. She looked at Lucia. "It's Mother. Let us be quiet and surprise her." She tiptoed so her leather sandals would not make a noise. She could not wait to see the surprised look on her mother's and her stepfather's faces.

She went down the little dark pathway and stopped behind a goddess's water feature. She sneaked a quick look and saw the back of her mother wearing her blue tunic and stola, a long, draped garment. The man was hidden behind her mother's embrace—both were whispering and chuckling.

Salome put her index finger to her mouth and whispered, "Shh, Lucia. Don't make a sound." She watched the amorous scene before her and smiled. "They love each other very much, Lucia. Isn't that lovely?"

She giggled again as the scene in front of her made her face warm. She did not want to watch anymore. Cautiously, she turned her back and tiptoed away, but the sudden name that came out of her mother's mouth made her head swirl around.

"Oh, Herod, I cannot live without you. I cannot bear the minute you leave Rome."

Salome gaped, and as her mother moved to one side, she saw the figure and face of her uncle, Herod Antipas! Her uncle had come all the way from Jerusalem to Rome to visit his half brother, Phillip Tetrarch. Herod had been in the villa for a few months. Salome frowned. How could her mother love two men? Did she still love Phillip? Her heart thundered in her chest as she listened to her mother and uncle talk words of love.

"I won't leave you, Herodias!" he declared, kissing both her hands. "I'm taking you back with me to Galilee!"

"What about Phaesali?" Herodias pulled her hands away and crossed her arms across her chest.

"I will divorce her! She isn't of any importance." Herod reached for one of her mother's hands. "What about Phillip?"

Her mother sighed, moved into his embrace, and wrapped her arms around his neck. "I will leave him and go with you. Nothing else matters to me but you."

Salome covered her mouth with both hands as little Lucia fell to the ground and broke into small clay pieces. Silent, fat tears rolled down Salome's face as she turned around and escaped the scene. Her heart ached for her aunt, Phaesali, and her stepfather, Phillip. She ran all the way to the villa and to the safety of her room. Sprawled on her bed, she cried herself to sleep.

Salome wriggled her face as another fly intruded upon her nose. She tried to swat it, but missed. Frustrated, she rested her head on Floriana's shoulder and stared through the openness of the palanquin, where she sat with her servant, Floriana, and her mother's servant, Drusa.

When Phillip found out about her mother and Herod's secret love, he became enraged and thrust them out of his villa. Only Salome could remain in the house while her mother and Herod moved into a nearby villa and made plans to sail to Tiberias near the Sea of Galilee. Her mother had insisted that she be allowed to bring both her servant girls, as she could not function without Drusa or Floriana.

Phillip had consented to the arrangements and said good-bye to his stepdaughter.

"You have brought me so much joy, my little princess. Do not forget me."

With tears in her eyes, she clung to the only dad she had ever known and promised she would never forget him.

"If you ever want to come to Rome, my house is always yours!" Phillip gave her one big hug, and then Floriana took her by the hand and walked her to the boat. Her heart cried for many nights.

"I can see the palace!" Her mother's excited voice brought Salome back to the present.

Her mother and Herod's palanquin came to a halt right next to Salome's. Herod grinned and pointed up ahead.

"This is your new home, my love and dear Salome. You will be happy here; I will make sure of that!"

Salome's eyes followed her new stepfather's pointed finger, and she drew in her breath at the magnificent palace with its endless towers. It was grand and so different from the buildings back in Rome.

They had been at sea for many months, and she missed her friends, her dear stepfather, Rome, and the villa.

As strong Ethiopian men hurled their palanquin forward, Salome vowed that one day she would return to Rome.

She looked down at her new clay doll that had replaced Lucia and hugged her close, waiting with anticipation of what lay ahead in her future.

Chapter One

25 AD, the kingdom of Herod Antipas

"Pay attention, Princess Salome! Your head is travelling the foreign lands again!"

Salome blinked a few times as Tabina's sharp tones brought her back to the present. She smiled sheepishly. "My mind has a power of its own, and I cannot concentrate. I apologise."

Tabina harrumphed. "Now, back to the dancing." She clapped her hands, jingling the dozens of bracelets she wore to complement her brightly coloured fashion. At her signal, the musicians began their low rhythmic sounds again.

"Move those hips. Now twirl. Twirl again so your gown flows around you. And again. Again." Tabina clapped to the rhythm of the music as Salome danced all around the spacious entertainment room of the palace. Feeling dizzy, she stopped suddenly and grabbed her head. "I need to stop." With an outstretched hand, she made her way to the reclining seat of the room.

Salome heard Tabina sigh, and with a click of her fingers, the musicians stopped their playing and scurried off. "Very well. I will be here tomorrow to continue your training."

Salome nodded and closed her eyes as she heard Tabina leave the room. It felt good to rest. She had been dancing for the last two hours and was exhausted. She did not understand why her mother insisted she take exotic dancing lessons with Tabina, a well-known Macedonian woman who travelled around teaching dancing to entertainers employed in houses of lords and kings.

"Salome! What is the meaning of this girl?"

Salome's eyes flew open at the sound of her mother's voice. She sat up straight.

"Tabina left. We are done for the day."

She watched her mother's elegant figure as she scanned the room with her big light brown eyes. "I have a feeling you are not telling me the whole truth."

Salome shrugged. "I do not know what you mean." She rubbed an invisible wrinkle from her long red dress and stood. She did not want to get into another argument with her mother about her dancing lessons.

"I know you think this dancing is a waste of time. But I can guarantee that it is essential." Herodias looked her daughter up and down. "Never ask Tabina to leave before due time. Is that understood?"

Salome rolled her eyes. "You were spying on me again, weren't you, Mother?" She folded her arms across her chest. Anger bubbled up inside her.

"I was coming this way because your stepfather wants to have a light lunch with us. He says he had a few things to discuss." Herodias walked around the room and touched the hand of a marble statue. "To my surprise, Tabina said you had dismissed the lesson early."

"I was dizzy and tired, Mother! Besides, princesses are not supposed to be dancers. It is degrading! There are dancing girls for that!" She also wanted to add that she hated that sensual dance she was learning. What was the purpose? Why was her mother so adamant she learn? She had stayed awake many nights trying to understand, but no answer ever came.

Herodias paused in front of her and lifted her chin with one long painted fingernail. "Dear, please do not crease your brow. You are such a beauty, and I do not want you to wrinkle early. Keep your features smooth."

Salome ran a hand over her forehead and tried not to frown again.

"Now, let us see what Herod wants to discuss with us." Without another word, her mother vacated the room in a flurry off her expensive dress and exquisite jewellery.

Salome walked slowly toward the door but looked at herself in the mirror. Her mother had insisted they had several mirrors installed throughout the palace. Besides the handheld ones, they also had this long mirror that reached the floor, a rare article of their time. The mirror's silver face had been polished, so she could look at herself clearly. Looks were everything to her mother. Did she think she was only beautiful because she had eyes the colour of topaz, skin as pale as ivory, and dark, wavy hair? She turned from one side to the other and sighed at her figure.

"Why am I not slim like Shira?" she said out loud, wishing she did not have such voluptuous curves. However, her stepfather's friends who visited always commented on how alluring she was.

"Hmm," she said, "maybe I am beautiful, after all!" With that, she left the room and hurried to catch up with her mother.

Chapter Two

They arrived at Herod's private room on the floor above the grand banquet hall. Her mother turned to Salome and shrugged when she saw that besides the furniture and food, the room was empty of servants and of Herod.

"Where is everyone?" her mother asked.

Salome noticed that the balcony door was opened. "He could be on the balcony." She pointed, and both women headed out there.

Salome suppressed the urge to tell her mother that whenever Herod was on his balcony, he was agitated. Something must be amiss, and to call them both made her more curious about what he would say.

Outside the breeze blew gently, cooling the midday's sun. Herod paced the balcony for a few moments without seeing them. His brow furrowed, showing that his mind was in knots. Herodias cleared her throat and waited to be acknowledged.

Herod stopped pacing. "Ah, you are both here. Very good."

Salome watched him reach over and take her mother's hand into his and kiss it. Her mother's cheeks turned the colour of the sunset. Salome looked away and thoughts of the first time she had seen them together, saying words of love, flooded her mind. She wondered what her mother loved about Herod? Was it his tall physique? His trim beard and dark eyes? Or was it the fact that he spoiled her and did everything she said?

Her mother was a strong, persistent woman and would get hysterical if things were not done the way she insisted they be done. Herod ruled the kingdom, but Herodias ruled him.

"Come, Salome." Herod stood at the door, waiting for her to go inside.

She smiled and followed them both.

The aroma of the food greeted Salome's senses, and she ate heartily while they talked about many things.

"What have you been up to today?" Herod asked Salome.

"Not much." She popped another juicy grape into her mouth and turned to her mother, who nodded her approval. She had forbidden Salome to tell Herod about her dancing lessons.

"Herod, my love. This has been delicious. Thank you for the invitation." Her mother batted her eyelashes and gave her husband a beguiling smile.

"Herodias." His face softened as he ran a finger along her cheek.

Salome glared at her mother. She knew what she was up to. Whenever she wanted something from Herod, she would become flirtatious and entice him to tell her *everything*. Since Herod had not told them yet what was on his mind and why he had summoned them, her mother was desperate to find out. Her coquettish manner always broke him.

"Tell me, my love, what is on your mind?" Herodias moved closer to him and ran one of her long, painted fingernails along his jaw.

Herod gulped, then exhaled. "It's John the Baptist."

Herodias withdrew her hand immediately. "John the Baptist?" she seethed.

Herod stood from the table and wandered to the opened doors of the balcony.

Her mother jumped up from her seat and marched over to Herod. "You know very well how I detest that man! How dare you bring him up and ruin such a pleasant time with you!" Her elaborate hairdo moved with each of her actions, and it looked like it would topple off her head. Salome concealed a smile. Her mother could be so dramatic. However, at this very moment, she was not being dramatic. The name John the Baptist brought out her mother's darkest side.

"I loathe that man!" she spat.

Salome looked away to the intricate tapestry that hung on the wall, pretending to study it. She did not want to get involved in this argument.

The reason her mother did not like John the Baptist was because he always preached about repentance. Whenever they were out in their palanquin roaming the Jordan River, John would be preaching. He was slightly strange, dressed in a tunic made of roughly woven camel hair. His leather belt was made of animal skin and worn about the waist to hold his long, flowing outer garment in place. He was spiritual and a prophet. Salome liked his direct speech and talk of repentance.

Herod always stopped to listen to John. Something about the man fascinated him. Whenever they stopped, John would turn to look at them and point.

"Repent, Herod!" he shouted. "Repent from your sins. Denounce your iniquitous union with Herodias, your brother's wife!"

Salome had watched many times how Herod trembled under the call to repent, and many times in the shadows of the night, she would hear Herod and her mother arguing about their union.

"He's a holy man, Herodias. A prophet of God. He is right. I took you from *my* brother!" His voice had quivered.

"Do not be a coward, Herod. What has been done is done," her mother's hard voice answered. "Besides, we are in love and nothing and no one can stand in our way!"

"But is lust the same as love?" Herod sounded exhausted. "You are an intoxicating woman, and I cannot yield. I have tried to forget you, but it is in vain."

"Then execute John so we can live our lives in peace!"

"Execute John? Are you mad? I refuse to slay John!" The sound of something shattering made Salome jump.

For the last few months, their shouts and arguments would wake Salome. Herodias tormented Herod to destroy John. However, her stepfather had been strong and not surrendered to her desire.

The last argument they had had, Herodias had been livid. She threatened to leave him and go back to Rome. To go back to Phillip and be away from John and his nonsense.

"You jest?" Herod said in disbelief.

"Do you think I jest? Do not test me, Herod. You might be the king, but nothing will stop me from doing what I desire!"

"Would you have the audacity to take Salome and leave me for Phillip?"

"Yes."

Salome could imagine her mother's angry face and crossed arms.

"I cannot lose you, Herodias." Herod's voice shook. "You have been my only delight."

"Then get rid of John." Her mother pushed him yet again.

"Cease with that woman! I will not kill John." Salome listened as Herod stormed out of the room.

Now, here they were again arguing about the same thing. Salome was tired of the whole situation. Why did her mother get infuriated? After all, what John said was true. He had done nothing wrong. She was on Herod's side, but, of course, she could never admit that to her mother. Her eyes adjusted back from looking at the tapestry and watched the lovers as they continued the John subject. Her mother's arms folded across her chest. Herod looked worn and confused.

"I know you despise John," he said in a soft voice.

He raked his fingers through his short, dark hair and walked out onto the balcony. Herodias followed.

"I have told you many times to kill him, yet you refuse. It's like you do not love me anymore."

Salome could hear the pout in her voice.

With curiosity building inside her, Salome stood and went to the balcony to listen and watch. She wanted to know why Herod had summoned them both to this luncheon, assisted by no servants. He obviously wanted privacy.

Herod paused in front of Herodias and took both her hands. "Herodias, my dove," he murmured.

Salome smirked.

Her mother had turned her grim face away from Herod, looking very much like a child who wanted a toy she could not have.

"Herodias, look at me."

Slowly, she lifted her surly face.

"John the Baptist is . . . I have . . . imprisoned him." The last words were barely audible.

Salome gasped and covered her mouth. Her mother had won! Her threat to leave him had worked, and he had to yield. Not wanting to hear or see her mother gloat, Salome left the room in a hurry and buried herself in her bed for the rest of the afternoon. Once she was ready, her maid, Floriana, helped her dress and put on a more comfortable gown. She breathed with relief as the figure-hugging red dress was off her body.

Chapter Three

The next few days were busy for Salome as she continued arduous hours of twirling, pirouetting, and swaying. Tabina was a rigorous teacher and made her work too hard. Salome was not used to so much physical activity; princesses usually spent a lot of time indoors and entertaining. This was new to her.

Some days, her mother would come in and watch her perform. She whispered instructions to Tabina, who voiced them to Salome. Salome grunted in frustration but remained silent. She knew her mother would slap her if she questioned her actions. Her hand went to her face as if the sting of her mother's handprint still ached on her cheek.

"Much better, Princess Salome. Much better." Tabina moved around Salome as she danced. "Sway your hips. You have curves that are envied by many women. Use them accordingly."

Salome tried again. This time Tabina approved.

"Remember, Princess, you must captivate your audience. Especially the men in the room."

Salome winced.

"Now, start again from the beginning. Perform to perfection," Tabina commanded.

Determination took over and Salome asserted she would show Tabina that she *could* do it. If Tabina saw her perform to her satisfaction, then she would tell Herodias and maybe let her have a few days off.

The music began again, and this time Salome closed her eyes and let the rhythm pulse through her body. She forgot about her mother. She forgot Herod. She forgot about John the Baptist. She forgot Tabina. All she could think about was the movements in her body. They needed to be flawless. Perfect. Captivating.

She did not realise when the song finished until a loud clap interrupted her concentration. A trickle of sweat ran down her back and across her forehead, and she huffed for breath.

"My dear princess, you have mastered the art of dance. Well done." Tabina inclined her head and smiled.

Behind Tabina stood her mother with a malicious grin on her face. She walked over to Salome and took her hands in hers. "No man will resist you now. Well done, my Salome. You are your mother's daughter, after all."

Salome wrinkled her brow. No man would resist her? She was her mother's daughter, after all? She did not understand what any of that meant, but she had an unsettling feeling that her mother had a devious plan. Maybe it was the fact that her eyes gleamed with a hidden secret. Or that her smile did not reach her eyes. Salome waited to see what it was.

The evening stars looked almost like silver stones shining from above. Salome stared at each one and wondered what it would be like to be a star. Although she had a lavish life filled with precious stones, opulent rooms, luxurious clothes from Egypt, Macedonia, Rome, and Greece, she lived with a sadness beneath her soul. What was missing in her life? A sudden sound from below made her stand and lean over her balcony to see what was happening. Lanterns illuminated the grounds and its surroundings, giving her a clear view of the happenings downstairs.

Below, she saw three men dressed simply in plain-coloured tunics. Their heads and voices were low as they left the back of the palace where the dungeons were. Even in the shadows, she recognised their simplicity—it was

John's disciples. Every day, men who followed his teachings visited him. Men who were faithful, strong in their beliefs, and loyal to each other.

She watched them walk away, deep in conversation, until they disappeared down the dusty road. She could only imagine how alone and directionless they felt without their leader.

Salome went back to her reclining seat and her stargazing. Her mind filled with too many questions and only a few answers.

"Princess Salome?"

Salome turned her head and saw her maidservant Floriana with her head inclined, waiting for her to reply. "Yes, Floriana?"

"The king has summoned you and the queen to dine with him tonight."

Salome titled her head. Hmm, what was he up to now?

With the help of Floriana, she dressed in a tunic of Phoenician purple from Tyre, a gift that had been sent to her from a distant aunt. She wore a gold necklace and gold bracelet and finished her hair with a Grecian hairstyle she had once seen another princess wear. Her long braid fell in curled tresses past her waist.

"You look a vision, my lady," Floriana gushed.

Salome laughed and thanked her. Before leaving her quarters, she had a quick glance at her reflection in the mirror. The dress emphasised every curve of her body. She wanted to take it off and put on a simple tunic, but Tabina's words about her curves being the envy of other women made her straighten, flick her hair, and walk out.

Soft music played in the king's dining hall as Salome entered the room. Today the king looked amused as he watched three dancing girls perform for him. Salome watched them and exhaled, remembering her own dance.

"Their dance is boring, if you ask me, my dear daughter. Yours will make any man insane." Herodias had walked behind her and whispered into her ear. Then, laughing, she sauntered to the king.

When the dance was over, Herod clapped and asked them to leave. He invited Herodias and Salome to sit next to him. As Salome walked up the little steps toward the seating area where the king sat behind an overflowing table filled with food, she noticed Herod staring at her.

"My dear Salome, you are a vision indeed." He tilted his head to one side. 'When did you grow so exquisite?" His eyes roamed her body, and suddenly she felt shy and self-conscious.

She looked away from Herod and turned her glance to her mother. Herodias's face was amused as she watched the scene unfold before her. Her beaming face did not have a trace of jealousy on it. Relief washed over Salome, and she relaxed and enjoyed the compliments of the king.

A few hours later, amidst the laughter and hilarity, Herod lifted his hand for silence. Salome, her mother, and the entertainers were all silenced immediately.

Herod stood. "It is with great pleasure to announce that I will celebrate my birthday this year with a grand banquet."

Salome heard her mother gasp. She looked over and noticed her mother's eyes dancing with . . . elation?

"Oh, my beloved, that is good news." Her mother lifted her golden goblet filled with red wine. "To you, my king." She blew him a kiss and took a long, thirsty gulp.

Salome watched in fascination. Something about her mother's indescribable joy bothered her. What was she up to? She titled her head to one side and stared at her with muddled thoughts.

After the king took a seat and the polite claps from the entertainers and servants ended, Herodias moved closer to her husband and put one arm around his neck.

"Let me be in charge of the food and entertainment, my love." She leaned over and kissed his cheek. "I will not disappoint you."

Herod grinned. "I trust you implicitly, Herodias. You can choose my food and entertainment. What kind of entertainment are you planning?"

Herodias inclined her head to one side and placed her hand on his chest. "One you have never seen before. Trust me . . . when it is over . . . you, my dear, will have your senses reeling in pleasure." With a sly grin on her crimson lips, Herodias turned to look at her daughter.

Hearing her mother's words and seeing the look she gave her made Salome's stomach flip. Somehow the dance she had been practicing for months, the sensuality of it, made her eyes narrow. Was *she* the entertainment? Is that what her mother had planned? Did she want Herod to have an affair with her?

Anger simmered in her heart. She took her golden cup filled with wine and gulped it down. If her mother wanted her to tempt and seduce Herod, then she would.

Her mother would regret the day she put her in a dancing lesson. Wine dribbled from one corner of her mouth, and she wiped it angrily with the back of her hand. She could not wait to see her mother's face on Herod's birthday.

Chapter Four

The days were filled with preparation for Herod's banquet. Invitations were sent to nobles, important government officials, and chief men of Galilee. Salome continued her dance training and Tabina had confirmed that Salome was going to gift her dance to the king. Her mother had requested it. Salome found the idea repulsive.

While she continued mastering her seductive dance, her mother worked on the banquet menu. One afternoon, as Salome made her way down the long corridor of the palace, she walked past the meeting room and heard Herodias speaking to Drusa, her personal maid of many years.

"The menu needs to be filled with luxurious and exotic foods and the most delicate wine available. I want to spoil Herod's appetite and indulge his passion." A soft, sinister laugh erupted from her throat.

"Yes, my lady," Drusa replied.

"I know what excites him and what will cause him to lose his mind. Herod will not know what came over him when the night is over . . . and then . . . I strike!"

Salome shook her head and continued on her way. In two days' time, she would know what her mother's secret plan was. Deep down, she knew it was an evil one.

The great day arrived with pomp and splendour, and before the guests arrived in the late evening, Salome snuck a peek at the grand banquet hall. They adorned the banquet table with outlandish flowers from Spain and platters of exquisite fruits and nuts. Lanterns of all sizes illuminated the room, making it almost magical and surreal. Ceramic white pots from Rome had been imported for the occasion and filled with unique indoor plants. Tapestries and draperies hung all around the room, creating warmth and intimacy for the guests. *Perfect.* Exactly what she wanted. Intimacy and warmth. With one last glance, Salome left the room and walked up the marble stairs to her bedchambers, where her provocative dress waited for her. A dress her mother had bought her for the occasion.

Her stomach bubbled with anticipation and nerves. She could not wait to have the whole thing over and done with. She would not be part of the celebrations tonight, just the entertainment.

A few hours later, a knock made her jump. Floriana opened the door. "My lady." The maidservant bowed and opened the door wider for Herodias to walk in.

"It's time, Daughter."

Salome sat up from her bed and looked at her mother from head to toe. She wore an ivory figure-hugging dress and a magnificent crimson cape held by golden brooches. Her hair was brushed in an elaborate outlandish hairdo that seemed to be a Grecian style. Her feet were covered in dainty golden sandals, and bracelets and jewels adorned her body. Her exquisitely painted face finished her glamourous look.

"Mother, you look breathtaking," Salome said.

Her mother did not acknowledge the compliment. Instead, she stretched her hand and pointed to the dress. "It's time. Make haste and put it on. The king and his guests await your arrival."

Salome glanced nervously at Floriana, and the maid gave her an encouraging smile. "I will help you, Princess. You will be a vision for sure."

"Do not let me down, Salome." Herodias stood in front of her. Her eyes narrowed. "This is a life-and-death situation." She twirled her cape and exited the room.

Life-and-death situation? Suddenly Salome's body trembled. She did not want to do this anymore. This was strange.

"Come, Salome, let's get you dressed." Floriana's soothing voice washed over her as it had done for so many years since she was a little girl. She turned to her maid and gave a faltering smile. Without a word, she nodded and lifted her arms to start the dressing process.

With each step Salome took toward the banquet hall, the more determined she became. Her jewels jiggled as she came to the last step, and she exhaled. Music and laughter echoed from down the hallway. She was close. Her mother had told her not to let her down, and she would not. She would make Herodias proud of her.

Before entering the grand hall, she stopped at yet another mirror of the palace and looked at her reflection in the shimmering lights of the night. She was decorated with costly garlands and flowers, sparkling jewels, anklets, and flashing bracelets. She had to admit that she was a vision of beauty and loveliness. With little covering and no modesty, every part of her body felt exposed to the public. Her full crimson lips smiled at her reflection. "Showtime, Salome. Make your mother proud," she added sarcastically.

She pranced into the room and waited for the musicians to begin the fiery rhythmic sound of their musical instruments.

A gasp erupted from around the room as the men admired Salome's beauty. She looked up and saw Herod gulp and his mouth gape at seeing her barely dressed body. She felt indecent and unscrupulous, like a lady of the night and not a princess, but this was what her mother wanted. She was going to give her more than she had asked.

The music began, and she started her sultry dance. She forgot about her mother. Forget about Herod and the guests and the servants watching. The music reeled at her senses, and she escaped to another world. A world of pleasure and happiness. A world where her mother did not exist.

Finally, the music ended, and Salome, breathless, came to a halt. She turned to Herod and bowed low, but she did not take her eyes off him. She gave him a seductive smile and watched his face. His eyes glowed with a fiery desire she had never seen in him before. His mouth was opened, his breathing raspy, and his hands outstretched. Then he burst into applause, followed by everyone around him. Salome turned to look at the guests' faces, and a feeling of satisfaction crawled over her. They all had the same look as Herod's. Desirous, irrational, driven by passion. Salome scanned the room for her mother and saw her leaning against a giant pillar toward the back of the room, watching her every action. Her mother inclined her head and blew her a kiss. Salome exhaled. Her job was done.

Her attention turned back to Herod, who was motioning for the roaring crowd of men to settle and let him speak.

"My darling Salome," he began. "You have pleased me beyond words. I will never forget the gift of your exquisite dancing."

Salome inclined her head.

"Today I make an oath to give you anything you ask of me."

Salome's mouth gaped and her eyes travelled to her mother, who had straightened and no longer leaned against the pillar.

"If you want half of my kingdom, it will be yours. Today your wish is mine to fulfill." Herod, in a drunken stupor, lifted his golden goblet. "To Salome," he shouted.

Everyone joined him, and more laughter erupted around the room.

"Now, what will it be?" Herod stared at Salome with intensity.

Salome blinked a few times. What did she want? She had everything she needed. Did she want half his kingdom? Her eyes flickered in confusion for a few seconds, and she felt unable to think clearly. What should she ask for? Her stomach lurched. She could not keep the king waiting.

In desperation she turned to her mother, who motioned to her with her index finger to come.

Chapter Five

Salome rushed to her mother's side. "I do not know what to ask for?" She felt her hands sweat. How humiliating to have the king and his guests waiting for her answer!

"Come, my petal, tell me the desires of your heart!" Herod hollered.

The crowd roared with him.

Salome turned back to her mother and waited for her to reply. She watched her mother's face flash with satisfaction as she leaned over and whispered in her ear, "Ask for the head of John the Baptist."

Salome blinked. Had she heard correctly?

"What did you say?" she asked.

"Ask for the head of John the Baptist."

This time she heard her clearly, and her heart thundered in her chest.

"John the Baptist?" she choked, her hand going to her throat.

Salome was astonished. She did not understand the hidden revenge in her mother's heart.

"No!" she said between clenched teeth. "I will *not!*"

She began to shake, and sweat broke through her body. She could not ask for such an inhumane act to take place. No! She shook her head.

"I will not, Mother. No."

Her mother moved closer to Salome and whispered venomously, "Ask for John's head, or I will ask for yours."

Salome's head shot up. The wicked look in her eyes made Salome tremble. She was serious.

"Hurry, Daughter, Herod awaits your decision." A smirk danced on her mother's lips.

Muted by her mother's action, Salome walked backward, watching Herodias's face the whole time. She could not tear her eyes away from her.

"Salome, my luscious rose of the desert, what is your desire?" Herod called again as he took another long drink from his wine cup.

Salome's nose tickled from the robust smell of wine. The faces of all the guests looked glassy and drunk. How could she ask such a thing when the king's mind was clouded?

Slowly, she reached the throne where Herod stood. Her uncovered body trembled. She opened her mouth to speak, but no sound came out. She cleared her throat. Her jaw felt rigid. Her eyes moved to her mother who stood with her hands on her hips, her mouth grim and eyes looking like snakes.

Salome tore away her gaze and looked up at Herod. "My only wish my king is . . . my only wish my king is . . ." Tears filled her eyes and rolled gently down her face. "I want the head of John the Baptist."

Under the flickering of the burning lights, Salome watched Herod's face turn the colour of ivory. His upper lip and hand shook. He frowned and spoke again. "My dear, I did not understand what you said. Speak louder."

Salome took a deep breath and rang out the words. "I want the head of John the Baptist."

The uncontrolled mirth ceased, and an ominous silence settled over every single guest. All Salome could hear was the thundering of her own heart.

Salome watched his face flicker with emotions. Although he was drunk, he understood the severity of the request. His eyes roamed the room until they settled on Herodias. Salome watched him clench and unclench his fists as he battled the demand. Frustrated, he hurled his cup to one side and let it shatter on a wall covered in tapestry. Red wine trickled down and onto the marble floor. A pool of red formed on the ground, and Salome grimaced. Red, like blood. John's blood. She turned her attention back to Herod, who was watching her intently.

She wanted to scream and yell that she did not want that request, but the look on her mother's face prevented her from it.

Finally, she watched Herod descend the stairs until he was towering over her. He lifted her chin with one of his fingers. "Your request is my command!"

He whirled around and back up the steps, his cape flowing behind him. He clicked his fingers to the soldiers at the door, and they scurried in. "Get me the head of John the Baptist, now!"

The two Roman soldiers dressed in their authoritative uniform saluted and tore out of the room.

Salome covered her face and tried to process what had just happened. The king, still standing in the same spot, looked numb and confused.

Salome's eyes travelled to her mother, who was the only one grinning from ear to ear. Salome felt sick.

The guests had gone back to talking in hushed tones. Salome knew they were all shocked. They stared at her and her mother and whispered to each other. She could only imagine the things they were saying about them.

It did not take long for the executioner to walk back in the door with the head of John the Baptist, covered with a cloth on a silver platter.

Loud gasps and chatter filled the room. Salome watched as everyone's face seemed to pale. Her mother was the only one who gloated.

The soldier said something to the king, and the king whispered back and pointed to Salome.

The king stood again. "Behold the head of John the Baptist." The king extended his hand toward Salome.

The soldier inclined his head and handed her the covered platter. Salome turned her face away, sickened. The heavy platter almost toppled to the floor, but she gripped it tight and slowly made her way to her mother. She did not look at the head once. Her body quivered.

As soon as she presented the head of John the Baptist to Herodias, Salome charged out of the room in uncontrollable tears.

The life of a good, innocent man had ended all because of her mother's malevolent desire. How could she have been so weak?

Up in her room she cried bitter tears, and nothing Floriana tried could calm her down. She knew her life would change forever.

Unable to sleep well, Salome woke up early and headed to the balcony to clear her mind. Her tears had stopped, but her heart remained heavy.

The light breeze of the morning made her shiver, and she wrapped the warm linen wrap closer around her shoulders.

Soft voices below made her walk to the edge and find out who was out there. Below were simply dressed men. It was John's disciples. They had wrapped what she could only assume was John's body and were carrying it out.

She sighed and turned away, unable to watch anymore.

One day, she would leave this place. One day, she would go back to Rome. That day, she made a silent vow to herself.

Epilogue

27 AD, the Jordan River

Salome sighed deeply as they carried her to the sailing boat one early morning. Her heart leaped with joy as she thought about starting her life over in Rome. She was of age now and could do anything her heart desired. When she had told her mother and Herod that she was going to leave, they had not opposed her wishes. On the contrary, they blessed her decision. Salome was relieved.

She wanted to start fresh and forget everything that had happened in those early years. Her mother seemed to have forgotten the atrocity of having John the Baptist murdered. But Herod lived with a guilty conscience. There would be days where he would be depressed and downcast—she had even overheard him telling Herodias how he regretted killing an innocent man. Her mother had brushed it off and told him not to worry about it anymore. That he had done a good thing.

"He reminds me of John!" The voice of Floriana brought her back to the present. Her head snapped around to where she pointed.

"John?" Her voice was breathless.

Near the Jordan River in a shaded spot that she usually used to see John preaching from, she saw a man preaching. His clothes were simple and different from John's, yet he looked similar to him. She squinted.

"Take me closer to that man," she ordered the manservants who carried her.

They took her close enough to see but not too close to cause distraction. On a closer look, she noticed he did not look like John at all. His features were softer and less rugged. His clothing was only a simple pale tunic, which was dusty from the roads. He looked like he was a Nazarene.

The man spoke with a strong, assured voice that rang out for miles. She wondered how he could project his voice so far. His eyes looked peaceful and kind, and his words of comfort washed over her soul. She watched with intent as people with many ailments came to his side. There was a blind man who walked to him with arms outstretched.

"Who is this man?" she asked no one in particular.

"His name is Jesus. Son of Joseph the carpenter and Mary," the manservant replied.

"Jesus." She let the name roll off her tongue. Even the name sounded soothing.

She watched as Jesus stood and walked toward the blind person and took hold of his shoulders.

"What do you need me to do?" Jesus asked.

"Rabbi." The old man's voice trembled. "I want to see." He stretched his hands and touched Jesus's face.

Jesus smiled. "Your faith has made you well." Then he placed his hands over the man's eyes and prayed while looking up to heaven.

Suddenly the blind man gasped.

The crowd waited in silence.

"I can see! I can see." The blind man jumped up and down.

A roar echoed in the fields as everyone around him celebrated—the man, suddenly remembering Jesus, fell to the ground and worshipped him.

"Thank you, my Rabbi. Thank you!" he cried, tears running freely down his face.

Salome wiped the corner of her eye at the touching scene. She liked this Jesus. He seemed compassionate.

Sighing, she tapped the side of the palanquin and motioned for them to leave.

As they moved away from the scene, she turned her head one last time and watched the man, Jesus, until he looked more like a grain of sand in the distance.

She did not know who this new preacher was, but it felt like she had witnessed something special.

Shaking her head, Salome told Floriana to tell her more about Rome when Salome was growing up. The maid smiled and began the stories.

Salome closed her eyes to enjoy the simpler times of her life.

Her mother forgotten.

King Herod forgotten.

Her guilt forgotten.

For now, she would enjoy feeling free.

If you enjoyed reading these stories, you can download my free eBooks, which are short stories about women of the Bible. Download them at www. gigistorylibrary.com.au.

About the Author

M.E. Mayorga is known to everyone by her middle name, Esther. She loves reading and writing books. If she could have her own library, she would.

Esther is the cohost of two popular podcasts: one for children called *Car Ride Stories for GIGI Kids* and one for teen girls called *GIGI Teen Radio*.

She enjoys cowriting with her younger sister Stephanie, and together they are creating an exciting Christian series for teen girls called *Charlotte Bay Girls*.

She lives in sunny Brisbane, Australia, and is looking forward to moving to the countryside one day, where she can find more creative inspiration in the beauty of the rolling hills and the quiet.

You can connect with Esther at www.gigistorylibrary.com.au or on Instagram @gigi_teen_girl, or you can email her at writegigi5@gmail.com. She will definitely reply to your email!

PS: GIGI stands for "Gorgeous in God's Image."